Stephanie P.

Down in the Dirty

BY

J.M. B

Copyright © 2006 by Jimmie .M. Benjamin

Cover design by Borel Graphics
Cover Photograph(s): Jerry Jack
Interior Design by Nancey Flowers
Edited by Chandra Sparks Taylor–www.chandrasparkstaylor.com
Edited by Tiffany M. Davis–www.phoenixblue.com

First Flowers in Bloom trade paperback printing 2006

For more information, or to contact the author, send correspondence to:

Flowers in Bloom Publishing, Inc.
2152 Ralph Avenue - #421
Brooklyn, New York 11234
www.flowersinbloompublishing.com

Library of Congress Cataloging-in-Publication Data
Benjamin, J.M.
Down in the Dirty/ J.M. Benjamin - 3rd ed.
Library of Congress Control Number: 2005938759

ISBN: 0-9708191-6-1
ISBN: 978-0-9708191-6-1

10 9 8 7 6 5 4 3
Third Paperback Edition

Printed in Canada

Acknowledgments

First and foremost, I want to give thanks to the Most High for providing me with a life preserver when I was drowning in an ocean of negativity surrounded by sharks. You are indeed the best of planners. Alla is Akbar.

Nancey Flowers, thank you for believing in me. With your guidance and assistance, I'm going to bloom in this game like Jack's bean stalk.

To my mother, you've always seen the good in me even when I thought I had none left, and always made sure that a light remained lit when I chose the path of darkness, in case I ever wanted to find my way back. It took a while, but I did. I love you for that.

To my father, finally the mold has been broken, and for what it's worth, I still love you too.

My children: You have been the motivational fuel that has kept me moving forward over the years. Let my mistakes, bad choices, and poor decisions be a learning experience and a reminder to you.

My sisters, Kima Shambry, Eisha, and Khadi; I want for you what I want for myself. I love you all. My brother, James (Peter Pan) Spann, to call us twins growing up would have been an understatement, but now as men, we have become individuals, and what we've been through in the past has strengthened us for the future. The struggle is ending in Akhi and progress is being made. Allah knows best, and for the record, Pete and Squirm 4 Life!

My nieces and nephews, Nafessa, Aaron, James Jr., Jakai, and our newest addition. To Daddy and Bonkey, for being the loving grandparents that I needed you to be. To my god-sent sister, Heather Jones. Sis, words can't express the love. I could write a book on how you held a brother down. Thanks for everything, and congratulations on your Sunshine Planning business.

Yolanda (Landa) Davis, lovers come and go, but friends are forever. The value of our friendship is priceless. Twenty years and counting. Also Eisha Singleton, Elyssia Boykin, Kejo Swingler, Teisha Braxton, and Monique Terry, I appreciate your love, concern, and support over the years. A special thanks to Ms. Salone Cameron. You are indeed a rare breed. Jacqui "Jai" Burwell and the Burwell family. God bless you all.

Ms. Susan Hampstead of *Don Diva* magazine: Sue, the love is deeply appreciated for real. Much success with Hampstead Publishing. Nikki Turner, the urban princess of street fiction, thanks for all the love and the opportunity to be a part of *Street Chronicles*. Not to worry, my joint "Charge It to the Game" is gonna hold its weight. Keep doin' what you do, ma.

Crystal Lacey Winslow, I look foward to "Keepin' It Gangsta" being a part of Melodrama Publishing's anthology, *Menace II Society*. I'm respecting your independent gangsta.

Wahida Clark, As Salaamu Alaikum, thanks for responding back when I was seeking guidance and advice. May Allah reward you for your efforts and your accomplishments. You have also been an inspiration to me and many other sisters and brothers who strive to be heard.

To my protege, Ms. Special Smallwood: stay focused and keep writing. Soon A Special Secret will put you on the map and you'll be the youngest in charge. I got you.

To the brothers on lock down, it's too many of you to name and my publisher just ain't having it. But before I lay my pen to rest, those who know they are worth mentioning in my book will be acknowledged respectfully. Much love to my strong peoples Vincent "Victorious" Jackson and Shawn Hartwell. You two brothers showed genuine love and opened doors for me in this book game when I was still knocking. You know I'm going to support Elizabeth's finest to the fullest. The book, the DVD. We shall remain friends and comrades for life. Union County stand up!

Keith "Twin" Wooten, you's a smooth cat, and all my peoples from The Field from the stat to the feds—stay up.

My man Prince Wint, I appreciate the plug, Big Dread. David "Puffy" Myrie, yo, dawg, whe gwan? Without your help Re-Entry with a Vengeance would not be the banger it is.

To my brother behind the walls busting their pens: Storm "Kasim" Weeks, Arnold Dorsey, Bey, Gary "Boo" Wiggins, my two crime partners in Six Feet Deep, Rock Hansen, Assante Kahari, Deon "Dee" Smith, J. Reddish aka Skinny, Peter Shue and Ben Okanume (author of *Motive for Revenge* and *Pilgrims of False Gods*), it was both an honor and pleasure to have met and built with you. Randy "Mo Deezy" Kearse, author of *Street Talk: Hip-Hop and Urban Slanguage*. To the homefront, Plainfield stand up! Check for the joint about the town, and to fallen soldiers and soldierettes from The Field (R.I.P.). My peoples 4 Life, Antwan Johnson, Charles Weatherspoon, Marcellus Richardson, and Rodney Dudley. You brothers have always kept it official with me regardless of whatever. Love is love, New Projects 4 life!

Last, but not least to The Dirty. You know I got nothing but love for y'all. A special thanks to the Jones family of Dunn, North Carolina. You will always be my extended family.

To the readers, without your support, I would not have a voice. I hope that this edu-tainment serves its purpose.

Please continue to support your African-American authors!

—J.M. Benjamin

Dedication

To my mother, Mrs. Jean Word, and children Yaseena, Jamillah, and Jameel, with love.

In memory of my grandmother, Mrs. Zella Vivian Bennett (May 1, 1919–February 15, 1995) and my nephew, Anthony Robinson, Jr. (May 31, 1989–November 21, 1989)

Down in the Dirty

BY

J.M. BENJAMIN

Prologue

"Keisha, come on!" Desiree nervously yelled to her friend as she stuck her head out of New York's motel room door to check to see if the coast was clear. She hoped that no one had heard the commotion that had just taken place and would come out of their rooms.

Everything happened so fast for Desiree that she hadn't had time to really stop and think about what she and her friend Keisha had agreed to do, but it was too late to turn back. The damage was already done, so she would have to live with the consequences.

When she first told Keisha what New York had done to her, Desiree had no idea that it would trigger Desiree's own past and cause Keisha to react the way she had.

She and Keisha had cried nonstop as they shared their stories, reliving the horrors of their ordeals, but as the tears began to dry up and their feelings began to transform from pain and shame into anger and wanting to seek revenge, Keisha proposed they go and confront New York.

At first Desiree was against the idea for fear of what could happen, but Keisha assured her that the two of them possessing baseball bats would be a match for New York.

Hearing how confident her friend was put Desiree somewhat at ease but at the same time, she was still scared. It wasn't until Keisha had actually gone and retrieved the two brand-new aluminum bats that had been left in her living room closet by one of her mother's many lovers that Desiree felt up to the confrontation.

She didn't know what to expect once they got to the motel, but Keisha's pep talk had her intrigued enough to want to see things through. Just as Desiree finished changing into one of Keisha's outfits, Keisha came back into the room holding a set of keys to her mother's burgundy 1979 Monte Carlo.

Taking her mother's car was not out of the ordinary for Keisha. She had always stolen—or, to let her tell it, borrowed—her mother's car whenever her mother had male company at the house. Her mother drank and got high so much that she had never noticed that the keys or the car were missing.

As they had driven to the Motel 6 where New York was staying, adrenaline was pumping a mile a minute through Desiree's entire body as Keisha ran down the plan to her again, making sure that she was clear on things. While Desiree was a nervous wreck, Keisha was as cool as an ocean breeze.

When they had arrived at the motel, Keisha had pulled into the back and parked like she already had a room there. They had exited the Monte Carlo and entered the motel through the back door. They hiked up the two flights of stairs to the second floor where New York's room was located.

As planned, once they had reached the floor, Keisha had waited at the end of the hall with the two bats as Desiree had cautiously gone and knocked on New York's room door.

Desiree was just about to walk away from the door, disappointed that New York hadn't answered, when she heard his voice coming from the other side.

"Whatcha doin' here?"

"I just want to talk to you, I know—"

"About what?" he had cut her off.

"I know you didn't mean what happened earlier," Desiree had managed to say, just as she and Keisha had rehearsed.

"Who with you?" he had asked with skepticism.

"Nobody. I'm by myself," Desiree had replied, hoping he believed her.

He had opened the door. Desiree could see New York was semi-erect through his boxers. She had tried her hardest to hide her look of disgust and flashed him a painful smile. New York had stuck his head out into the hallway, looking left, then right, to confirm that Desiree was actually alone. Convinced, he had let her in and walked back to the bed. Desiree had closed the door behind her.

"So what you want to talk to me about?" New York had asked as he rubbed his dick.

"New York, I thought you cared about me. Why you do me like that?" Desiree had questioned as she fought back the tears.

She and Keisha had discussed what she should say, and Desiree thought she could handle being in front of him again, but now being face to face with New York released all the pain Desiree had endured from him earlier.

"Bitch, that's what you want to talk to me about? Get ya li'l dumb ass outta here before I—"

That was as far as he had gotten before Keisha had burst through the unlocked door, holding the two bats.

Before New York could really react, Keisha had closed the door and handed one of the bats to Desiree.

"What the fuck you country-ass bitches think you doin'?" he had asked, laughing aloud.

To answer his question Keisha had rolled up on him and swung the bat.

"Oh shit," New York had yelled, throwing up his hands up to protect himself. As Keisha had tried to knock his head clean off his shoulders.

She had connected with New York's forearm, and he fell to the floor.

"Bitch, you broke my arm," New York had spat, looking at Keisha.

Crack. Crack. Keisha had caught him again, once in the stomach and once on his left kneecap.

Desiree had stood there in shock as New York had spit blood. She had never seen Keisha act so out of control.

"Nigga, shut the fuck up. You want to take pussy without permission? Huh, muthafucka?" Keisha had asked.

Crack. Crack. Crack. Keisha had hit New York over and over, trying to knock his dick off, while New York screamed in agony.

"Des, get something to stuff in his mouth before somebody hears him," Keisha had commanded.

Desiree had found one of New York's socks and stuffed it in his mouth while their eyes met. Desiree didn't feel pity for him, because he had violated her and now he had to pay.

"Des, bust this muthafucka in his head," Keisha had barked. Desiree had just stood there, watching New York squirm in pain.

"Des, you hear me? Bust this nigga's shit." Keisha had repeated, but still Desiree stood there in a daze.

It wasn't until the blood spattered her face that she had snapped out of the trance. Keisha had done what she told Desiree to do.

"Where this nigga keep his shit at?" Keisha had asked herself as she began searching the room.

"Keisha, let's just go," Desiree had said as she used her shirt to wipe New York's blood off her face.

"Fuck that. Wait a minute. This nigga need to know that he can't just fuck with a bitch in the Dirty and think it ain't gonna cost him. Just wait for me at the door. I'm comin'."

"Okay, but hurry up." Desiree was anxious to get out of the room.

Desiree had headed toward the door. As she began to walk away from New York's body, she was stopped in her tracks. She felt the resistance on her leg, and without having to look down, she knew what immobilized her. New York had grabbed her by the ankle as tight as he could. More afraid than anything, Desiree had turned around and began beating New York's helpless body with her bat.

With each swing, images of what New York had done to her played inside Desiree's mind. Tears streamed down her face, and without realizing it, she had slipped into a blind rage.

Keisha had to call her girl's name six times before she had ceased her attack on New York's lifeless body. It didn't take a medical examiner to determine that it was over for New York. Keisha had counted at least fifteen times that Desiree had hit him directly in the head with the bat.

Once Desiree had come back to her senses and realized what she had done, the pit of her stomach began to boil, and she had run to the bathroom to vomit. She had reached the toilet just in time. Seeing New York's bashed-in face had sickened her. She could not believe she had beat him beyond recognition, but she was not in her right state of mind, so she really didn't know what to believe. She had reached for a towel and wet it, then wiped her face. When she had looked, the towel was soaked with blood—New York's blood.

She wasn't sure whether it was out of fear or habit, but Desiree began wiping down the bathroom area, making sure nothing could be traced back to her or Keisha.

She had headed back to New York's body. Still somewhat discombobulated, Desiree had looked around as Keisha continued her search. As she scanned the room, Desiree's gaze had zeroed in on the black-handled 007 blade that lay on top of the nightstand. New York usually used it to split his Dutches.

Judging by the smell of him when she entered the room, Desiree was sure New York hadn't taken a shower after he had raped her earlier that day. She knew her pubic hair and fluids were mixed with his, and she knew enough about DNA to know this incident could be linked to her because people knew about her and New York's dealings. Without hesitation, she had snatched up the 007 along with the gold lighter that lay next to it and walked over his body. She had kneeled and pulled New York's stained boxers off to expose his limp penis.

Keisha had searched high and low but still couldn't find what she was looking for. A movement from the corner of Keisha's eye caused her to turn her attention to Desiree. Before Keisha could even guess what her friend was about to do, she had watched as Desiree had sliced New York's manhood clean off. Her homegirl had stood over New York's body with his shriveled-up dick in her hand. Keisha had managed to keep down her lunch at the sight. She had turned away from the scene right before Desiree replaced the blade with the lighter.

There was not a lot of blood like Desiree thought there would be when she cut off New York's penis, which made it easier for her to burn off all his pubic hairs. She thought she was going to be sick again as the hairs crackled in the fire until she had burned them down to the skin. Once she was done, Desiree had gotten up with New York's dick still in her hand, walked to the bathroom, and flushed it down the toilet. She used the same towel from earlier to wipe off the 007 and put the blade and lighter in her pants pocket. She had also wiped down her bat and tucked both it and the towel under her arm to take with her. She then headed to the motel room door, partially conscious of what had just taken place. "Keisha, come on."

Keisha checked all but one place for New York's stash. There was no doubt in her mind now that it was there, and she was determined not to leave without it, especially now that New York had no use for it.

When she dropped to the floor and pulled back the covers, she smiled. "Jackpot!" she said to herself as she pulled the duffle bag from under the bed. She jumped up, placed the bag on the bed, and unzipped it. Once she saw the money, drugs, and the gun, she zipped the bag back up and threw it on her shoulder. As she was exiting the room, she remembered something.

Desiree still waited impatiently at the door, peeking in and out to be sure the hallways were clear.

"Keisha, what you doin'?" she had asked, growing more impatient with her friend when Keisha stopped at the bathroom.

"Hold on for a sec," Keisha had told her, coming out of the bathroom with a towel in her hand. Keisha began backtracking their every move, wiping down any and everything she thought she and Desiree may have touched. It was times like this Desiree knew why the two of them got along so well. They were just alike. When she was done, Keisha snatched all of the linen from the bed and stuffed it into New York's duffle bag, then picked up the bag and headed back over to the door.

"Des, did you clean up the bathroom?" Keisha had asked.

"Yeah. Now let's get the hell outta here," Desiree had answered.

"Alright, come on. We out."

Chapter One

"Shit," Desiree cursed as she looked at her watch on the bathroom sink. The ice-bezeled Marc Jacob read ten to twelve, which meant she was running late.

Had she been on schedule, she would have already been pulling up in front of the Taj Mahal club at 12:00 A.M. where her crew was waiting for her. Instead, Desiree was just hopping out of the shower, naked as the day she was born.

There was no way she could be on time. It would take at least twenty minutes for her to dress and be out the door, and another forty to reach the Durham hot spot, putting her arrival at well after one o'clock in the morning.

Desiree snatched the towel off the shower rack and wrapped it around her dripping-wet body, tucking it in at her cleavage. Once in her bedroom, she unwrapped the towel and quickly began to dry off.

It never failed. She had always been the one out of the four of them to either be the last one ready or the latest to show up whenever it came to her and her crew hooking up. Despite them being accustomed to her tardiness, Desiree knew she wouldn't hear the end of it from Keisha, Pam and Tasha.

As she slipped into her powder-blue lace thong and fastened its matching bra, Desiree couldn't help but notice herself in the full-length wall mirror.

"Damn, I look good," she complimented herself aloud, admiring her own beauty. At twenty-seven, she was satisfied with her God-given features. Her butter-pecan skin was flawless and as smooth as a baby's bottom. Her natural auburn shoulder-length hair highlighted her soft light brown eyes, giving her a look that could easily be mistaken for a Spanish *mami*. Her breasts, often referred to as a "mouthful" by men, still possessed the youthfulness of a teenager. She bore a flat midsection that had a trail of silky auburn hair, which started at the bottom of her navel and faded into her neatly trimmed bush. Her waistline was petite, but her hips protruded on the sides, and her apple bottom was nice and firmly shaped. She could give the video vixen, Ki Toy, a run for her money.

It was the same features that kept her pockets laced, Desiree thought, as she turned around. She looked over her shoulder to check out her backside. Careful not to disturb her perfectly laid hair, Desiree pulled the black tightly fitted Christian Dior T-shirt over her head before fighting to zip and fasten the matching black painted-on jeans. The radio alarm clock read 12:21 A.M. by the time she slipped on her black, red, and white Manolo Blahniks. Seeing that it had taken her a little over half an hour to get dressed, Desiree hurried to the bathroom, sprayed herself down with Obsession perfume, and grabbed her watch. She snatched up her Dior sunglasses, keys to her Honda Accord, and her baby nine-millimeter off the nightstand. Picking up her matching Dior bag, she threw the gun inside before she bolted out the door.

"Where the hell this hoe at?" Keisha asked no one in particular as she, Tasha, and Pam all sat in her Honda Civic smoking weed.

"I don't know, but I wish she'd bring her ass on, so we can get up in there before all them bitches snatch up the ballas," offered Pam, who sat in the passenger seat in front of her sister, Tasha, and pulled on the blunt. "Look at all these muthafuckin' Benzes and SUVs out this bitch with New York and New Jersey tags. It gots to be some potential up in that muthafucka."

"You ain't neva lied, sis," Tasha joined in from the back. "But when you gonna pass the blunt? You hogging it all up and shit."

"I know, right?" Keisha said in agreement. "Puff, puff, pass, hoe. You know that." Pam laughed as she passed the weed back to her sister. She was known in the clique for being a blunt hog, which was why the complaints didn't come as a surprise.

Normally she didn't have to worry about sharing her weed with her sister or her girl because she would have driven her own car to the club, but that night they rode in Keisha's Honda Civic.

They all owned Hondas, and when they sometimes traveled back-to-back, one would think they were Honda models they looked so good in them. Desiree had a cherry-red Accord, Keisha a pearl-green Civic, while Tasha had a canary-yellow Prelude and Pam had a royal-blue one.

"I hope we run across some niggas like we did two months ago, when we caught those clowns from Philly slipping. Okay," Keisha replied, giving Tasha a high five.

"Keish, did you hear about them new niggas over in Dunn making some noise?" Pam asked. "I heard they getting money and tryna fuck every skank that'll open her legs up to 'em."

"Yeah, I heard. Them niggas kill me from up north. They think just 'cause they from out of state, they some type of celebrities when they come down to the dirty. Actin' like they Jigga Man or some damn body, and we supposed to just drop our muthafuckin' panties just 'cause they from New Yawk, or wherever the hell they from."

"I think most of them niggas that come down here be frontin'," Pam added. "You see the way they be actin' all hard, like they some killas, and then when they get a couple of dollars they think they kingpins? I bet they come down here 'cause the real gangstas ran them from their own hoods and they can't get no ass back home."

"That's alright though, 'cause if we run across their asses, they gonna see just why they call this shit *the dirty*," Keisha said deviously.

"I'm wit' you on dat, gurl. I could use a couple more dollars anyway, 'cause my stash getting kinda low," Tasha added.

"Your stash always kinda low," Pam retorted.

"Shit, it takes money to live how I like to live."

"Exactly. You need to slow ya ass down and start savin' dat shit," Keisha spat. "This shit ain't gonna last forever."

Over the years, Keisha found herself getting on Tasha's elaborate spending and flashy lifestyle. She tried not to be so hard on her childhood friend because she was aware of the reason for her behavior. Keisha could still remember as if it were yesterday how Tasha always cried about the boys in school teasing her about her homely-looking clothes. Of course Keisha, who played the role of big sister, did what she had to do to protect Tasha, just as Keisha had also done for Desiree. Sensing that she had offended her crimey, Keisha attempted to soften the blow.

"Don't worry about it, Tash. We gonna be straight in a minute. They got niggas posted up in hotels all around us, and some niggas even coppin' trailers and opening up shop. As long as these simple muthafuckas keep comin' down here thinkin' they housing shit, not knowing the real deal about the south, we gonna be a'ight. We gonna show they asses some real southern hospitality. With our looks and these bomb shots we got between our legs, we bound to come up on some decent licks, and when we do, we gonna handle our business. Yo, Pam, where you get this weed from? This some good shit. I'm feeling it already."

"Yeah, I see. Talking about me, bitch. You damn near took the rest of that shit to the head," Pam replied.

"Fuck you." Keisha laughed as the weed continued to have its effect on her.

"I got it from one of them Jamaicans that be pumping out of Meadowlark Apartments."

"How much you get from him?"

"He sold me an ounce for half price 'cause he think he gonna get some pussy."

"Shit. Keep him in the cut, gurl. We might need him for something down the line 'cause I know he gonna blow off sellin' this shit. And you know them Rasta muthafuckas be having this shit by the trailer loads. He could be a potential vic."

"I got it," Pam interjected.

"Look, there go dat bitch right there." Tasha pointed in the direction of where Desiree had just parked.

Keisha began flicking her high beams to get Desiree's attention once she saw her step out the Accord. "Look at this heifer, thinking she's cute," Keisha said.

Upon seeing the flashing lights, Desiree started toward Keisha's Civic. "Damn, where the fuck you been?" Keisha asked, rolling down her window once Desiree was at the car. A cloud of smoke smacked Desiree dead in the face as it poured out of the car window.

"We been out here for more than an hour, waiting on your ass," Keisha complained.

"I know. My bad. I'm here now. Hey, Pam. What's up, Tash?" Desiree greeted her partners in crime.

"Hey, Des," Pam replied.

"Hey, gurl, witcha slow ass," Tasha greeted.

"Whatever. Damn. What y'all smoking? That shit smell good."

"Some trees Pam got from some Jamaican nigga," Tasha answered, taking another pull.

"Tasha, let me hit some of that," Desiree said.

"Here." Tasha leaned over and handed Desiree the nearly finished blunt.

"Um, stay on this nigga, Pam. We may need him for something," Desiree said after hitting the weed.

All three women in the car looked at one another then at Desiree and burst into laughter.

"What's so funny? Y'all some silly bitches," Desiree barked. She was completely clueless.

"Nah," Tasha replied, catching her breath, "Keish had said the same thing to Pam just before you rolled up."

Tasha wiped the tears of laughter from her eyes. Now it was Desiree's turn to laugh. It was no secret she and Keisha had a habit of thinking alike. They'd been saying the same thing at the same time ever since they were little girls. Although Tasha and Pam were sisters, it was Desiree and Keisha who people thought were blood relatives.

"Hurry up and finish that so we can go in. There's money to be made," Keisha reminded as she, Tasha, and Pam exited the Civic.

Chapter Two

The Taj Mahal in Durham was the place to be on Sunday night, especially if you wanted to be where all the moneymakers and some of the South's best-bred females were. As usual, the club was jam-packed—men and women were wall to wall. Everybody who was somebody was in the house, from athletes and entertainers to hustlers and gangstas, not to mention the low-budget and high-maintenance chicks. The club could have been a duplicate for the infamous Tunnel in Manhattan on Sunday nights. Everywhere you turned, there were people flossing Prada, Gucci, Fendi, Coogie, Iceberg, Christian Dior, Timberlands, Air Force Ones, gators, and even ostrich. Between all the platinum and ice that was being worn, the club was lit up like the Hollywood billboard.

As the girls all slid toward the bar with the intention of getting their drink on, Desiree took a quick scan of the crowded room, her gaze skipping from table to table. She pretty much had an idea who was who and what was what.

She noticed people sitting at the first couple of tables. Niggas rocked iced-out white-gold chains—fake platinum wannabes, they were called. Others chipped in to cop a bottle or two of Cristal or Moët. They had beer money with champagne taste.

The next few tables were the brothers who looked as though they had spent their entire stash on the jewels and the four bottles that sat before them. Desiree continued her evaluation of who was really balling and who was really frontin', and her gaze landed in the VIP section. It was apparent to her who the true number-one stunners were in the house. "Bingo," she uttered under her breath.

These were the brothers who had on the official "Big Boy" status platinum and diamonds, with the bug-eyed headlights in their ears and below-zero-degree wrists. They were the ones with the assorted drinks like Belvedere, Armandel, and Hennessy by the gallons, the yellow bottles of Cristal and Moët at their tables and throngs of females hovering around them.

Any chick with even half an eye could see those were the niggas to cut into, and Desiree had two perfectly good eyes with 20/20 vision. Although there were several groupies lingering, Desiree saw no possible threats. She didn't think any of the women could stand next to her and her squad. She and her crew were indeed the hottest bitches in the spot that night, she thought.

Sipping on the Absolut and cranberry juice Tasha had passed her, Desiree was caught up in figuring out the best approach to make their way over into the VIP section. Her train of thought was broken when she noticed one of the guys signaling for her. *Oh no this nigga ain't,* she thought. She didn't care who he was—or who he thought he was— or how much paper he probably had, nobody signaled for her with his hand like some traffic cop. There was no way she was going to go over there so he'd think she was just some average chickenhead clucking for the night. She signaled for him to come over to her.

A grin came across his face. He stared at Desiree for a minute, leaned over to whisper something to one of his boys, then got up.

"Des, you see that fine-ass nigga coming over here?" Tasha said, trying to be inconspicuous.

"Chill. I see," Desiree mumbled.

"Work ya shit then, bitch," Keisha said with her back to them, not even bothering to turn around.

Pam didn't utter a word. She was too busy ordering her third drink.

"What's up, lady?" the kid spoke after walking up on Desiree.

At first sight, Desiree rated him fine as hell, but she tried not to get caught up into looks because she figured all money looked the same. However, she couldn't help but admire him, because lately, the niggas with the money had been looking like trolls and monkeys. This guy was light-skinned with deep brown eyes, dimples, nice teeth, low-cut hair, and he was short and stocky, like he worked out. *Probably been to jail before,* she thought.

"What's up wit' you?" she asked back.

"I was just over there trying to enjoy myself when I seen you and figured I'd call you so we could enjoy ourselves together, but you shot me down and made me walk over here."

"You sound like you mad you had to walk over here."

"Nah, not at all. It was definitely worth the walk."

Desiree had to smile, 'cause just like the rest of them, this nigga thought he was smooth with his shit and slick with his tongue.

"Why didn't you come over there when I asked you, though?" he asked.

"'Cause it looked to me like you had enough groupies over there occupying your space, and I'm far from a groupie."

He laughed. "Alright, I respect that, but if you woulda came over, it woulda been all about you, 'cause them shorties wasn't doin' nothing but drinking up all me and my people's shit."

"Um-hmm, I bet," Desiree said, giving him attitude.

"Forget that back there though. I'm over here now, so what's up? What you trying to get into for the night?"

Desiree couldn't believe this cocky-ass nigga, pressing her like he knew he was going to get some after just five minutes of conversation.

"I ain't trying to get into nothing besides my bed after I leave here and get something to eat from the Waffle House," she told him.

"Nah, I didn't mean it like that. I was just asking 'cause I was trying to see you again, either later or another day. As a matter of fact, let's start over. My name's Stacks. What's yours?"

"Desiree."

"Nice to meet you, Desiree."

"You too," she replied.

"Who you wit'? I mean, I know you ain't wit' your man, 'cause any nigga that'll leave something as hot as you by yourself is either crazy, careless, or both."

Stacks made Desiree smile again, but not to the point that she let down her guard. "You right. I ain't here wit' my man, and I don't have a man either, which you should've just come out and asked rather than beating around the bush. I'm here wit' my girls. This is my girl Tasha and her sister, Pam, and that's my girl Keisha," she said, pointing to each of them.

On cue, they all hit him with their million-dollar smiles. They had been through this type of scene thousands of times with one another.

"Nice to meet you," Stacks replied, observing the other three women. "Those jokers over there is my brother Styles, wit' the blue Yankees fitted hat, and my man Don is next to him. Like I said before, we were over there sipping on something. The four of you are welcome to come through and join us, if you want to."

Both Tasha and Pam looked like they were ready to take him up on his offer, but before they got the chance, Desiree spoke up.

"No, thank you. Like I said, it looks like you and your peoples have enough groupies over there occupying your space, and we're not groupies. We're never last choice sweetheart, always first."

"Shorty, I told you it wasn't even like that, but since you put it that way, where I come from, I always save the best for last."

Desiree gave credit when credit was due. This nigga was definitely smooth with his shit, but not smooth enough to make her change her mind.

"Maybe some other time."

"Yeah, no doubt. Ladies, enjoy the rest of your evening. It was nice meeting you." He turned his attention back to Desiree. "It was a pleasure. I'll see you." Stacks walked back to his table.

"Damn, bitch. What was your problem? That nigga had money written all over his forehead," Tasha said.

"Yeah, the nigga even smelled like that shit," Pam added.

"Desiree, what was up wit' that, baby girl?" Keisha asked.

"Nothing. Why y'all buggin' the fuck out? Did you see the way the nigga was looking at me? Did you hear the way he was trying to holla at me? I ain't blow nothing. That nigga feeling me, and I know he ain't gonna stop until he get to know me. How long have we been doing this? How many times you bitches know me to fuck something up? Never, 'cause I haven't. If we would've went over there drinking wit' them niggas, then we wouldn't have been no different than them other dumb-ass, free-pussy-giving-away-ass bitches. We ain't goin' out like that. Trust me, I'll see him again, and when I do, I'll give him some play."

"Yo, son, who was them bad muthafuckas you were over there hollering at by the bar?" Styles said to his brother.

"Fuck who they are. Why the fuck you ain't bring'em over here?" Don asked.

"Nigga, don't you think I tried that? Shorty I was trying to holla at was fronting, but a few of her partners acted like they wanted to come through though."

"I know that ain't Mr. Mac talking like that," Don teased. "Not the nigga who thinks no shorty can resist his G, the nigga that bag the baddest bitches in the world. You let some country chick shut ya shit down? No good." Don laughed.

"Nigga, shut da fuck up. Just 'cause I ain't bag her tonight don't mean I ain't gonna never bag her. Shit ain't over. Believe that."

Chapter Three

"Bitch, wake ya ass up," Keisha shouted through the receiver.

"Hey, girl. What's up? I'm woke. Whatcha doin'?"

"Nuthin'. Just chillin', smoking some of that shit Pam got from that dread."

"Yeah, that's some good smoke," Desiree agreed.

"This is the best shit we had down here in a minute. I told her to give that nigga some ass and find out as much as she can, so we can knock him off."

"I hear that, but Keisha, you know them Jamaican niggas are crazy and they keep a lot of guns wit' 'em."

"Yeah, you right, but like every other nigga that think they invincible, them niggas would never think a bunch a pretty bitches like us could get at them," she said as she took another pull of the blunt.

"Girl, you crazy," Desiree said, laughing. "But you know I'm down wit' you all the way. You spoke to Tasha today?"

"Yeah, I spoke to her trick ass. She's in Charlotte wit' that nigga from Jersey with the 750 she met at Flavas last month when we were in Fayetteville. Sometimes I wonder how we stayed friends this long, 'cause she ain't on it like we on it. I don't understand why Tasha and Pam keep giving their pussy away. You know niggas ain't gonna buy the cow if they getting the milk for free. I told her ass if by the end of the month she ain't producing shit, then whether she wit' it or not, we gonna get that nigga, with his fake cool ass."

"I know what you're saying, but maybe they do be getting broke off when they be fucking with them niggas."

"If that's true, then why the hell Tash was complaining to me last weekend about how she's with another lick 'cause her stash low? How she gonna be fucking a nigga pushing a new 750 Beemer and doin' big things, and her stash low? Come on, Des. You do the math."

"Yeah, that is fucked up, but those are our girls, and whenever we need them, they always come through for us on some nice licks."

"Oh, that reminds me. Remember that short, stocky, light-skinned nigga you shot down that night at the Taj Mahal?"

"What about him?"

"Him and them two niggas he was with is the niggas we been hearing about over in Dunn."

"Stop playing."

"I ain't bullshitting, girl. I heard that night we were there, after we left, every bitch in the club was trying to leave with them. I was getting my manicure and pedicure at the nail shop, and I ran into Tomeesha—you know how she likes to run her mouth. All them bitches out there do, but anyway, I overheard her saying how all the bitches was sweating them 'cause they all had Range Rovers, and how them two niggas Styles and Don snatched up Monique and Tangie from Raleigh. I wouldn't've even knew who she was talking about if she wouldn't have said Stacks. She was saying how the nigga Styles and Don left with Monique and Tangie but the niggas Stacks left by himself. Then she went on running her dumb-ass mouth, talking about why they be riding around out there in rentals when they got Rovers. How dumb can that bitch be? Little as Dunn is, everybody know if you come through in some shit like that, ya ass is goin' to jail. One bitch said that the nigga Stacks had hooked up with Rachel, but when he heard his name in the streets from fucking with her, he cut her off. Other than that, they don't know any other bitches he ever fucked with. They said that Styles and Don ran through the whole town, though. And that the most they break a bitch off with is Waffle House money. I heard they got a bunch of young-ass niggas pumping for them over on Elm and Vance and Grove Park, and they sell weight to a lot of other niggas that hustle. From what I hear, though, that nigga Stacks is the mastermind behind their whole little team. Them niggas sound like some vics to me. What you think, girl?"

"It sounds like them niggas cheap to me, at least two of them anyway, and as far as that nigga Stacks, he don't sound like much either. For all we know, them Rovers could be rentals, too, or tagged up. You know how niggas be stunting 'cause they out of state, but if you think there's something there, you know I'm down for whatever."

"Yeah, I think it's something there. Why else would that nigga name be Stacks? I know they don't call him that for nothing. He must be known for sitting on stacks or stacking his dough or something."

"Bitch, you shot the fuck out. That weed got you bugging."

"Nah, this weed got me right. Matter of fact, let me give Pam a call and see what she found out about that Jamaican nigga."

"Alright, girl. I'll talk to you later."

"Okay. Page me when you step out, and think about how you gonna get close to that nigga Stacks."

Chapter Four

"Styles, count this. Don, count this one." Stacks threw them each a stack of dough. "Don't forget to separate all that shit, either. You know how I hate having all those singles and fives up in there. That shit be too bulky when I'm going up top to cop, and plus, that nigga Nike be wanting me to wait until he count all that shit before I leave, so I ain't taking no small bills no more. I don't even want any tens up in there, if you can help it. We'll keep all that shit and split it between the three of us. Styles, where that paper at I told you to go get from them niggas over on Elm and Vance?"

"I got it. It's in the back already, rubberbanded up," Styles answered.

"How much was it?"

"Altogether it was eighteen Gs and some change. Like about three Gs of it is singles, fives, and tens."

"Alright, just give me the fifteen, then. Don, you picked that dough up from them niggas on the other side yet?" Stacks inquired.

"Yeah. I went through and scooped what they had. Them two niggas Marcy and BB told me they'd have theirs later tonight, but on the tally it was a little over eight Gs. I gotta separate it, though. I just counted it on some quick shit," Don replied.

"Where's it at? Give it to me. I'll do it."

"Aye, yo, Stacks?" Styles called.

"What up?"

"Why don't you let me take that trip up top? I'm homesick like a muthafucka. This south shit is fuckin' with me, son. It's been a minute since I've been down here, and shit getting boring, kid," Styles complained.

"Nigga, what you talking about, shit getting boring? This ain't no vacation. We trying to get paper, not have fun. You can go back up top anytime you want, but when you do, don't try to come back down. I can't tell ya ass is bored, all these country chicks you and Don fucking. You niggas think more about pussy than you do paper, but if you wasn't getting paper, you wouldn't be getting all that pussy."

"Yo, why you coming at us like that, Stacks?" Don stepped in the conversation. "Like we ya shorties or something. We suppose to be a team, but here it is, you trying to chastise us, dawg. What's good?"

"What's good? I'll tell you what's good. You niggas down here getting all comfortable and shit with these chicks, fucking crazy like it's going out of style instead of staying on top of things. Since when we ever let a muthafucka dictate when they gonna pay us and you let that slide? You know what I think? I think you probably fucking one of them niggas' sisters or something, and on the strength of that, you rolled with that shit. Them niggas probably fucking our work up, and now we might have to make examples out these niggas and blow this spot, all because you letting ya dick do the thinking."

"Bro, it ain't even like that," Styles said.

"Yeah, we be fucking mad chicks, but me and Don don't let that interfere with what we suppose to be down here doing. Ain't nothing changed. M.O.B—money over bitches—son. If them niggas fuck our work up then we gonna handle that, that's all. You know I ain't just gonna up and bounce on you and Don. It ain't even like that. I was just saying that I miss the yiddy, that's all, but if it ain't meant for me to go up top, then fuck it, I'll get there when I get there. You my big brother, nigga, and I know you know what's best. If you want me to chill on the chicks, then that's what I'm gonna do. Fuck these bitches. I'll wait until we get back home."

"Yo, I'm not telling you two niggas not to fuck with no chicks. I know you some li'l horny muthafuckas."

Styles and Don laughed a little.

"I'm just saying, we gots to be careful. You been seeing that shit on the news, how they been finding niggas from Jersey, New York, Philly, and Connecticut bodied up in some of these tele's down here, and you been hearing about niggas from up top getting set up and robbed. Trust me, it ain't just these country niggas we gotta watch out for. It's these chicks too. I bet money that out of all that shit that's been happening in Charlotte, Durham, Raleigh, and even around this area, some, if not all them shits involve a chick. That's why we gots to be on point at all times 'cause like niggas, bitches can have cold hearts, too, and you best believe that the word is out that we getting paper, especially after bringing our Ranges down here and taking them to the club that night. I knew that was a bad idea, but I did it on the strength of you two niggas wanting to show off and floss. Now damn near every nigga and broad in the area know we seeing some type of paper 'cause Ranges ain't cheap. I just hope that shit ain't get us hot, 'cause we don't need that type of heat."

Don spoke up. "Yo, Stacks, my bad, son, you right. I shouldn't've took offense to what you said. I know you only looking out for us and like Styles said, if them two niggas fucked our dough up, we gonna handle that. I'm gonna handle it personally. I ain't even gonna front. You hit that shit right on the head. I'm fucking both them niggas' sisters, that's why I probably let them lame-ass excuses they hit me with ride."

"Don't worry about it, kid. It happens to the best of us, and I knew ya little dirty-dick ass was knocking them niggas' family," Stacks said, laughing.

They all laughed.

"Let's do what we came down here for and stack this paper. Distractions, especially pussy, come with a penalty," Stacks cautioned.

"True dat," Styles and Don said in unison.

Chapter Five

"Pam, you sure this nigga sitting on what you say he is?" Keisha asked.

"Girl, you know I don't be bullshitting when it comes to shit like this. The last time I was with that nigga, he got a page from somebody and called them back. He must've thought I was still asleep 'cause he didn't even get out of the bed so I couldn't hear his conversation. I really couldn't catch everything 'cause he was talking all that Jamaican shit, but I caught when he said forty grand was nothing. He told whoever was on the phone to come get that. When he hung up, he climbed out of bed, went to this Bob Marley painting on the wall, and kept looking back at the bed at me to make sure I was sleep. I was laying there with one eye opened just enough to see what he was doing. When he moved the picture, the nigga had a wall safe behind it, and when he opened it, the first thing I saw him pull out of it was a chrome piece, some big ole shit. I think it was a .45 or something. Then I watched him take out some stacks and stuff 'em in a drawstring bag. Right before he closed it, I caught a glimpse of what was left up in the safe. That muthafucka had stacks of money piled up in that bitch. If I had to guess, it was more than a hundred grand up in there."

"Bitch, get the fuck outta here," an unbelieving Keisha said.

"Pam, are you serious?" Desiree said, and her eyes lit up.

"Why wouldn't I be?"

"If that's true, we gonna have to put that dread head to bed for that shit," Keisha retorted.

"Keisha, let's think this thing through before we make any decisions," Desiree responded. "Pam, how many times you been to his house?"

"Umm, let me see. Five, no, this last time makes six."

"Not including the one you seen him take out the safe, have you ever seen him with any other gun, or did you see any lying around the house?"

"Desiree, you acting like I'm new to this. I peeped everything out every time that nigga took me to the crib. I could walk in that muthafucka blindfolded and point out everything in that nigga house. I never said he ain't have no guns. Yeah, that nigga got guns all over. He has his own little arsenal up in there. We fucked in every room in that piece, and he got a joint for every room. Soon as you come in, you in the living room. The nigga got a pump right behind the door next to a coat rack. He got a Glock stashed in the couch, and in his kitchen he keeps a Tech on the side of his microwave. This muthafucka thinks he's the Jamaican Scarface, too, always pulling his AK out from up under the bed, wiping it down, trying to sound like Tony Montana, talking about, 'say hello to my little friend.' Yeah, girl, that nigga got some guns."

"Okay, well, we know we can't be half-stepping when we run down on his ass, that's all," Keisha said. "Niggas like him is going to go all out, so most likely it's gonna get ugly. Pam, you just gonna have to play your part to a tee if we gonna make this happen. I got this all mapped out once we get inside. You just gotta get us up in there. First thing you do when the nigga let you in is get close enough to make sure he ain't got no heat tucked under his shirt or nothing. Your main objective is to get the door unlocked for us once he let you in. Then keep the nigga occupied. I need you to run that nigga whole layout down to us from front to back and top to bottom so we'll know how to move once we get inside."

"I got you," Pam said before she began to describe the dread's crib.

Then Keisha told them all what they were supposed to do, as the three other women listened closely.

Chapter Six

"Damn, nigga. You tried to rip my shit in half just now with all that rough shit," Pam said to the dread.

"Mi a punanny murderer, ya know. Yardman ah murder the pumpum 'nuff times. Dat's why all de gyal dem love mi."

Pam let out a fake laugh. "Dread, you crazy. Shit, my pussy sore as hell. I need some ice for my shit."

"Go look inna di fridge. Mi have an ice pack inna di freezer."

"Yeah, that'll work. I'll be right back."

"Yuh hear me. Hurry up and come back. Mi have a big spliff waitin' fi yuh."

"I'm with that."

Pam climbed out the bed, snatched up the sheet, and wrapped it around her naked body. "Dread, why you putting another condom on? You might as well take that shit off and throw it away."

"Weh yuh mean? Mi no done wid it yet, just hurry back, yuh hear?"

"Nigga, you ain't getting none of this for at least a few hours. I'm serious. My shit is sore."

Pam wasn't serious about her coochie being sore, but she was indeed serious about the dread not getting anymore, not only for a couple of hours, but forever. Not from her or any other female.

She climbed out the bed, grabbed her panties, then headed toward the kitchen. When she reached the kitchen, instead of grabbing the ice pack from out of the fridge, she went straight to the microwave and searched for the Tech-nine she remembered seeing on the side when she and the dread had sexed on the kitchen counter. Once she located it, she ran with it to the front door and unlocked it.

"Damn, bitch, it's about time," Keisha said as she, Tasha, and Desiree entered the living room. "I thought you fell in love with the nigga's dick and crossed us."

"Keisha, shh. You want that nigga to hear you?" Pam whispered, sounding somewhat paranoid.

Desiree grabbed the pump from behind the door and checked to see how many shells were in it.

"Did you move the nigga's gun from up under the bed?" Desiree asked.

"Yeah, I took care of that. The nigga was so caught up in me sucking his little Jamaican dick he didn't even notice me reaching for it. I got it right here." Pam unwrapped the sheet, revealing the AK. "I didn't know how the fuck I was gonna get it up outta there butt-ass naked, but then it dawned on me to grab the sheet off the bed." She pointed to the other gun. "This is the Tech I told you about that be in the kitchen," she said, holding up the other weapon.

"Pam, what you do so long? Da spliff almost done," the dread yelled from the bedroom.

"Oh shit, I gotta go 'fore that nigga come out here," Pam said.

"Go 'head. We got it from here. We right behind you, sis," Tasha said.

Pam started back toward the room, stopping to grab the ice pack. When she returned, the dread was still lying in the bed with the condom on, puffing on a blunt that looked like it was once a phat one.

"Damn, you wasn't bullshitting when you said the shit was almost done," Pam said as she approached the bed.

"Wheh ya mean? Mi a big ganja blowa. Mi nuh wait for no one," Dread said as smoke escaped his mouth and nose.

"Nigga, let me get some of dat." Pam reached for the L.

She took a few pulls, held it in for a minute, then let some smoke go from her mouth up through her nostrils. "Umm. This shit is the bomb." She took a couple more tokes and passed it back to him.

Dread took the blunt. "Yo, yuh nuh know how fi smoke ganja. You haffi tek long pulls, not short ones. You no smoke right," he said as he took a pull as if to show her.

He leaned his head back, enjoying the effect the weed had on him. The dread momentarily closed his eyes to enjoy his high.

Boom! Keisha kicked the door open, holding the dread's Glock.

"Bumbo clot," the dread yelled as he tried to reach under the bed for his AK, only to find out it wasn't there.

"Nigga, if you move, I'll blow ya muthafuckin' dick off," Keisha told him as Desiree and Tasha entered the room.

"What ah gwan? Dem gyal mussi mad, comin' up in 'ere like dem a murderers," he said, looking around the room.

"Shut the fuck up," Desiree said. "Pam, put ya shit on, bitch. We ain't got time to be bullshitting."

Pam hopped out of the bed and got dressed.

"Blood clot, skettel set up da rude boy, trying fi kill mi off. If mi live through this, ya dead, all oono dead!" he yelled.

"D, point that Tech right at that nigga shit. If he say one more thing funny, shoot his dick off," Keisha told Desiree.

"I got you," Desiree said, taking her position.

"Now, nigga, I'ma ask you one time and one time only. What's the combination to ya safe?"

"What safe? Mi nuh know weh yuh a chat 'bout."

"Oh, you don't know what I'm talking about, huh? Pam, move that muthafuckin' painting," Keisha demanded. When she did, there was the safe, just as clear as day.

"You still don't know what safe I'm talking about, nigga?" Keisha asked again as she cocked the Glock back, but the dread said nothing.

"I see we might have to go to plan B, because this nigga ain't telling us nuthin'. Tasha, break out that drill, 'cause that shit look like them same cheap-ass safes all them other niggas be having."

Tasha opened the duffle bag and pulled out the drill. Then she went to the safe.

"You can make this shit a whole lot easier if you just give up the combination, and we'll be up outta here," Pam tried to reason with him.

"Pussy hole, nuh chat tuh mi, guh suck yuh madda," the dread said to her.

"Oh shit," Tasha yelled.

"What? What's wrong?" the girls asked in unison.

"This muthafuckin' shit was already open."

"Get the fuck outta here," Keisha said.

"I ain't bullshitting. Come look at this shit," Tasha urged.

When they went to see the safe, they all had a look of surprise on their faces.

"Holy shit," Keisha said stunned.

"Damn," Desiree responded, shaking her head.

"Yeah, this what I'm talking 'bout," Pam followed.

The four of them were so hyped about the stacks of hundred-dollar bills in the safe, they almost forgot about the dread. Keisha saw him try to make a move for something near the bed, and when he turned around, she planted a bullet right in his chest. The noise startled Desiree and Pam, and they immediately turned to look at the dread.

"Bitch, didn't I tell you to watch that muthafucka?" Keisha screamed at Pam.

"I was until this bitch started yelling," Pam said.

"Don't fucking put that shit on me," Tasha barked.

The dread was bleeding from the chest, but he wasn't dead. He had snuck into the drawer of the nightstand and pulled out a snub-nosed .44 Bulldog, which was still in his hand.

"Both of y'all chill the fuck out," Desiree said as she walked over to the dread and put two more in his head with the .38 she carried. There was no doubt about it now, the dread was definitely dead.

"Damn, Desiree. You had to do it like that?" Tasha asked, a little shaken.

"Fuck you mean, bitch? Wasn't the plan to rob and kill this Jamaican muthafucka?"

"Yeah, but..." was all Tasha could get out.

"But nothing. That nigga dead now, so don't worry about him. Worry about getting all that shit out that safe and putting it in that muthafucking duffle bag."

Tasha just started taking the money out the safe.

"Keisha, make sure you find the shell," Desiree told her friend. "Pam, go all around the house and wipe down everything you touched in this spot, and the shit you can't remember if you touched, too. We gonna get up outta here. You know where we'll be. We'll meet you there."

"Okay, I'll catch up to y'all later. Be careful getting up outta here, 'cause somebody might've heard the shots," Pam advised.

"I doubt it, but we will, and you be careful too. Don't leave nothing behind," Keisha instructed.

"I won't."

"Alright. See you when you get there."

Chapter Seven

"What's up, Stacks? You're looking good. Where you been hiding at?" Vanessa asked.

Vanessa was one of the baddest chicks around Stacks' way, and she was also one of the few who were getting money around there, too. Although she was a couple of years older, she and Stacks had practically grown up together and traveled in the same circles.

Vanessa was a thorough chick—she put mad work in around the hood. She was definitely a bitch you didn't want to fuck over. Back in the day she did stick-ups with niggas from the block then switched to hustling when crack hit the scene. She used to beat just as many niggas' asses as she did females, and she'd cut or shoot somebody just as quick.

One time she got into a beef with another thoroughbred chick, and they went blade for blade. Vanessa sliced the girl up like she was a Japanese Samurai. The girl did manage to catch Vanessa on the side of her face, but Vanessa only ended up with fifteen stitches. When the cut finally healed, it looked like a little scorpion on the left side of her cheek, which made her look even sexier and harder. Niggas on the block nicknamed her "The Scorpion Queen."

There were only a few dudes she fucked with, all heavyweight niggas in the game. For some reason, something always happened to the cats she messed with. Either they got murdered, or got cased up so bad that they weren't going to see the streets for a long time. Nobody around the way really tried to push up on her or fucked with her like that because they knew about her history with men and thought she was bad luck, but as far as everything else, Vanessa was like any other nigga or chick in the hood who was getting money. She was part of their street family.

"I was away on vacation down south," Stacks replied.

"Vacation, my ass, nigga. I heard about you. You trying to get that OT money, huh?"

Stacks smiled. "Oh yeah, that's what you heard?"

"That's the word on the street, but I don't believe everything I hear anyway. Besides, your business is your business, so do you 'cause I'ma do me."

"It's like that, V?"

"Yeah, nigga, it's like that." Vanessa smirked. "You the one acting like ya shit's top secret."

Stacks laughed. "Nah, it ain't even like that. I just don't be wanting my business out in the street like that. You know how niggas get when they hear a muthafucka doing their thing. They start hating and shit, and you fucked me up when you said that's the word on the street, that's all."

"My bad, Stacks. I feel where you coming from. I was playing with you. It was just nice to see a good nigga after dealing with all these snakes out here, but I did hear that you was blowing in the dirty, though."

"Li'l something," Stacks said.

"I ain't mad atcha. You deserve it."

Bzzz. Bzzz. Bzzz. Stacks' cell phone vibrated.

"Yeah, what's up?" he answered.

"Yo, Stacks, guess what, son?" Don's voice was laced with tension.

"Don, what? What's good, son?" Stacks asked, becoming alarmed.

"Yo, some fucked-up shit happened, B."

Instantly thinking the worse, Stacks responded, "Don't tell me that, kid. What happened to my brother, dawg?"

"Nah, nah. Styles right here. Everything good with us."

"Well, nigga, why you calling me like this, sounding all crazy and shit, like something happened to my fuckin' brother?"

"My bad, son, I ain't mean to scare you like that, but some shit did happen though. It's crazy down here right now."

"What happened?"

"Yo, you know the dread we be fucking with down here? They found that nigga up in his crib, slumped with two in the head and one in the chest, butt-ass naked."

"Say word?"

"Word. The ill shit though is that the nigga still had a condom on his joint when they found him, so he must've been up in some guts when somebody clipped him, but it wasn't no bitch at the scene, so you know what that means."

"Yeah. Shorty was down with it."

"No doubt. It had to be a setup on some stick-up shit 'cause it wasn't no forced entry or nothing like that, I heard. I was watching the shit on the news, and they ain't mention nothing about no guns, money, or drugs being found, so whoever robbed him wiped him out. I just seen the nigga the other night when I got at him about the material that I had, and I remember asking him when he'd have the paper to cop it. The nigga was sitting on the forty Gs at the crib right then and there, so ain't no telling how much more he had up in there. Plus, the nigga had a chrome four-pound tucked in his pants when I got there, and when I was walking out to leave I saw a shorty laying up in the bed, sleep. Shit was definitely an inside job, and whoever it was did their homework on the nigga," Don said.

"Damn, B. That's fucked up. Son was a good dude and an even better cutty. Where you two niggas at right now?"

"We out in the country at the trailer. I told you shit is crazy hot in the town right now. We just laying low until you touch back down. When you reach the area, breathe easy when you coming through."

"Yeah, I feel you. Good looking. Yo, put my brother on the phone."

"What's the deal?" Styles asked, getting on the phone.

"Everything's good on this end. How you?"

"I'm alright. That shit with the dread got me a li'l fucked up 'cause that's a nigga we know and we fuck with, so that shit was kinda close to home. Feel me?"

"Word. I know what you saying, but you gots to shake that shit off, 'cause shit like that happens. I ain't saying that it was the dread's fault, but somewhere along the line he was sleeping and got slept on. That's the type of shit I been trying to tell you and Don about them money-hungry-ass hookers down there."

"I know."

"Yeah, I know you do, kid. Listen, I'll be there in a minute. Until then, you two just sit tight. Mommy and them send their love and told me to tell you they miss you. I'm around the way right now so I'mma cut this shit short. You know I don't really like being out in the 'hood like this, so I'll see you when I get there, alright?"

"Yeah, I'll see you when you touch down, bro. Yo, any of my hoes ask about me while you were up there?" Styles joked.

"Nigga, ain't none of these chicks around here thinking about your punk ass."

"Who dat Stacks, Styles?" Vanessa asked.

"I can't tell, nigga. Who dat in the background?" Styles asked.

"Nigga, that's just Vanessa."

"Oh, tell her I said what up."

"Stacks, what you mean 'that's just Vanessa?' " she asked with a little attitude.

"Nah, he thought you was one of his little groupie chicks he can spit his weak game to."

Stacks and Vanessa laughed.

"Yo, son, why you blowing me up like that?" Styles asked, getting defensive.

"Nigga, chill. I'm just fucking with you. If I see any of your hoes, I'll let 'em know you still alive, and you'll have that money for them when you get back," Stacks said, still laughing.

"Yeah, whatever nigga. Yo, what you doing with Vanessa anyway?" Styles was curious.

"Fuck you talking about? Ain't she from around here? What type of question is that?"

"Damn, nigga. Now you the one getting all defensive like you trying to hide something. Let me find out, bro," Styles said, playing with his brother.

"Nigga, get the fuck outta here. Matter fact, holla back."

"What was that all about?" Vanessa asked after he hung up.

"That wasn't about nothing. Nigga Styles bugging out, talking about what we doing together."

"I'm not talking about that. I'm talking about when you first got the call. It sounded like you had problems down there or something."

"Nah, I ain't got no problems down there. Don and Styles was just filling me in on something that happened to a nigga we knew down there."

"What happened?"

"Somebody bodied the nigga in his crib and left him butt-ass naked."

"Damn, that's fucked up. I heard they be getting down like that in the dirty though, especially the bitches."

"Yeah, I know how they get down out there. That's why I keep it on some strictly business shit when I'm out there."

"Yeah, right, nigga. Fine as your yellow ass is, I know them country bitches be throwing the coochie at you, and you just be catching it left and right." Vanessa laughed.

"Yo, do you know me for fucking with a lot of chicks up here?" Stacks asked.

"I ain't gonna front. I don't be hearing your name out there like that, but all that proves is that you a li'l slicker with ya shit than the next man. That's all. It's in ya nature. All you niggas around here are dogs, straight D-O-G-S."

"That's fucked up, V. How you gon' judge me without even knowing how I roll? I admit I ain't no angel, but I ain't no dog, either. I'm real selective with my women. I ain't trying to catch nothing from no chick. I ain't trying to knock two and three chicks up and go through that baby-mama-drama shit, and I ain't trying to fuck with no chick who can't understand what I'm into and what shit is all about. I don't need a hundred chicks. If I can just find one that I'm compatible with, then fuck all the other chicks that exist, and that's my word."

"Umm. Listen to you, trying to sound all intellectual and shit. I'm scared of you." Vanessa had a funny look on her face.

"You better be," Stacks said back.

"Why is that?"

"Because you ain't ready for a nigga like me."

As soon as the words came out of Stacks' mouth, he wondered why he had said them. Not only that, he wondered why he was even having this conversation with Vanessa.

"Nigga, please. Ready for a nigga like you? What type of nigga is that?" she asked.

Stacks hesitated for a moment. "Yo, I'm just fucking with you. I know the type of niggas you fucked with, so I know you can handle anything that comes ya way."

Vanessa just stared at him. Her expression showed how disappointed she was that Stacks discontinued his conversation. Stacks was unaware of the fact that this was the first time in years that a man had come on to Vanessa or even attempted to hold a male-female conversation about something other than the streets.

"Yeah, I thought so, nigga," Vanessa said, downplaying her true feelings. "When you leaving to go back down?"

"I don't really know, maybe tonight or tomorrow. It depends on how tired I am after I make a few rounds."

"I know it's probably nice as hell down there this time of year. I wouldn't mind going down there for a little bit, just to get away from all this city bullshit."

"Word?"

"Yeah, nigga, I be getting tired of New York sometimes. I've been here all my damn life. I never really been anywhere else besides Jersey a few times and Connecticut a couple. If my dough was right, I'd leave this raggedy muthafucka in a heartbeat and wouldn't look back. Ain't nuthin' here for me. All my family either died or I don't fuck wit' 'em anymore, besides my grandmother. Yeah, I got some good memories, but I got twice as many bad ones, so I wouldn't miss this shit, you know what I'm saying?"

"I feel you, V. When I'm down there, shit is just different. I can think better, sleep better, and all of that. I don't have to worry about a lot of the bullshit I do up here. I still gotta be on point at all times when I'm down there, but it's different than how I gotta be up here."

The more Vanessa talked, the more thoughts went through Stacks' head. He had talked to her many times in the past, but not like this. Today he saw her differently. This was the first time he was really attracted to Vanessa while holding a conversation with her.

"Yo, I ain't making you no promises or nothing, but take down my cell number and store it in ya phone. Give me about a week or two then holla at me. If everything's love at the time, you might can come cool out with me, Styles, and Don." Stacks made sure to include his boys so it wouldn't look like he was inviting Vanessa for himself.

"Okay, I'm feeling that. What's the number?" Vanessa took down Stacks' number and stored it in her phone.

"Make sure you call," Stacks said.

"Nigga, I will. I told you, I'm tired of New York."

"Alright, I'll holla at you then. I'm out."

"Okay, travel safe," she said, and they parted ways.

Chapter Eight

"Yo, that shit that happened to Dread hurt us a little," Don said.

"Word. That nigga was good for at least 30 Gs a week," Styles said.

"It's fucked up, what happened to the dread and all of that, and his dough was love, but we ain't starving. We got paper and besides, it's mad niggas out there like him who we can fuck with. We just gotta find them niggas and cut into 'em, that's all," Stacks told them.

"Yeah, you right, bro, but shit is getting crazy down here. Muthafuckas is getting slumped left and right, and ain't nobody getting knocked for none of that shit. That means whoever doing it is still out there. We don't know whether it's a nigga or a bitch. So while we trying to cut into niggas, we gots to watch out for the snake shit, too," Styles said.

"Yeah, I'm with Styles on that, Stacks. It's a lot of snaky shit jumping off out here, and it's hard to know who to fuck with and who not to. It's bad enough these country niggas don't like us on the low. You know what they say about niggas from up top. All we do is try to come down here and fuck all their chicks, make all their dough, and take over their towns. Niggas might act like they got love for us, but they ain't really feeling us. They just waiting for us to slip up and make a wrong move so they can try and creep us," Don said, supporting Styles.

"Don't you think I know all that?" Stacks said. "We ain't down here to try to win no popularity contest. We down here to get that money. It's greasy niggas in the game up top, too, and what do we do when they try to cross us or step on our toes?" he asked, answering his own question. "We handle them niggas. Ain't nothing changed but the area we in. That's my word. If I even think somebody trying to clip us, it's over for 'em. I ain't playing no games with these niggas down here, and I'll push their shit back. That goes for bitches too."

Ever since they had heard about what happened to the dread, they had all been a little worried about becoming another statistic. The only one who really didn't seem worried was Stacks. He kept his worries to himself. Instead, he reassured his team there was nothing to fear.

"Stacks, we still going out tonight?" his brother asked.

"We can go if you want to. It doesn't matter to me," Stacks answered.

"What's popping tonight?" Don asked Styles.

"They suppose to be having some album release party at Kamikaze out in Raleigh. I don't know who shit it is, though."

"Kamikaze hot too. I'm with dat," Don said.

"Yeah, we can bounce out there, but check, if you two niggas meet some chicks that you trying to hit for the night, make sure you keep it basic and simple. Don't be stunting for them broads and talking no Big Willie shit, telling none of our business. Feel me?" They both nodded.

"And don't leave up outta here with a lot of paper on you like you usually do. Just take enough to cop a bottle or two, and enough to get something to eat and to cop a room, that's it. I got a funny feeling that those niggas that's coming up bodied all let their guards down 'cause of some grimy bitch with a fat ass and pretty face."

"We got you, bro," Styles said.

"Yeah, we feel you," Don responded.

Chapter Nine

"Damn, this line is long as hell. Who up in this piece, Scarface or something?" Desiree complained.

"I thought Tasha said she know the nigga at the door," Keisha said, annoyed.

"She do," Pam said in her sister's defense. "But you see the bitch ain't here yet, and I know him, but not like that."

"Talking about my ass being late," Desiree added when Tasha walked up.

"Hey, y'all. Sorry I'm late," she apologized.

"You were supposed to have been here twenty-five minutes ago," Pam said to her sister, as she looked at her watch.

"Bitch, what you doing with that on?" Keisha spat, noticing the brand-new female Rolex Pam was rocking.

"What? It's mine. I bought it."

"I figured that out already, but what the fuck you doing with it on right now? I thought we agreed not to be splurging on nothing until shit blows over? Now ya ass out here sporting a twenty-five-thousand-dollar watch on ya muthafuckin' wrist, and you ain't got no job, no nigga in ya life that's getting it like that, and ya dumb ass still live in the projects. You tell me what's wrong with that picture?" Keisha said.

"Dag, why you gotta talk to me like that? It's my bad for wearing this shit tonight. I know we said shouldn't draw no unnecessary attention to ourselves, but it's been almost three weeks now. You don't think shit blew over by now?" Pam began whispering. "Dread is long gone, and that shit ain't even making noise on the news no more."

"That ain't the point," Desiree said. "The point is we all agreed not to do no dumb shit to draw suspicion, and then you go do something like this." She lowered her voice so that no one in line heard besides her crew.

"Just take it off," Keisha said. "We know you ain't meant nuthin' by it, you just wanted to treat yaself, but you know better; we've been doing this for a minute now. Maybe the payday never been like this, but we ain't new to this."

Pam knew she was wrong and took the watch off and put it in her Coach bag.

"What's up? What y'all doing back here?" Tasha changed the subject, while trying to come to her sister's aid.

"Waiting for ya slow ass, bitch," Pam said.

"You ain't have to wait on me. You know Big Mike, just like I do," Tasha retorted.

"Yeah, I know him, but I ain't fucking him. Ya pussy is our E-Z Pass up in this piece."

Everyone started cracking up.

"Shut the fuck up and come on." Tasha laughed aloud.

When they stepped inside the club, the music was pumping, and the dance floor was jam-packed. Everywhere they looked, there was alcohol, and the women outnumbered the men three to one, if not more. Niggas and chicks were wall to wall on both levels.

"Tasha, you must've sucked the skin off that nigga Mike's dick, girl," Keisha said as she laughed. "When he saw you, he lit up like a Christmas tree. I could see the bulge in that nigga's jeans."

"Fuck you, I ain't suck that nigga dick. That muthafucka just feeling me."

"I don't care if you sucked the nigga shit or not," Desiree said. "Whatever you did to him, I'm glad you did because tonight this is the place to be. Look at all these niggas up in here stunting, waiting for some fine-ass bitches like us to step on the scene."

"I know it's some heavyweight muthafuckas up in here," Keisha said.

"Okay. I hear that," Desiree said.

"You two bitches are one in the same, always scheming," Pam said. "Y'all some greedy-ass hoes."

"Oh, bitch, please, don't act like ya ass ain't always looking to get in a nigga pockets, especially after you done went and wasted twenty-five Gs on that fucking watch. Tell me you wouldn't want to replace that shit if you could," Keisha said.

"Huh, you think I wouldn't? But I'm just saying, we just came off lovely on our last vic, and already you bitches scheming on the next one."

"Bitch, how long you think that paper gonna last you?" Keisha asked. "I keep telling you this shit ain't forever."

"Yeah, we came off, but it's still money to be made. We live high-maintenance lifestyles, and I know y'all like this shit, so I'm gonna do whatever it takes to maintain mine."

Keisha was right. They had come off. In fact, they came off more than they ever had before. The dread was holding more than Pam expected, and they wound up splitting more than two hundred grand between the four of them. They had also found seven pounds of smoke stashed in the closet, and sold five of them at two thousand a pound, keeping two pounds for themselves.

"Keisha, why you always trying to bark somebody out when they say something?" Tasha asked, coming to Pam's aid.

"Bitch, what are you talking about? Ain't nobody trying to bark her out. She asked a question, and I answered it. What the fuck you getting all defensive and shit for, anyway? Miss me with that bullshit."

"All of y'all chill," Desiree said. "We all girls, and we suppose to have one another's back and shit. We a team, and y'all at one another's throats like y'all don't know one another. Pam, you know Keisha always fly off at the mouth. That ain't nothing new, so why you tripping now? And Keisha, you know Pam take the shit we say to heart sometimes, so y'all beefing over nothing. We came here to have a good time and scope some niggas that think they got it going on, and see who we can catch. Let all that other shit go, 'cause you bitches blowing my high," she said, deading the conversation.

"You know what? You right, girl, I'm bugging," Keisha said. "Tash, Pam, my bad. Y'all know y'all my dawgs."

"I'm sorry, too, girl. I know you ain't mean nuthin' by what you said," Pam replied.

"Me too," Tasha agreed.

"That's what I'm talking about. Now kiss and make up so we can get our party on," Desiree told them.

"Ooh wee. It's some honey's up in the house tonight," Don said.

"Word up. Shorties is deep up in this piece," Styles added.

"Yeah, no doubt, but remember what I told you," Stacks said to them.

"Stacks, chill, son. We got you. We on point. Right, Styles?"

"Yeah, bruh. Chill. We here to have a good time, and we know what time it is."

Stacks had heard them, but he wasn't listening. He was more focused on the familiar face he'd spotted coming out of the rest room. She was with the same clique she had been with that night he had met her at the Taj Mahal a month earlier, and like before, she was looking hot.

"Nigga, did you hear me?" Don asked, tapping Stacks on his shoulder.

"What?" Stacks turned his attention away from the woman when he felt the tap on his shoulder.

"Yo, Stacks, what the fuck wrong with you, man?"

"Nothing, nigga, I'm good. I just saw somebody I knew—I mean, met before."

"Who?" Styles asked.

"Remember that shorty I was hollering at at the Taj?"

"You mean that chick that shut your shit down?" Don corrected him with a laugh.

"Whatever, nigga, if that's what you think, but yeah her. I just seen her and them other chicks that was with her that night right over there."

Stacks went to point in the direction he had just seen the woman, but she and the rest of her crew were already gone.

"Damn, shorty was just over there by the bathroom. Fucking with you two niggas, I didn't see which direction she went in," Stacks said.

Both Don and Styles looked at each other, then they looked at Stacks, reading each other's minds.

"Sounds to me like you need to be the one on point, the way shorty got you open," Don joked.

"Don, get the fuck outta here. Picture shorty having me open. Nigga, I stay on point," Stacks said seriously.

Styles laughed at his brother. If anybody knew when he was feeling a chick, it was Styles. The way Stacks was acting, Styles knew his brother wanted to get at shorty.

"Bro, if you feeling her like that, go find her and holla at her, and see what's good," Styles said.

"You two niggas bugging the fuck out. It ain't that serious, B. If I see her again before we bounce, I'll get at her. If not, then I'll see her when I see her. I ain't gonna be chasing down no chick with all these other bad shorties up in this spot. You must be crazy," Stacks said.

Neither Don nor Styles responded.

"Yo, son, I know what I'ma about to do. I'm gonna hit the bar 'cause my alcohol level real low right about now," Don said.

"Yeah, kid, a nigga on E, and my throat feeling a li'l dry," Styles said.

"Alright, I feel you. I'ma slide to a table over there, cop a bottle of

Moe for me," Stacks said to Styles as he pulled out his dough.

"Chill, bro. I got you. First bottle on me, the next one on you," Styles told him.

"That's cool. I'll be over there." Stacks pointed to the other side of the club where there were a few empty tables.

"We'll meet you over there," Don said.

"Desiree, ain't dat that nigga who stepped to you at the Taj Mahal, that be out in Dunn?" Keisha asked her friend.

"Where?" Desiree asked, looking around the club.

"Right there, sitting over there by his fine-ass self," Keisha said.

Desiree's gaze followed Keisha's finger, and when she focused in there he was, sitting by himself, looking as good as the first time she had laid eyes on him. Something inside of her was triggered. Her stomach started to tighten, but she didn't know why. Maybe her period was coming. The more she stared at him, the tighter the knot in her stomach got. When their eyes met, she could tell he was glad to see her because his face lit up. She didn't blame him because she was looking good. Any man with a pair of eyes could see that. Even a nigga with only one good eye could see this truth.

"He is looking like something," Tasha said.

"What's up, girl? You gonna give the nigga some play, or are you gonna front on him like you did the last time?" Pam asked.

"Pam, kiss my ass," Desiree told her, but she knew Pam was right. Tonight was the night when she'd have to make up her mind. There was a lot of females in the house who could easily get his attention, including her own girls.

"What are you gonna do, though, Desiree?" Keisha asked.

"Girl, that nigga probably fucked so many bitches since that time we met that he probably forgot about me," Desiree said, knowing it was a lie.

It was obvious by the look he gave her he hadn't forgotten her.

"Bitch, please. I saw the way that nigga was just clocking you and the way you was looking at him too," Tasha said, sipping on her drink.

"How the fuck you see all that when you got ya drunk ass buried in ya drink?" Desiree asked.

"Desiree, damn all that. Are you gonna get at this nigga or you want me to step to him?" Keisha asked.

"It don't matter to me, if you wanna holla at him go ahead." Desiree tried to sound convincing, knowing she really didn't want Keisha or any of her girls getting at him. "As a matter of fact, I'ma give 'im some play."

"Umm-hmm. Yeah, I bet, bitch. With ya frontin' ass," Keisha said laughing. She knew Desiree wouldn't pass up the opportunity to see if the nigga they called Stacks was holding it down like his name, not only in the stash department, but in the bedroom as well.

"There go those same two niggas that was with him before at the Taj," Pam said.

"Who'd he say they were, again?" Tasha asked.

"The one on the right is his brother. I think he said his name was Styles or something, and the other one on the left he said is his boy, Don."

"Let's go over there before some lame bitches beat us to the punch," Keisha suggested.

"If we go over there, what will that make us? Desiree asked.

"Hopefully, it'll make us some money," she answered.

"Okay," Tasha and Pam sang, snapping their fingers.

"You bitches are crazy," Desiree said with a smile as they all grabbed their drinks and headed for Stacks' table.

"Yo, son, you see what I see?" Don asked Stacks.

"What you talking about?" Styles asked, but Stacks already knew.

"Yeah, I see," Stacks answered.

"What's up?" Styles asked again, sipping on his glass of Moët.

"If you look, nigga, you'd see. Here comes that shorty Stacks met at the Taj that night, with them three bad-ass bitches she was with," Don said.

Stacks had been laid back, enjoying his drink while nodding to the music but when Don spoke, he instantly sat up and became alert. He couldn't believe this chick was coming over to his table, although he was curious to know why.

"Are we interrupting?" Desiree said to Stacks.

"Nah, not at all. Sit down," Stacks replied. "Styles, snatch them chairs up right there," he told his brother, so there would be enough room for everyone.

"Thank you," Keisha said to Styles as he placed a seat next to her.

"No problem, sexy," Styles replied.

They all sat down. Don got up so Desiree could sit next to Stacks, and he sat between Pam and Keisha while Styles was on the opposite side of Keisha, who sat beside Tasha.

"What brings you lovely ladies over to this corner to grace us with your presence?" Stacks asked, breaking the ice.

Desiree responded with a smile. "We thought you three looked kind of lonely over here, so we came to keep you company."

"Oh, this must be Good Samaritans night, huh?" Stacks asked.

They all laughed.

"Nah, it ain't like that."

"So how is it?" Stacks asked Desiree.

"It ain't easy to find three fly-ass brothas in a club full of bitches sitting alone with more than one bottle of Moët on the table, so we figured we'd come over before they noticed."

"A'ight, I'll roll with that." Stacks smiled. "How you ladies doing?"

"Fine," they all said.

"I know we all met before, but you never got to personally meet my dawgs." Stacks introduced his crew. "That's my brother right there, Styles."

"What's up?" Styles said, raising his drink as if he was toasting.

"And this right here is my peoples, Don P."

"What's going on, ladies?" Don said.

One by one the women spoke. It was that easy for them to get into any role they were playing. They had mastered the art of manipulating the situation, making the men think that they were in control, when actually they weren't. Every one of them had their game faces on as they went into action.

"Y'all don't dance?" Pam asked, directing her question to Don.

Don smiled. "A li'l something," he responded.

"So what's up? Show us something," Keisha joined in. "Styles, come dance with me."

"Yo, I got a bad leg. I got shot before," Styles replied as he touched his left leg.

"Nigga, please. You look fine to me. Don't front on me like that. Come on," Keisha insisted. She pulled on his right arm as Tasha grabbed his left one.

"Yeah, come and dance with us, or are you scared you might get dogged by us?" Tasha taunted.

Styles began to laugh. "Scared? Ha, nah, never that. A'ight, I'll dance with you two, but take it easy on me out there." A grin covered his face.

Don, Tasha, Pam, Keisha, and Styles all got up to head toward the dance floor while Desiree and Stacks remained at the table.

"Desiree, what's up girl. Y'all coming?" Keisha asked.

Desiree looked at Stacks. "You wanna dance?"

"Nah, I don't do the dancing thing," Stacks said.

"Why not?" she asked.

"No particular reason. I just don't."

Desiree stared at Stacks for a moment. Her expression showed how much she really wanted to dance with him. She hoped he'd give in, but he didn't.

Desiree realized that Stacks wasn't going to break easily, but she felt that it was just a matter of time before he did. It would take more effort, but she knew all men had a weakness, and it was usually her. Desiree was good at playing the damsel in distress and no man could resist her charm. She turned to answer her girls.

"Okay. Nah, y'all go ahead. We chilling."

After the others left, Stacks sat sipping on his drink.

"You just gonna sit here all night and sip on that drink and not say nothing?" Desiree asked to break the silence.

Stacks put his drink down and grinned. "My bad, pardon me," he said. "I just didn't wanna keep yelling back and forth over the music."

"Oh, I can hear. If you can't hear me, then I'll move closer." Desiree slid so close her thigh was up against his.

As before, Stacks could smell her perfume. It was the same sweet fragrance from their previous encounter. His muscles became tense, and his manhood began to stiffen. Between her rubbing up on him and her scent, Desiree was driving him crazy, but there was no way he was going to let her know that.

"So what's good?" Stacks asked. "I see you in a better mood than the last time we were in each other's company."

"Why you say that?" Desiree asked, trying to sound innocent.

"Come on, yo. You know you gave me attitude at the Taj Mahal."

Desiree smiled then she chuckled seductively. "Okay, maybe I did, but you the one who was flagging me like you work for the airport."

"Oh, you got jokes, huh?" Stacks said with a grin.

"Nah, I'm just messin', but you did have a lot of hoochies all up in your face, and I wasn't trying to be thrown in that category."

"Never that, shorty."

For the next twenty minutes Desiree and Stacks got to know each other.

"Yo, you want something to drink?" he finally asked.

"Uh, alright. You can get me a strawberry daquiri," Desiree replied. She purposely ordered a conservative drink, but her choice drink was cranberry and vodka mixed.

"A'ight. Pardon me," Stacks yelled over the loud music, addressing the waitress who was passing by.

"Yes, may I help you?"

"Yeah, can I get a strawberry daquiri and a glass of Hennessy?"

"Will that be all?"

"Yeah."

"Okay, I'll be right back with your drinks."

As they were finishing up their beverages, everyone returned from the dance floor.

"Gurrl, these niggas wasn't playing," Tasha said, breathless.

"Yeah, girl. I think these niggas some Chippendale dancers," Keisha added. "These niggas dance better than Usher and Ginuwine. We couldn't even keep up with 'em and shit."

"For real. We just stepped back and watched from the sidelines," Pam said.

Styles and Don laughed.

"Yo, I'ma bout to hit up the bar. Ladies, what you drinking?" Styles asked.

"Oh, I'll have an Alabama Slamma," Tasha responded.

"I'll take a Cosmopolitan," Pam said.

"And I'll take a Sex on the Beach," Keisha said, running her fingers through her hair.

"That can be arranged," Styles joked.

Keisha flashed a phony smile.

"Shorty, how about you?" Styles asked Desiree.

"No, I'm okay. I just got finished with one."

"That's nothing," Styles said, looking at her almost empty glass. "Whatcha sippin?"

Desiree smiled. "Daquiri—strawberry."

"Got you. Bro, what up? Three bottles and some Hen?" Styles asked, acting giddy.

"Yeah, that's cool," Stacks replied. "Matter of fact, get a gallon."

"Oh, no question."

For the next hour or so everyone drank and got acquainted. Three empty bottles of Cristal and a gallon of Hennessy later, Stacks was ready to call it a night. He could feel the mixture of the cognac and champagne taking effect on him, and since Desiree showed no indication that she was leaving with him, he just wanted to make it to his crib and crash.

"Yo, it's been fun, but I gotta bounce," Stacks said to Desiree, hoping she'd ask to go with him.

Instead, she replied, "Okay. Well, here, take my number."

They exchanged cell numbers. Stacks could see both Styles and Don doing the same with Keisha and Pam. That being done, the three women rose to leave.

"You gonna call me, right?" Stacks asked.

"Are you gonna call me?" Desiree retorted.

"There go that attitude again," he said with a smile.

"Shut up, boy. I'ma call," Desiree said.

Everyone then said their good-byes, and the men headed toward the entrance of the club.

"Yeah, we got us some real-live winners," Keisha said slyly as they watched the three ballers walk through the crowd.

"You ain't neva lied," Pam agreed.

"I hope so," Tasha added.

Desiree remained quiet as she replayed her conversation with Stacks over and over in her head.

Chapter Ten

Stacks woke up to the strong smell of weed. He thought he was dreaming at first, until he opened his eyes. There was Don, leaning over him, blowing the smoke from his blunt in his face. Stacks reached out and mushed Don.

"Nigga, what the fuck I tell you about doing that shit, huh?"

Don and Styles cracked up at Stacks' reaction.

"Cool out, nigga. That shit can't fuck with you if you don't inhale. You heard what Bill Clinton said." Don laughed.

"I told you that nigga was gonna be tight, son," Styles said to Don.

"You muthafuckin' right I'm tight. Last time you did that dumb shit, I had the munchies and shit, nigga," Stacks said.

"What's wrong with that, bro?" Styles asked.

"What's wrong with that is I don't need any extra shit to help me eat more. I do that on my own. I don't know why you niggas be smoking that shit anyway, especially while we in the dirty and all that shit that been popping off. We just talked about why we down here, and you niggas still acting like you back home."

"A'ight, a'ight. Yo, chill. You ain't gotta keep going on and on about the same shit. Damn. We can't even play with ya ass no more, son."

"Don, I ain't trying to hear that shit, B."

"Yo, both you niggas chill. For the past couple of days that's all we been doing is beefing. Bro, lately you been on some hot-and-cold shit. What's good?" Styles questioned.

Stacks didn't mean any harm. He was just concerned about their well-being. He didn't feel Don and Styles were conducting themselves properly, and whatever they did while they were in North Carolina, or anywhere for that matter, would affect him as well. They were a team.

"Yo, I might flip sometimes, but it's all love. I just don't want anything to happen to either one of you two, that's all. I brought you down here, and it's on me to see to it that nothing goes wrong, feel me? How the fuck I'm supposed to explain some shit like what happened to Dread to Mommy or Ma Porter? Huh? I'd feel fucked up if something happened, kid. That's my word. Not only that, I love you niggas. You my heart."

"Damn, son. That's deep," Don said. "I ain't look at it that way, but I see where you coming from. If something was to happen to either one of you niggas, I wouldn't know how I'd live with myself either."

"Bro, I feel you, too, but ain't nothing gonna happen to us, kid," Styles said.

"I hope not, son."

"It won't," Don said.

Stacks changed the subject to lighten the mood. "Yo, anyway, how shit turn out with them two shorties last night?" Styles and Don had hooked up with two women as they were leaving the club.

"Oh, son, shit was love. Those chicks were straight-up freaks, kid. We did 'em something dirty. We were just taking turns, switching on 'em, and the whole nine, but that ain't the half. We was chilling up in they crib watching this smut flick, puffin' on a L, and out of the blue, these broads do the illest shit and start eatin' each other the fuck out." Don's voice said he was still bugging off the previous night's scene. "Styles and me were fucked up."

"Word," Styles agreed.

"Get the fuck outta here."

"That's my word on everything I love, son," Don said.

"No bullshit, bro." Styles co-signed Don's version of events.

"So what you niggas do?"

"Nigga, fuck you mean what we do? We joined in," Don said as he and Styles started laughing.

"You two some muthafuckin' freaks, too, nasty-ass niggas."

"Stacks, stop fronting. If you was there, you would've did the same thing."

Stacks started to laugh too. "You muthafuckin' right," he said as they all fell out.

"Yo, them chicks that were with us at the club last night was official, though. I'm feeling that chick Keisha," Styles said, changing the subject.

"Oh yeah, no doubt. I got that chick Pam's number. I'ma get at that. Shorty got a banging body, and she sexier than a muthafucka," Don said.

Styles looked at Stacks with a knowing grin. "Bro, I see you was digging that chick you was hollering at, and it look like shorty was digging you too. I saw how she was all up under you. What up? You in there?"

"Yeah, everything looks good. I'ma see what's up, set something up on the one on one and see how she acting when her girls ain't around, nah mean?" Stacks played it off nonchalant; he didn't want them to know that he was really digging Desiree.

"I feel you." Styles knew his brother, and knew that he was playing it cool. It was best to let things ride for now.

"Yo, we about to dip out," Don said to Stacks. "Them niggas out in Fayetteville called us on our way back to the crib, so we gonna go see what the deal is out there, then we gonna shoot to the mall. What up? You rolling?"

"Nah, I gotta slide out to Raleigh and check on them li'l niggas over in Walnut Terrace," Stacks replied. "I was supposed to pick that dough up yesterday before we hit the club, but it slipped my mind."

"A'ight. Well, yo, we'll meet you back out here later. You want us to stop off and collect that paper from them niggas at the pool hall and over on Elm?" Styles asked.

"Yeah, do that, and I'll get at them dudes out in Benson on my way to Raleigh," Stacks said.

"Cool. We out then," Don said.

"Catch you on the come around. Travel safe," Stacks told them. "Styles, hand me that phone off the charger before you go."

After his boys left, Stacked checked his messages. The automated voice said, "*You have four messages. To review your messages, press one.*"

"Hey, hon. It's your mother. Just calling to see how you and your brother are. Haven't heard from you two in a couple days, and I had one of my dreams. Call me when you get this message. Love you." Stacks smiled and deleted the message.

"Yo, Stacks, what's up, my nigga? This Dre. Get at me, man, when you get this. Peace." Stacks made a mental note to call Dre and deleted the message.

"I don't really like talking to answering machines, but this is the only way you'll know that I called you first. I thought you said your phone was always on. Well, anyway, I just wanted to let you know that I enjoyed hanging out with you last night, and I hope we can do it again sometime. Call me when you get the chance. Okay, bye."

Stacks saved the message as a smile crept across his face.

"Damn, I can't believe she called already. I knew I should've left my shit on last night," Stacks cursed himself as he continued to check his messages.

"What's up, Stacks? It's me. I bet you thought I wasn't gonna call…well, surprise. I know you not still sleeping. You know if your ass was up here, you'd be on the block right now. Let me find out the south making you lazy. If so, maybe I shouldn't come down there. Nah, I'm just messing with you. I'm still interested, if the offer still stands. Call me back and let me know what's up."

Hearing Vanessa's voice brought Stacks back to reality. He was still dwelling on the fact that Desiree had called him so soon. He had forgotten he had even told Vanessa that she was welcome to come down. Stacks couldn't understand why he was bugging over Desiree. He thought maybe letting Vanessa come down would be the best thing for him to do in order to keep his head straight.

Stacks figured if he had her bring some product down and helped her get a little paper while she was there, he'd be too busy schooling and holding Vanessa down he'd have no free time to think about Desiree. There was no doubt in his mind he was feeling Desiree, but he was far from stupid. Stacks knew there had to be a reason why a woman of her caliber didn't have a man, and until he found out that reason, he decided it was best that he dealt cautiously with her. No matter how much he was digging Desiree, he had to watch his back.

Stacks hopped out of bed and got ready to jump in the shower. He had a long day ahead of him, but first he called Vanessa back and let her know his decision and his intentions.

Chapter Eleven

"Did that nigga call you back yet?" Keisha asked her friend.

"Nope. I ain't heard from him today," Desiree answered.

Keisha heard the disappointment in her voice. "Don't worry. That nigga will call. I saw how he was all into you and shit."

"I'm not worried. I know he's gonna call. I just think I should've waited until he got at me first, that's all. I don't know why you wanted me to call him like that so early, like I'm sweating him or something."

"Desiree, why you acting like you new to this? We've done it like this a million times. You know how niggas get when they think a bitch on they dick, and you know what we trying to do. I called his brother already and left him a message saying that we could hook up. I ain't playing no games. I'ma give that nigga some pussy, 'cause a bitch gotta get hers, too, but when I do give him some, Styles gonna be all on my shit, and I'ma make him think he King Kong. Those two niggas is brothers, so I know he gots to know what's popping. Shit, he might be sitting on something his damn self, with all that ice he had on. Either way, them niggas gots to get got," Keisha said.

"I know," was all Desiree said, feeling a little uneasy.

She wanted to tell Keisha right then and there to forget about their plans for Stacks, Styles, and Don, and move on to some different victims, but she couldn't bring herself to say it. She knew her friend would see right through her and think she was getting soft—or even worse, falling for Stacks.

A person wouldn't know it unless she said something, but Keisha despised men. She wasn't a lesbian or anything like that. She just hated the way men were.

Starting with her father, Keisha had been dogged all her life by men, and was taught to believe that women were inferior. Desiree was the only one out of the whole crew with whom Keisha really shared her past, because Desiree was the one Keisha trusted the most and felt understood her. When she was a little girl, Keisha's father, who was born in Bronx, New York, used to molest her when she lived in Greensboro. That was the reason her mother left and migrated to a different part of North Carolina. She wanted to take Keisha away from the bad memories, but Keisha viewed her moms as weak. She had grown up watching her mother get treated badly and get dogged by man after man, and she put up with it, claiming that it was in the name of love. Keisha thought if that's what love was, then she didn't want any parts of it. Keisha promised to never let a man handle her the way she saw her mother get treated, and made a vow to never fall in love with one either. A few years earlier her mother had passed away from cancer, but Keisha believed that she died from a broken heart.

Desiree didn't find out what Keisha had been through until one day when Desiree was fifteen and was raped. Up until then she had been a virgin. She had met a guy from Staten Island, for whom she had instantly fallen. Everyone had called him New York. He never bothered to tell her his real name, but she didn't care. The only thing that he told her was that he was twenty years old and where he was from.

One day Desiree went to his room at the motel he was staying at, to hang out and spend some time with him. When she knocked on the door and it opened, she was hit in the face with a cloud of smoke. When

New York had reached to hug her, she could smell the alcohol coursing through his body. He had kissed her, and she could taste the liquor on his lips. She'd been around him before when he had been smoking weed and drinking, and had even smoked and drank with him a few times, but something was different and just didn't sit right with her this time. Her first reaction was to go with her gut instinct and make up some excuse to leave, but she had brushed off the notion. It was a decision she would later regret.

New York closed the door behind Desiree and locked it, putting the safety latch on as well. He had come and sat on the bed next to her and told her how he had been thinking about her while he had kissed on her neck. She attempted to push him away, but he grabbed her hands and put one arm behind her back while pinning the other one down with his body. Desiree tried to resist, but New York was far stronger than her. Desiree cried, kicked, and screamed as New York put one hand over her mouth, and used the other hand to go under her skirt, snatch her panties off, and climb on top of her. New York had forced himself inside her. Desiree felt a sharp pain that she had never felt before. She continued to cry and put up a fight, but New York kept raping her. When he finally loosened the pressure on her mouth, Desiree had bit him with all her might. New York screamed in agony and reflexively backhanded her across the face repeatedly until she was unconscious.

When Desiree woke, she was lying in the park half naked with blood on her skirt, and her body ached. She was confused and ashamed and felt responsible for what occurred. She didn't know what to do, who to turn to, or where to go. If she had gone home, her mother would've ridiculed and blamed her, so she decided to take a chance and visit Keisha's house. It was Keisha whom she chose to confide in and in return, Keisha disclosed what she had gone through with her father. It was then that Keisha came up with the idea of making New York pay for what he had done to her friend.

They never told anyone else what had happened to Desiree or what they had done to New York. From that day forward they began making any hustler from out of state pay for what New York and Keisha's father had done to them. Desiree would never think of going against Keisha. They had been through too much together.

Chapter Twelve

"Yeah, who this?" Vanessa asked.

"Yeah, who this?" Stacks mocked. "That's how you answer ya shit?"

"Oh, hey, what up, Stacks?" Vanessa sounded surprised.

"What's up with you?"

"Nothing. Just trying to do my thang, you know?"

"Yeah, I hear you," Stacks said. "I just got ya message. I see you were serious about coming through."

"Yeah, I was serious, boy. Were you serious when you said I could come?"

"No doubt. I wouldn't play with you like that. When you trying to come?"

"As soon as you say I can."

Stacks smiled broadly. "Okay, I got a few things to tie up, but it shouldn't take me no more than a day or two. Let me see, today is Sunday. How 'bout this Wednesday?" he asked.

"That sounds good. That'll give me enough time to get shit up this way situated," Vanessa replied.

While she was talking, Stacks was trying to think of a way to get Vanessa to bring some work so she could get money while she was there. He didn't want her to think that was the only reason he invited her, and he also didn't want to talk reckless over the phone.

"Yo, how long you plan on staying?" he asked.

"How long you gonna let me?"

"It's up to you. Whatever you decide. "I'm just saying, you know you gonna need paper to really enjoy yourself while you down here, but I got you though if you fucked up," he said.

"Nigga, please. I don't need you to have me while I'm down there, I got my own dough. If I'm down there that long and run out of paper, then we'll come up with something, know what I mean?" she said.

Stacks knew exactly what Vanessa meant and was glad she knew the majority of the tricks of the drug trade. He was trying to figure out how he could say the same thing and be discreet about it.

"Yo, why take that chance and wait for it to happen? Why not just come down prepared? It'll be love when you get here," he said, hoping she caught what he was telling her.

"Yeah, you right. I'm feeling that, but I don't know how to get there. What's the best way to travel?"

Stacks had trekked back and forth every way possible and knew the best option for a female to take with the least amount of risk. "Hop on the train. That's about your best bet. It's kinda long, but it's a smoother route to take than the bus or plane, nah mean?"

"Yeah, I follow you."

"Soon as we hang up, call and make the arrangements and get back at me. When you touch, I'll come scoop you from the station."

"Alright, I'll do that," Vanessa said. "How prepared should I come, though?" She wanted to know how much work she should bring.

"However you want," Stacks answered.

"It's like that?" Vanessa asked, impressed.

"Yeah, it's like that."

"Okay then, let me make this call, and I'll hit you back later."

"No doubt."

"And Stacks?"

"Yeah, what up?"

"Thank you." She changed the tone of her voice to a much more sensual one.

Stacks had never heard Vanessa sound so alluring, but he liked it. If he didn't know who he was talking to, he would've mistaken her for someone else.

"Thank me for what?"

"For everything."

He was lost. All he had done was invite her to come down south and get a little money while she was there. To Stacks that was nothing, but to Vanessa it meant a lot.

"Don't worry about it. Just get down here safe. I'll see you when you get here."

"Alright. See you then."

Stacks turned his attention to Styles and Don who had returned from their errands.

"Yo, how everything go in Fayetteville?" Stacks asked.

"It was worth the trip," Don answered.

"Word. We damn near moved two bricks out there," Styles added.

"Word?"

"Yeah. Niggas was kinda dry out there on the powder tip. Altogether we knocked off sixty onions, plus a pound and a half of trees," Don reported.

"That's decent," Stacks replied. "Niggas came correct out in Benson on the dough tip, and I got rid of twenty-one ounces while I was in Raleigh. How much you let them go for when you was out there?" Stacks asked, referring to the ounces they had sold.

"Nothing under a G a whop," Styles answered.

"Yeah, that's what I charged niggas too. Ain't no need trying to move 'em for twelve hundred unless niggas just copping one and ain't trying to come back."

"We only made an eight-hundred-dollar profit off the smoke, though. We charged the niggas twenty-three hundred for it," Don said.

"That's cool. That's better than nothing," Stacks replied. "Let's count all this money and put it up. I'm tired as hell from driving all day."

"Word. I was just telling Styles that on the way home. I almost dozed off and smacked that muthafuckin' rental up," Don said.

"Yo, bro, I know what I meant to tell you. That chick Keisha called me earlier. I talked to her ass for like an hour straight, kid. Shorty a freak on the low, and she on my dick."

"Oh shit, you just reminded me," Stacks exclaimed. "I gotta call her partner. She left me a message this morning when I was sleep. I almost forgot about that shit."

"How you forget to call that chick, son?" Don asked. "She bad as hell."

"Yeah, no doubt. It ain't that I really forgot to call. I was just kicking it to Vanessa, and it slipped my mind."

"Vanessa?" Styles said with surprise. "What you doing talking to her?"

"We were making arrangements for her to come down."

"What? Come down where?" Styles asked.

"Here, that's where."

"For what?"

"'Cause I asked her to and she wants to, that's why."

Both Styles and Don looked at each other, not knowing what to make of what Stacks had just said. One thing they were certain of was that if Stacks invited Vanessa down, then there was a good reason for it, and more than what he was telling.

Chapter Thirteen

Knock. Knock. Knock. Vanessa banged her fist against the metal door.

"Who is it?' an elderly voice asked.

"It's me, Nana," Vanessa yelled to her grandmother through the thick steel door.

She could hear the locks being undone and the chain sliding off as her grandmother started opening up the door.

"Hey sugah," her grandmother greeted with open arms.

This was the only person in the world that Vanessa truly loved. For as long as she could remember, her Nana had always been there for her and loved her unconditionally. Even when her own mother turned her back on her and disowned her when she found out what Vanessa was doing out in the streets, her grandmother was there for her. She was an only child, so she had no siblings to turn to, and she had never known her father. Nonetheless, her grandmother showed Vanessa enough love to pardon the absence of both parents.

"Where you been at, chile? I ain't seen you in over a week. What? You don't love ya grandmother no more?"

"Nana, don't talk like that. You making me feel bad," Vanessa said. "You know I love you to death, and you far from being an old woman, so cut it out. You're looking younger than me," Vanessa teased.

"Chile, please. I look a mess, but I don't care about that. I ain't got nobody to impress. I leave that to you kids with all that fashion and stuff."

Vanessa laughed. "Nana, you crazy."

"I ain't crazy. I got good sense, girl. I might be old, but I ain't slow. You ain't just come over here to tell me how good you think I look and all that mess. Remember, I raised your black butt, so I know when something's on ya mind, even before you think it. Now come on in here and tell me what's wrong."

Vanessa followed her grandmother into the kitchen. After all these years, her grandmother still could read her like a book.

"Nah, it ain't nothing wrong, Nana. I'm just going away for a little bit, and I needed to come get some of that money. You still got it, right?"

"Of course I still got it. What you think I woulda done with it, spend it all up?"

"I didn't mean it like that, Nana. I don't care if you spent it. I told you to use what you needed, anyway."

"Chile, I don't need ya money. Just what you gave me is what I put up. I ain't touched one penny of it. That's your money, and you did whatever you did to get it, and I don't want any parts of it. I only agreed to hold it for you because I love you like no other and you my grandbaby. I only hope you come to ya senses and stop what you doing before something happen to you. The streets ain't no place to be for nobody, let alone a young woman. You're only twenty-eight and got a whole life ahead of you. You can still go back to school and do something with ya life, baby. I pray to the Lord every night that He shows you the way before it's too late."

Vanessa knew her grandmother meant every word she said, and everything she said was out of love. She was used to her grandmother being straightforward with her. There was never a time when Vanessa came to see her that her grandmother didn't plead with her to leave the streets alone. Although she had all the love in the world for this woman, still Vanessa never listened, but she told herself that one day she would surprise her grandmother and tell her that she was out of the game.

"That's enough preaching though," Nana continued. "You never listen, anyway."

"Yes I do, Nana," Vanessa said, sounding like a little child.

"No, you don't, but I still love you anyway. You said something about going away. Where you going?" her grandmother asked.

"I'm going down south."

"Wit' who?"

"By myself, to visit some friends."

"What friends, chile? Since when you got friends down south?"

Vanessa smiled. Her grandmother had always been suspicious and wouldn't drop a subject until she got to the bottom of it. "They're not originally from down south. They're from around here, but stay down there now."

"If they from around here, then I know 'em or I know their kin folk. Who is they?"

Vanessa knew that would be the next question. "You remember Mrs. Bennett's grandsons, Stacks and Styles?"

"Who, Bunkie's boys?"

"Yeah."

"They names ain't no Stacks and no Styles. Them must be some ole street names. You mean Darren and Andre? I know their mamma, Jean. They call her Sissy. "

Vanessa hadn't heard their real names in so long, she had to think for a minute because she had forgotten them. "Yeah, that's them."

"What they doing way down there?"

"They bought a place down there," she said, hating to lie to her grandmother. She knew she had seen right through it.

"Um-huh. Them boys 'bout round the same age as you and been

out there in them streets just as long as you, if not longer. Don't gimme that crap about they bought some house down there. I don't even wanna know why you going or why they down there. The less I know, the better. You just make sure you're careful, you hear me?"

"Yes, Nana, I hear you, and I will."

"I'll be right back." Her grandmother got up and went into her room and came back with a shoebox. "Here's that money."

"I'm not taking it all. I just need some," Vanessa said as she opened the box.

She had been hustling for eleven years and from day one, she had always saved some of her profit. When it was a nice amount, she gave it to her grandmother to hold. Back in the day Vanessa had spent a lot of money on clothes and jewelry. Still, she was able to save for a rainy day. This was her rainy day, and it was time to dip into her bank. Stacks was cool, but she couldn't go down south with empty pockets. Vanessa wanted to come with her own trim. She had managed to stash a little over eighty-five thousand dollars. Vanessa had already made up her mind to take half a brick down, which would only cost her twelve grand. She had three days to move almost four Gs worth of work, so she only took thirteen thousand from the stash and left the rest.

"Here, Nana," she said, handing back the box.

Her grandmother went to put up the money and returned to the kitchen.

"Nana, I don't know how long I'm going to be gone, but just in case I'm not back by next month, happy birthday." Vanessa handed her grandmother one of the thousand dollar stacks.

"Chile, what I tell you before? I don't need your money. Besides, what I'ma do with all of that?"

"Nana, I don't know, whatever you want, but please don't turn this down. It's a present, and it's all I have. If you love me, you'll take it."

Her grandmother's eyes became misty, and she reached out and took the money. "Baby, you know I love you. You all I got in this world. I'ma miss you, but you a big girl now. I know you gonna be alright. You take care down there, and call me when you get there, understand?"

"Yes. I will."

"Now get outta here before I won't be able to stop crying," her grandmother told her.

"I love you, Nana," Vanessa said as she got up to leave.

She had never cried in front of anyone before, not even her grandmother, but as she headed for the door, two tears fell. She wiped her face and walked out of her grandmother's apartment.

Chapter Fourteen

"Hi. You've reached the voice mail of Desiree. Sorry I missed your call, but if you leave me a message at the tone, I'll get back with you at my earliest." *Beep.* Desiree's voice mail activated.

"What's good, Desiree? This Stacks. I got your message earlier, and I'm returning your call. Pardon me for the delay. I had to take care of some things today and lost track of time. I guess we both tried to catch each other and still didn't get to hook up. Hopefully our timing will be better and we can link up. Whenever you get this message, hit me back 'cause I really wanna get at you. Alright, I'll talk to you, and again, I apologize for waiting until the end of the day to return your call. I hope you understand," Stacks ended.

"What do you think, Keisha? Should I call him back or wait until tomorrow?" Desiree asked after listening to the message.

"It's up to you, girl, however you wanna play it. But you know what we trying to do. I'd call his ass back right now. Shit, I already got something set up with his brother, and I think Pam with that nigga Don right now, so we already on our jobs."

Even though she hadn't directly come out and said it, Desiree knew

Keisha was basically trying to tell her she was bullshitting. This was the first instance Keisha had ever seen her friend procrastinate so much. Any other time, Desiree would be slick-talking a nigga and setting up her plot, but now she was slow rolling. She had known Desiree for a long time, and because of all they had gone through, she knew they shared the same views on what they were into and what they were about.

"Yeah, you right. I'ma call him back now," Desiree said to Keisha.

"Alright, well, I'm about to see what's up with the rest of these hoes. See if they been putting something together. Knowing them bitches, they ain't met no ballers. Gimme about three hours and call me, and let me know how it went with you and that nigga. I should be home by then," Keisha told her.

"I'll call you."

"Okay, girl, I'll talk to you later. I'm out." Keisha left. As soon as she walked out the door, Desiree picked up the phone and dialed.

"Yeah, hello?" a voice on the other end answered.

"Hello. Is this Stacks?"

Stacks sat up, recognizing the voice.

"Yeah, this me. Wassup, lady?"

"Nothing much. I got your message. I was in the bathroom when you called and couldn't get to my phone," Desiree lied.

"That's alright. I'm glad you called."

"You not busy or anything, are you?"

"Nah. I was just watching a movie, eating some pizza. I should say the movie was watching me. I dozed off until the phone woke me up."

"Oh, I woke you?"

"That ain't nuthin'. I needed to be up anyway."

"I guess our timing got better," she said, repeating Stacks' message.

"Yeah, no doubt. Like I said, I would've called you earlier, but today was kind of hectic for me. When I called, I was just really getting some free time to get at you. I didn't want to be talking to you having to rush, nah I mean?"

"I understand. It's alright."

"So what you do today?" Stacks asked.

"Nothing really. Went to the mall with one of my girls, then we came back to my place and cooled out. I been here most of the day waiting for you to call," she teased.

"Ah, I see you ain't gonna let me live on that one, huh?"

"Nah, I'm only messing with you. What did you do today?"

"A lot of running around. Something I really don't like to do, but it had to be done. I had to dip out to Benson, then shoot out to Raleigh, and that shit took all day. But I don't wanna talk about that. I wanna talk about you."

"What about me?" Desiree cooed innocently.

"That's what I want to know. Whatever you're willing to tell me."

"Okay. Ask me a question, and I'll decide whether I want to give you an answer or not."

"Still feisty. I like that."

Desiree laughed into the receiver. "I'm not feisty. Why you say that?"

"Because you talking about 'I'll decide whether I want to give you an answer or not,' " Stacks teased.

"I wasn't trying to sound feisty. I was just saying," Desiree replied, still laughing.

"Okay, I got a question. How come someone as sexy as you don't have a man?"

Desiree became quiet. She knew that would be his first question. It was always the first one men asked her. Normally her well-rehearsed answer would roll off her tongue, but for some reason, she was stuck. She pulled her thoughts together before responding.

"I don't need a man to be happy, and I don't need a man who's no good either. I can do bad all by myself. Most niggas come at you the same way, and they all want the same thing. Having a man is too much aggravation, and I'm not beat for the bullshit." That was the best she could come up with at the moment.

"So did I?" Stacks asked curiously.

"Did you what?"

"Did I come at you the way every other nigga does?"

She paused to think about it.

"Honestly, no," she told him. "You were original wit' ya thing. I give you that."

"Oh, thank you, your highness."

"Shut up," she said, laughing. "You know what I mean. When you stepped to me, you seemed like you were being your own smooth self," she said, attempting to stroke his ego.

"Well, let me ask you another question. If I was so original and smooth, and you were digging me, then why'd you shut me down that night at the Taj?"

It was a good question, and Desiree hadn't anticipated him asking. She had no intentions of answering him directly.

"I didn't shut you down. You and your peoples already had a bunch of groupies around you, remember? Maybe you weren't into them, but your boys were. I wasn't trying to intrude, 'cause if I would've come over to your table, my girls would've had to come, and since y'all already had company, it woulda been too crowded. Besides, I never said I was digging you," she finished with a smile.

"Oh, my bad for assuming."

"No problem. Just try not to do it again," Desiree replied.

"Yo, you cold."

"I'm only playing, boy," she said, laughing.

"I know."

"Oh, you do?"

"Yeah."

"How you know that?"

"'Cause if you were for real, we wouldn't be talking right now," Stacks answered confidently.

"You ain't never lied."

"So, what's up? When can I see you?" Stacks asked.

Desiree knew she was taking a chance, but she had prolonged things long enough, so she was ready to turn it up. She was beginning to feel like her old self again.

"That's up to you. Tonight, if you want."

Stacks was caught off guard. He didn't expect Desiree to be so forward, but there was nothing more he'd rather do than to be with her. He always placed business before pleasure, and as bad as he wanted her, he had to decline the offer—for the moment.

"As much as I wish I could come through tonight, I can't. I gotta take care of something important that's gonna take the rest of the night and then some. How about I come scoop you this weekend and we do something?"

"Alright, that's cool," Desiree answered.

Stacks detected the disappointment, but he had to take care of his business.

"Cool. I'll get at you, and we'll set something up, okay?"

"Okay."

"Well, yo, I'ma let you go, and I'll speak to you some other time."

"You better," she said.

"Don't worry, I'ma make it my business to. Oh shit, I just remembered something."

"What?"

"My cousin is coming down in a couple of days, and I promised I'd show her a good time while she's down here," Stacks said, referring to Vanessa. He didn't know why he blurted out the lie about Vanessa being his cousin, but he decided to let it be. He doubted Desiree and Vanessa would ever meet anyway, so it really didn't matter.

"How long is she staying?"

"Maybe two weeks."

"Okay, well, whatever. Whenever you get the chance, you got my number."

"Yeah, I'll work out something. I promise."

"Alright. Talk to you soon, then."

"Definitely."

"Bye," Desiree said and hung up.

"Damn," Stacks said to himself. Out of all the times in the world to invite Vanessa down, why did it have to be that week? He was a man of his word and would have to work around Vanessa once he got her settled in and set up in town. Either way, it didn't matter, because Vanessa was like a cousin, and Desiree wasn't his girl, so what the worse that could happen?

Chapter Fifteen

"What does the P stand for in your name?" Pam asked Don.

"Perignon," Don said, smiling.

"No, it don't. Stop playing, boy." Pam softly hit him in the chest. "Besides, it's called *Dom* Perignon," she corrected.

"I know dat. I was playing."

Don and Pam had spent the night together at the Comfort Inn, smoking blunts, sipping Hennessy, and sexing until the sun came up. Don was really into her. He had been with at least a hundred different chicks since the three of them had been getting money in the south, and it was always just a fuck to him, but he really enjoyed being with a shorty from the Dirty. Just having her under him felt good. Pam wasn't like any of the other females he'd met. She was different and didn't ask him what type of whip he pushed back home, how much paper he was making, or to take her shopping. She wasn't up in his personal business, and he liked that. Not to mention she was his type physically. He had never been attracted to redbones or chocolate females, so Pam was right up his alley. He was feeling her caramel complexion, dark brown eyes, and long wavy hair. When they first met, Pam had worn her hair in a ponytail, but now she sported eight neat cornrows down her back. She had a prominent nose and a set of luscious lips, and her lip gloss enhanced their fullness. She was fit with small breasts, a shadow six midsection, petite waist with hips and ass to match, and muscular thighs and calves. Even when Don was sexing her, he could feel her muscles contracting on his Johnson. Pam and her sister had a strong resemblance, but to him she was the badder of the two.

"Nah, P's the first letter of my last name," he told her.

"Oh, so what's Don short for?"

"It ain't short for nothing. That's my name," he lied.

Don had never told any chick he met his real name, which was Donnell Lamar Porter. The older heads from his block started calling him Little Don Juan back in the day because he had a lot of shorties sweating him. As he got older, he eventually just went by Don.

"I know you lying, but it doesn't matter. I don't mind. If you wanted me to know, you would've told me, so it's not meant for me to know."

Pam was good at what she did. She knew how to make a man feel comfortable with being around her. In the past she had gotten some of the so-called thoroughest niggas to open up and share with her, behind closed doors about some of the most personal shit. Niggas who were supposed to be strong and tough in the streets, she had found to be some of the most insecure and weakest muthafuckas in the world. Pam even knew how to make niggas talk about their money without having to ask them shit about it. One of the things she realized they all had in common was the fact that whoever she dealt with who hustled and got money did it to make themselves feel good. Ironically, that was also the story of her life. Back in the day she was considered an ugly duckling. Niggas couldn't stand to look at her, but now she was the baddest bitch in the pond. She used her looks to her advantage.

"I dig how you think," Don said. "A nigga could get use to being wit' a shorty like you. Why you don't have a man?"

"Who said I didn't?" Pam answered in a serious tone.

Don looked at her not quite expecting that answer.

"Ha! I got you." She laughed. "I ain't got no man. It's hard to find a good nigga down here."

"Yo, you had me fucked up for a minute wit' that shit. Not that it would've mattered. That nigga's relationship would've been in jeopardy, 'cause that wouldna made me stop fucking wit' you," Don told her. He thought back to what she'd just said. "What you mean anyway, a good nigga hard to find down here? You saying I ain't shit?" he asked, smiling.

"You said it, I didn't," Pam joked.

"It's like that?"

"Nah, I'm just messing wit' you. It ain't like that. You seem like you cool and all, but you ain't from down here, and plus, we just met, so it's too early to tell, know what I mean?"

"Yeah, I know what you mean, and you right, but you'll see, though." Don said this as if he was determined to prove just how good of a dude he was. "Yo, light that blunt back up," he said to her. "That's some good smoke right there, the type of shit we be blowing up top. God bless the dead. This taste just like the shit my man Dread use to pump down here."

Pam almost choked as she was lighting the blunt. She was sure it had to be a coincidence. It couldn't be the same Dread they had robbed and put six feet under, but to be on the safe side she had to find out. If by chance the dread was one in the same, Pam and her crew were playing a dangerous game fucking with these new vics.

"You a'ight?" Don asked, patting Pam on the back.

"Yeah, I'm okay. Fucking smoke went down the wrong pipe."

"Yeah, right. That shit too strong for you. You can't handle it."

Pam flashed a fake smile. "What happened to your man?" She tried not to sound too curious.

"Who?" Don asked, forgetting what he had just said.

"You said your man use to pump some smoke down here like this."

"Oh, you mean my man Dread? Yeah, he got killed out in Raleigh a few weeks ago."

Pam was eager to learn how he'd been killed, but knew better than to ask.

"The nigga got bodied and robbed right up in his crib, and whoever did it left him butt-ass naked with a condom still on his joint, so it definitely had to be a chick involved because that nigga was up in some guts before he got murdered."

Pam's heart nearly burst out of her chest as she listened to Don. She thought she was going to have a heart attack right then and there, and wondered if Don could tell something was wrong.

"Did you hear about something like that on the news?" Don asked.

Pam tried to speak, but the words wouldn't come out. She finally answered "no" barely loud enough for him to hear.

"What's wrong? You a'ight?" Don asked again.

Pam was still stuck on stupid behind the coincidence that Don, Stacks, and Styles were cool with her and her girls' last victim, Dread. Her guilty conscience began to overwhelm her, and she started to wonder whether Don and his boys had figured out what happened to the dread, and if they planned on finding out who had killed him. She knew it wasn't the time to be falling to pieces, and she had to keep herself together. One false move or one wrong word could cost her and her girls their lives. She had to think of a way to get up out of there—and fast.

"I'm alright," she said, beating on her chest. "My asthma fucking with me, and I don't have my inhaler on me," she lied. "I need to get home and clear my lungs before I die out this muthafucka."

"A'ight, let me get dressed and I'll take you," Don offered.

"No, you don't gotta do that. I can make it home all right. I'll just call you when I get there to let you know I made it in."

"You sure?"

"Yeah."

"Okay, I'ma roll with that this time, but if something happens to you, I'ma feel fucked up that I let you drive by yourself like that. You better call me as soon as you get in."

"I will." Pam rushed to put on her pants and shoes.

"Yo, you sure you good?" Don asked again, watching her get dressed.

"Yeah. I told you, I'll be alright. I'll call you later," Pam said, reaching for the doorknob.

She had rushed out of the room so fast, she didn't even realize she had left her purse on the side of the table.

Chapter Sixteen

"Bitch, what was so important that you had to drag all of us over here to your crib like this? Why you couldn't say what you had to say over the phone?" Keisha asked.

Calling Don to let him know she had made it safely was the farthest thing from Pam's mind when she arrived home. There wasn't anything wrong with her in the first place besides wanting to get away from him. Instead of calling him, she called her crew. Now they were all at her place, stressing her to hear what she claimed was so urgent.

"Yeah, what's up, sis?" Tasha wanted to know.

"If y'all let me talk and stop asking me all these damn questions, I'll tell you."

"It better be good, the way you talking," Keisha snapped.

"Everybody chill, and let her talk," Desiree said.

Everyone got quiet and waited for Pam to continue.

"Thanks, girl," she said to Desiree. "I just got back from hanging out with that nigga Don."

"You called us over here to tell us you just got some dick?" Tasha asked, cutting her off.

"Tasha, shut the fuck up," Keisha barked, wanting to hear what Pam had to say.

"I was only fucking with her. Dag," Tasha whined.

"Well ain't nuthin' funny about what I'm talking about. This shit is serious," Pam responded. "You know that dread muthafucka we knocked off? That's Don and them other two niggas' boy."

"What?" Desiree said, surprised. "How you know that?"

"I told you, I was just with the nigga Don, and we were smoking some of that weed we took off the dread, and then outta the blue this nigga start talking all this bless-the-dead shit and that the smoke tasted like the shit his man Dread use to pump down here. At first I thought it was just a coincidence, but when I asked him how his man died, he went into the story about the police finding him butt naked with a condom on his dick, and how a chick gotta be involved because he was in some pussy when he got bodied. I almost choked when the muthafucka brought that shit up. Then the nigga gonna ask me, did I hear about it on the news."

"What did you say?" Keisha asked.

"You know I said no, but I don't know if he bought it."

"Do you think he knew you had something to do with it?" Desiree asked.

"I don't think so, but I don't think we should take any chances and keep fucking with them niggas like that."

"What the fuck you talking about? Why not?" Keisha wanted to know.

"I just think it's too close, and the way he was talking, you can tell they probably been thinking about it and trying to figure out what really went down."

"It doesn't sound like that to me," Keisha said. "It sound to me like that shit was just a coincidence. Ya ass all paranoid. The smoke could've come from anywhere. Them niggas way over in Dunn. We all the way over here in Durham, and that nigga got bodied like an hour from where we at. So how the fuck could we be linked to that shit when it's grimy bitches everywhere? Huh?"

"I'm just saying."

"Saying what, Pam?" Desiree asked. "Keisha's right. That shit was just a coincidence. Plus, you said it yourself you were blowing trees with that nigga. You know how ya ass get when you high."

"Yeah, maybe." Pam was unsure. Maybe her girls were right and it was just a coincidence. But her instinct told her otherwise.

"Maybe, my ass. That's exactly what it is, and we ain't backing down from this. We sticking to the script. If you wanna stop fucking with that nigga, then Tasha can get on him. The nigga probably would think he did something slick by fucking two sisters anyway. But either way, it's going down," Keisha said.

Everyone waited to hear how Pam was going to respond. If she wasn't up to working on Don, Tasha would easily step up to the plate and pick up where she left off. At one time or another they all had to fill in for one another for whatever reasons, so it wasn't a big deal.

"Nah, I don't need anyone to step in for me. I can handle it," Pam said. "You know I'm riding with my girls 'til the end. I just got a funny feeling about these niggas, that's all."

"Don't worry about it, sis. This ain't no different than any other clique of niggas we done got before," Tasha said to her sister, trying to assure her that there was nothing to be worried about. "Remember those niggas from B-more? It was four of them, and that shit was like taking candy from a baby. Now they were supposed to have been some rough-ass muthafuckas, but we got it like that."

"You right, girl. I'm probably bugging out. I'll be alright, and we gonna get these niggas," Pam said, regaining confidence. "How things going on your end?" she asked Keisha and Desiree.

"Shit in play. I'm suppose to hook up with that nigga Styles tomorrow, and Desiree got something set up with his brother, but it'll probably be a week or two from now for her," Keisha said.

"Damn. Why so long?" Pam asked.

"'Cause he got one of his female cousins coming down from up top, and he gotta be her baby-sitter while she here. At least that's what he said. I don't think the nigga lying 'cause he sound like he really wanna get at me," Desiree said.

"She? Girl, that nigga is frontin'. You know that bitch coming down here is probably his muthafuckin' girl. You know all them niggas that be coming down here getting money got a wifey up top. She probably one of them bitches that be pressing her man so much that he figured it would be less stressful to bring her ass down here. That's why we ain't really heard shit about him fuckin' with a lot of chicks like we did about them other two niggas," Pam said.

"You might be right," Keisha said. "But he definitely feeling Desiree, and if that's the case, and that bitch really his wifey, then we gonna make sure that nigga coughs up some of that paper and throws it our way."

Desiree just listened. She hadn't really thought about the fact that Stacks could've been lying to her about the female coming down from New York. It bothered her that he would lie about it. It shouldn't have made a difference if they were involved because he was supposed to be just another victim. However, it did matter, and the possibility that he may have lied about the girl or that he might actually have a girl, bothered Desiree. The more she thought about it, the more she realized she had also lied to him, and everything that she was about to try to establish with him would be all one big lie, too, just to get his paper. She wished she had agreed with Pam when she first started talking about changing their plan and moving on to the next vics, but it was too late.

"It don't even matter if that's his girl. She ain't coming down to stay for good. When she bounce, I'm gonna play him so close you gonna think I'm his wifey," Desiree said, trying to sound convincing.

"Okay. I hear that," Pam said.

"In about thirty days if shit go the way I think it will, then we should come off just as lovely as we did with that dread muthafucka, if not more. Our pockets will be blessed, and those niggas will be a distant memory," Keisha said to her friends. "This one right here could put us over the top, and we might not ever have to do this shit no more."

Everybody nodded in agreement. At one point they all had second thoughts about being involved in their schemes. None of them wanted to spend the rest of their lives using their bodies to get ahead, especially if it included robbing and taking lives. They had done so many setups together in the past that they'd become numb and would do whatever it took to get that money, get away safely and scot-free, even if it meant leaving no witnesses behind.

"Alright, I'm taking my ass back home, but Tasha, what's up with that nigga from Jersey?" Keisha asked.

"Honestly, that nigga ain't broke me off with shit. I'm getting tired of his ass. I'm ready when y'all ready," Tasha replied.

"That's my girl." Keisha was satisfied with her answer. "We'll handle that while that nigga Stacks is playing house with that bitch."

They all agreed and called it a night.

Chapter Seventeen

"How was your ride down?" Stacks asked, taking Vanessa's bags from her.

"It was cool. A little boring, but cool."

"Yeah, I know what you mean. I usually chill in the dining cars and sip on something until they close, then when they open up, I go sip again. By the time I start feeling nice, it be time to get off," Stacks said, smiling.

Vanessa laughed. "Stacks, you shot out. All you niggas from around the way alcoholics, anyway."

"What about yo' ass, you weed head?"

She laughed again. "You got that right. I love my trees. I was so bored on the train I slid up in the bathroom and blew one. That shit was crazy, 'cause I was trying to blow the smoke in the toilet and flush it out, but I don't think that it worked 'cause when I came out, everybody was looking at me all funny. I know the conductor smelled it 'cause every time he walked past me, he had this little grin on his face, but he ain't blow me up though. He was cool. He was an old black dude. He probably wished he could've smoked wit' me, the way he was looking,"

Vanessa said with yet another laugh.

Stacks didn't see the humor in the situation.

"Yo, that was some real dangerous shit you did, especially traveling the way you was. V, it's a different ballgame down here, baby. You can't be moving reckless like that 'cause one foolish move can cost you. Dig where I'm coming from?" he asked.

Stacks didn't enjoy having to talk to Vanessa the way that he did, but it had to be said. She had to understand how serious shit really was down in the Dirty South, and it was his job to make sure she knew. Vanessa was his responsibility while she was visiting, just the same as Styles and Don were.

"Don't take what I'm saying the wrong way. I'm just letting you know, a'ight?"

"Stacks, I ain't take it the wrong way. I know where you coming from, and you right, that was reckless of me. That could've gotten knocked and would've been my own fault," she said, admitting her mistake.

"Yeah, you could've, but don't talk like that, though. You made it down safe, and you here now. The hard part is over with. Shit gets easier from here on out. While you down here, you gonna get some of this paper, and you gonna have some fun. I'ma show you how the ballers ball in the dirty," Stacks told her.

"I like the sound of that."

Stacks closed the car trunk after he put Vanessa's bags in. He watched her as she opened the door to the rental. In spite of Vanessa's rough street attitude, Stacks thought she was definitely nice to look at. He admired her beauty and her shape. She turned back and caught him staring as she entered the car.

"What?" Vanessa asked, wondering why Stacks was staring at her.

"Nothing." Stacks got in the driver's side of the car. His cell went off, and he removed it from his hip clip.

"This Stacks. What's good?" he answered.

"This Desiree, you tell me," Desiree shot back in a mocking tone.

"Oh, what's up, yo?" Stacks cut his eyes at Vanessa.

"Nothing much. Just calling to see if your cousin came down yet?" Desiree said.

Stacks continued looking at Vanessa as Desiree talked. Instantly he began to feel guilty, but he didn't know why. After all, neither of them was his girl, and neither was giving him any pussy—yet. Stacks had never even kissed either of them. He couldn't understand why he was feeling like he'd just been caught out there by his wifey. He still hadn't figured out why he had lied to Desiree about Vanessa being his cousin. Even though his mind told him to tell the truth, his mouth was set to tell another lie.

"Yeah, I just picked her up."

Vanessa immediately turned her attention to Stacks' conversation, knowing he was referring to her with his last comment.

"Who's that, Styles or Don?" she asked.

Stacks put his hand over the receiver so Desiree couldn't hear what was being said.

"Nah, it's a friend. You don't know 'im." He made sure not to indicate that it was a female.

"Stacks, is everything all right?" Desiree asked.

"Yeah, everything's good," he replied, removing his hand from the phone. "We're on our way to my crib. She kinda tired, so I'm gonna take her to get settled in. I'll get at you a little later, a'ight?"

"That's cool. I'll talk to you then," Desiree responded.

"Definitely," Stacks said before he hung up.

"Who was that, one of your little down-south groupies?" Vanessa asked with a grin.

"What? You buggin'. I ain't got no down-south groupies or no up-north ones, either. I told you, it was a friend."

"Umm-hmm. Whatever, boy."

Stacks felt even worse. Though he had nothing to hide, he believed it was best that Desiree and Vanessa knew as little as possible about each other.

Chapter Eighteen

"So what's up? That bitch made it down here?" Keisha asked Desiree after she hung up the phone.

"Yeah, she down here."

"You think that's his cousin or what?"

Desiree hesitated for a minute. She was convinced the girl Stacks claimed to be his cousin from New York was definitely not. If it were his cousin, why would he cover the receiver during their conversation? Even though the two of them were friends, there was something in the way Stacks had emphasized she was "just a friend," when the girl in the background asked him to whom he was talking. Not one time did he ever refer to the girl as his cousin. Desiree was sure that this chick was no kin to him, but it still didn't prove that she was his wifey. She was definitely going to find out though, because that would determine how she'd vibe with him moving forward.

"No, I don't think she's his cousin, but I don't know if she's his girl either," she finally anwered.

"If she ain't blood, then she gotta be his wifey, or he at least fucking her. Why else would he send for her ass to come down here if they ain't fucking?" Keisha asked.

"You probably right," Desiree replied, not completely convinced.

She was digging Stacks. She felt in her heart and believed in her mind that he was one of the good ones. These thoughts caused Desiree to struggle with the fact that he was going to be their next victim. She always saw herself being with someone like Stacks, and she could tell if he had a girl, he would treat her the way a woman deserved to be treated. *Maybe that's why he sent for the girl he's calling his cousin, because he couldn't stand to be away from her so long,* Desiree thought.

Desiree wondered if Stacks thought about her the way that she was thinking about him at the moment. If he did, then that would change things, too, because guys like Stacks were hard to come by, and she didn't want to do anything she might regret later.

Desiree knew she had to find out where Stacks' head was before she revealed to Keisha and the rest of her partners that she was feeling him. First she wanted to know what the real connection was between him and the girl he had brought from up top before she did something she'd later regret.

"I'm gonna work on his brother and see what I can find out while that nigga entertains that bitch. It shouldn't take me more than three days after I give him some to get the nigga to start spilling his guts. No nigga can ever resist my shit and my head game. By the time I finish sucking the skin off that nigga dick, he'll be practically showing me where they keep their stash at," Keisha said proudly.

"You shot the fuck out, girl," Desiree said. "I'll still see what I can find out and see how close I can get, even though he got that chick down here. Maybe I can get him to creep off with me."

"Yeah, do what you can, but don't try too hard and blow it. You don't want the nigga to get too suspicious. If he feel you coming on too strong, he might think something funny. Don't forget, you dissed him a little the first time you met him, so it wouldn't look like your style if you always the first one to make a move. Let that nigga make the next move, then take it from there," Keisha told her.

Keisha was right. If Desiree started doing anything out of the ordinary, it might make Stacks suspicious, and the whole plan would be blown. She didn't know why she was speeding. She had never rushed with a vic before. For a quick moment Desiree thought she was slipping. She decided to take Keisha's advice and wait until Stacks made the next move.

Chapter Nineteen

Vanessa had just gotten out of the shower. It had been a long trip, and all she wanted to do was rest. The train ride down had worn her out. Stacks had settled her in and told her to make herself comfortable and rest up, because they were going to hang out later. He promised to return after he took care of a few things.

Vanessa wrapped the towel around her body and went into the room that would be hers for as long as she liked, according to Stacks. *It definitely feels good to be out of the hood,* she thought, smiling.

The bedroom was a spare that Stacks and his boys had hooked up. Vanessa would be the first to ever use the room. Everything in it was neatly situated. It was a nice, plain, comfortable room containing the basic necessities.

Vanessa went over to the stereo and turned on the music.

After finding a station that played R&B, she went to the bed and popped open one of her suitcases. She began pulling out her panties, bras, and cosmetics, laying them on the bed. She picked out the outfit she intended to wear for her night out on the town, and she found a drawer to put the rest of her things in. She then opened her other suitcases to pull out what she would put on the following day. Just then Vanessa heard one of her favorite songs by Jodeci on the radio.

"Oh, this is my cut right here," she said, snapping her fingers to the beat. She went and turned the music up, then took her towel off as she began grooming while she danced to the beat.

Stacks had a habit of rushing out, forgetting something he really needed, and he wouldn't realize it until he reached his destination or was almost there. He had just driven for twenty minutes and had to turn back around because he had forgotten to snatch up the digital scale.

Stacks pulled in to the yard and saw that Vanessa's bedroom light was still on. He thought she would've been asleep. When he got out the car, he could hear the music blaring from inside the house. He smiled, because he normally fell asleep with the music blasting. When Stacks walked into the house, he went straight to the kitchen and saw the scale on the table right where he had left it. He snatched it up, then opened the fridge and got a Corona before leaving. Stacks almost forgot to turn off Vanessa's light, but her slightly cracked door jarred his memory. He cracked the beer open, took a sip, then went to Vanessa's bedroom.

As Stacks pushed open the bedroom door, he stopped dead in his tracks in disbelief. There was Vanessa, naked, with her eyes closed, singing and dancing along with the music. Stacks knew she could dance because they had been up in the same clubs up top before many times. He used to enjoy watching the way she did her thing on the dance floor, especially when she dogged some nigga who tried to get up on her and couldn't hang. But to be standing there able to see the way her body moved in the nude had him mesmerized.

Her body was flawless. He had always wondered what she looked like up under the jeans and sweatshirts she wore. She was immaculate. Her chocolate skin looked as smooth as silk, and her frame resembled a beautifully carved sculpture. Everything was indeed in order, he thought, and seeing the way her body moved as she danced while applying the lotion to her nakedness, only heightened how sexy she looked. Stacks just stood there, continuing to watch Vanessa as he sipped on his Corona. He couldn't move, even if he wanted to.

Vanessa finished lotioning as the song was coming to an end. She reached for her deodorant on the bed, and when she opened her eyes, she noticed something in her peripheral vision. "Oh shit. Stacks, what are you doing?" she asked, startled, trying to cover herself up with her hands.

Stacks was so absorbed in watching Vanessa's peep show that her statement didn't register until the song went off and he heard the commercial. "Huh?" he answered.

Vanessa laughed at having caught him off guard.

"Boy, you heard me. What you doing here?"

"Oh, nah, I forgot something and had to come all the way back," he said, trying to stay focused. Vanessa continued to stand there naked while she talked. She had placed her hands on her hips. Stacks thought she looked even better standing still as he ran his eyes up and down every inch of her body, admiring her beauty some more.

"Well, I know it ain't in here, and it sure ain't down there where you looking, nasty." Vanessa smirked because Stacks' eyes were glued to the lower part of her body.

"What? Oh, you real funny. Ain't nobody looking at you. Anyway, put some clothes on," he said, trying to keep a straight face.

"I will if you get outta my room, nigga."

"Yeah, I'm out anyway. I'll be back later, like I told you," Stacks said.

"Bye," Vanessa replied, fanning her hand at him.

"Next time shut this door. I could've been anybody coming up in here catching you like this," he said, closing the door behind him.

After Stacks left, Vanessa sat on the bed, put her hands beneath her head and fell back. She knew this trip was going to be a long one, one she'd never forget.

As Stacks drove away, visions of Vanessa clouded his mind. He couldn't get over the fact that he was feeling her the way he was. He knew that it was best for him to just cool out and breathe easy because he didn't know how Vanessa felt about him. If he tried to make a move on her and she rejected him, he could mess up their whole friendship, and that's the last thing he wanted. He decided to be on his best behavior while she was in town, show her a good time, and help her get up her dough. Stacks knew it wasn't going to be easy with the way he was feeling. Aside from Vanessa, he had another chick on his mind that he was feeling. He didn't know how he had gotten himself into this sticky situation and didn't know how to get himself out of it, either.

Chapter Twenty

"I thought you wanted to hook up tomorrow, but I'm glad you called me tonight," Keisha said to Styles.

"Yeah, I was thinking about you and ain't have nothing to do, so I figured I'd call and see if I could come scoop you so we could cool out or something," Styles said.

"Well, you here. Now what you wanna do?" she asked.

"Whatever. It's up to you."

That's all Keisha needed to hear to take control of the situation. She knew that once she told Styles where she wanted to go, he'd have no problem taking her there. He probably would be feeling himself for how easy he thought it was to get her there in the first place.

"Let's go get a room and cool out," she said.

Styles couldn't believe it. He had hoped the night would end up that way, but he never thought it would be the first and only destination. Styles already had his mind set on wining and dining Keisha with the hopes she would give him some. He didn't have to worry about the wining and dining part anymore. He was ready to go straight to dessert. When Keisha stepped out her crib to get in the car, his joint started throbbing just from her looks. *She is a bad piece,* he thought. With her golden complexion, mouthful breasts, high butt with hips to match, and long legs, what more could a man ask for in a woman? Yeah, it would be a good day for Styles, and he had every intention of enjoying every moment of it.

"Yeah, we can do that. I'm wit' dat," Styles told her as he popped in Tupac's *All Eyes On Me* CD. He pushed play and pulled off.

As soon as they got into the room, Keisha sent Styles on a mission.

"Why you need these ice cubes? You gonna put them in your Henny?" Styles asked with disapproval. "All that on-the-rocks shit is for them bougeouis muthafuckas that can't handle it. You got to drink the Henny straight up wit' no chaser."

"Who said the ice was for my drink? I ain't putting no ice in my Henny. I'm putting the ice on you," Keisha said. She grabbed a cube from the bucket, put it in her mouth, and crunched.

Styles' eyes lit up as he smiled. Each time he heard Keisha's chewing the ice, his joint got harder. He had heard about chicks going down on niggas with ice, but he never had it done to him before.

"Yeah, I like the sound of that," he said.

Keisha knew that Styles would be open once he found out her intentions. She had mastered the technique of giving head with ice cubes in her mouth. That night she planned to do to Styles what she had done to several men in the past. And just like all of them, he was going to both enjoy and love it. After that night, she knew she'd have Styles chasing her the same way all the other men before him did. Keisha never had any complaints with the way she freaked niggas. Just on the strength of her head game alone, she had been lavished with all types of gifts, money, and trips. Some niggas had even proposed to her, but it always ended the same way. *Bitches get paid and the niggas get played, and soon Styles and the rest of his little team will be added to the list,* Keisha thought.

Later on Styles fell asleep, drained from the fucking Keisha had put on him. She had sucked and sexed him until he was out of gas. To her surprise, Styles had lasted longer than the others. She thought he'd never cum. She had given him head so long that her jaws locked up and began to cramp, but she got the job done. Keisha was quite pleased with her performance as she sat there puffing on an L.

"Yeah, nigga, rest up. Ya ass gonna need it," she whispered to herself. Keisha's goal was to whip it on Styles so good that he'd feel comfortable telling her anything she wanted to know so she could figure out the best way to execute her plans.

When he awoke, she planned to give him a repeat performance just as soon as her mouth loosened up. No nigga could resist double portions of her sex, even if they couldn't hang. Thanks to her father, she knew at a young age she had something special between her legs that would drive men crazy and this nigga Styles was no different.

Chapter Twenty-one

"Yo, Stacks, you the only nigga I fucks wit', dawg, and you still be taxing me. In a week, I done copped at least four pies from you, and nothing under ten onions a whop, and you can't do me better than a G an ounce?" Jalon, one of Stacks' regular buyers, asked.

"Son, you know it ain't even like that, B. Nigga, I be showing you mad love. You just don't be appreciating that shit. You one of the few muthafuckas I be fronting shit to and don't be sweating how long it takes to pay me. Now if you wanna fuck wit' them niggas that got them bullshit ounces for eight hundred dollars from Florida, then do ya thang. I ain't gonna be mad at you, but if you do that and then decide to cop from me again, you gonna have to pay twelve hundred an ounce like I be charging them other inconsistent-ass niggas."

"Nigga, you know I'm just bullshitting wit' you. You my muthafuckin' dawg, baby, and I ain't trying to fuck wit' nobody but you. I know you been showing love. Don't think I ain't appreciate that shit," Jalon said.

"I know you do, kid, and I know you a loyal muthafucka too. Matter of fact, I'll make a deal with you," Stacks said as a thought popped into his head.

"I got a half of brick that I need moved. I'll front you the whole half, and instead of giving me fifteen hundred off every onion for fronting it to you, just give me thirteen hundred. The only thing I want you to do is hit me with half a week from when I give 'em to you, and the other half the following week after that, unless you move it all before that. But I need the paper no later than two weeks. You think you can fuck wit' it?"

"Man, that's love, dawg. That's a bet. I got you covered. You got it wit' you now?"

"Nah, but I'll come check you tomorrow, and we'll set up, a'ight?"

"Yeah, that'll be cool. Good looking on that, my nigga," Jalon said.

"Don't worry about it. Just make sure you come through for me on that."

"I told you, dawg, I got you covered. Yo, ain't that ya boy's ride right there?" Jalon asked, pointing to the latest rental that Don drove.

"Yeah, that's him. Yo, listen, I'll catch you tomorrow, so be on point. I'll call before I come through. One."

"A'ight, my nigga. Peace out."

Stacks started toward Don's rental, and he got out of the car when he saw Stacks.

"What's good, B?" Don asked.

"Everything's good. What up wit' you?"

"Business as usual, you know."

"How you know I was out here?" Stacks asked him.

"I was just at the house, and Vanessa told me you said you were going to take care of something, and I remembered you saying Jalon got at you yesterday about rein-up. I figured this where you'd be. Yo, Vanessa looking good as hell, son," Don said.

Stacks didn't respond and switched the subject.

"Yo, where Styles at? The house?"

"Nah. He called me not too long ago and told me he was at the tele with that chick Keisha he met at the club."

"Desiree's homegirl?" Stacks asked.

"Yeah, that's the one. He called me from the hallway and told me how he hooked up with shorty and was ready to take her out and shit, but when he asked what she wanted to do, she said she wanted to go get a room and cool out. He said he think shorty a freak on the low. They probably all some freaks. You know I knocked off that chick Pam that be with them, right?"

"Word?"

"Yeah, son. Me and shorty got busy all night long, sexing, puffing, and sipping," Don said.

Now Stacks was curious. He wanted to know if Desiree was like her girlfriends, and whether she was just looking for a nigga to sleep with. He was usually a good judge of character, and nothing about her gave him that impression. He didn't take her as the type of female who slept around. Still, he couldn't be sure, since that old saying "birds of a feather flock together" usually rang true, but he was living proof it wasn't necessarily true since he wasn't anything like Don. Although Styles was his brother, he was nothing like him either. In fact, he and Styles were complete opposites.

"What up wit' you and that chick Desiree? You ain't hit that yet?" Don asked him.

"Nah. We parlayed a few times, but I ain't try to set nothing up. I knew Vanessa was coming down, and I ain't wanna get caught up wit' fucking wit' Desiree and not be able to show Vanessa a good time, nah mean?"

Don gave Stacks the same look he and Styles shared when Stacks first mentioned Vanessa's coming down.

"Nigga, what's the deal wit' you and Vanessa?" he asked. "I mean, she looking all good and shit, and I know she ain't just leaving the city because she heard so many good things about the South. What's really going on?"

"I told you before, ain't nothing. She wanted to get away from the yiddy, and I told her she could come chill wit' us. Then I told her since she coming down, she might as well bring some work and get some of this South money. That's it. No more, no less," Stacks said.

"Yeah, a'ight. That's what ya mouth say. I bet ya jimmy saying something else." Don smiled.

"Nigga, shut the fuck up. Yo, what you need? Why you looking for me anyway?"

"Oh, I almost forgot. Niggas out in Goldsboro got at me. They wanted a whole, man, so I dipped out there, and the muthafuckas talking about they want raw, not rock. I wanted to smack the shit outta them cats because they could've told me they was switching up. They normally get rock, and I charge them thirty-five grand for a brick. Since they wanted powder, though, I told 'em our bricks of powder go for thirty-eight."

"So why you ain't just go get a brick of raw and sell it to 'em? Why you need me?"

"Why you think? 'Cause you the only nigga out of us that can stretch that shit. I ain't trying to give these niggas a whole brick like that," Don said.

It made sense, but Stacks wasn't in the mood to put in the work required. He had too much other stuff on his mind, but he knew there was no way Don would let him get out of doing it. He made a note to remind himself to teach Styles and Don how to stretch the coke.

"A'ight. I'll meet you back at the crib. I gotta stop off at the store and get some come back and some other shit," Stacks said.

"A'ight, we'll link up at home, and I'll have all the stuff out for you by the time you get there so you can handle ya business. Then I'ma go make that delivery and collect that dough from them niggas in Goldsboro."

They both hopped in their rentals with the intention of meeting up at the house.

When Stacks arrived at their crib, everything was set up as Don promised.

"Don, go get them two pieces of plywood I got out back," Stacks said.

"I brought them in already. They in the living room."

"A'ight. Cool."

Stacks had everything laid out in the kitchen that he needed to stretch the coke. The kitchen resembled a chemistry lab. Ever since he'd been in the game, he had learned ways to expand his drug business and get more dough. When he was younger, his best friend's father had taught him how to stretch product, and it had served him well.

"Stacks, what you doing?" Vanessa asked as she walked into the kitchen.

"I'm about to hit this brick right quick."

"What?" Vanessa said, confused.

"I'ma about to stretch this brick and make an extra two to three hundred grams," he explained.

"For real? I heard you knew how to do that, but I thought niggas use to be fronting."

"Nah, they wasn't fronting. This how I really got back on after I came home from my bid, and this how I stay strong down here."

"Can I watch?" she asked.

"Yeah, no doubt. I don't care."

Vanessa pulled up a chair.

"Here, put this on." Stacks handed her a facemask. "This shit is strong, and when I bust it open and start fucking wit' it, it's gonna be even stronger. If you don't wanna get high, you better put it on."

Vanessa put the mask on as Stacks took a razor and slit the plastic in the middle of the packaged key. He burst it open and began pouring it onto a cake pan.

"Hand me that spatula over there by the sink," he said.

Vanessa handed Stacks the spatula, and he began to chop the rocks of coke up the way a chef diced an onion. After Stacks chopped the rocks to a manageable size, he grabbed a box of acetone, known on the streets as come back, poured some into a sandwich bag and weighed it. After he reached one hundred grams, he poured the acetone over the coke. He did this three times, dumping a bag of come back into the coke. He took the spatula and mixed it.

Stacks then got a spray bottle filled with water and adjusted the tip. "Close your eyes," he told Vanessa as he started to spray the water all in the air over the coke.

Vanessa did as she was told.

"You can open 'em now," he said a few minute later.

"What's that for?" she asked Stacks as the mist fell onto the cake pan.

"That's to help that shit I added to the coke to mix in without having to shave the rocks all the way down. If niggas get a brick of powder wit' no rocks, they gonna know a muthafucka hit it, but with this, they'll never be able to tell, 'cause I'ma put this baby back together the way it was before I busted it open."

"What's that you mixed in it?"

"That ain't nothing but acetone. You can buy that shit in any hardware store."

Stacks used the spatula again to mix the product, repeating everything until he had all 250 grams of come back mixed in with the coke.

"Plug that lamp in for me and slide that stool over here," Stacks said.

Vanessa plugged in the lamp and handed it to Stacks. He took it and set it on the high stool that he had slid as close as possible to the table. The lamp was an adjustable goose-neck heating one used to dry the product.

"What's that gonna do?" Vanessa asked.

"This gonna dry this shit back up, 'cause it's too moist right now from all the water I sprayed. You could either use one of these lamps or let it air dry, depends on how quick you wanna get it done."

"Oh."

"I hope you learning something, all these questions you asking," Stacks grinned.

"You want me to tell you everything you just did?" Vanessa said.

"Oh, you think it's that easy, huh? Okay. Well, I ain't done yet, but we'll see."

"Boy, shut up. I ain't saying I know what I'm doing. I'm just telling you that I was watching everything you did, that's all," Vanessa said.

Stacks hoped she was paying attention because niggas in the hood would kill to learn what he had just shown Vanessa.

"Why you got that separate from that?" she asked him a few minutes later, pointing to the Ziploc bag of drugs he had taken out and weighed earlier.

"I'ma take this 250 and whip it up and make about an extra three-and-a-half Os of hard off of it. I only needed 750 grams of the brick to turn it back to a whole brick of soft," Stacks said. He continued to check to see how the new key of coke was drying. "Yeah, this is what I'm talking about. This a good batch right here."

"How can you tell?" Vanessa asked.

Stacks pointed to the product. "Look at that right here. You see that? You see how you can still see the crystals in the coke and how everything looks one color?"

Vanessa studied the drugs for a minute. She tilted her head to the side, trying to see what Stacks saw. After taking a good look, she knew exactly what he was talking about.

"Oh yeah, I see it now. That's how you can tell?"

"There's other ways, but that's how I judge my shit."

"So now what you gonna do to it?" Vanessa asked, eager to learn more.

"Just watch. You'll see."

Stacks reached for the Saran Wrap and began spreading it across the kitchen table.

After taking a long piece of plastic, he grabbed the spatula and started scooping the coke from the sheet pan onto it, trying to put it as close as possible to the middle. Once he had transferred everything, he wrapped it so it didn't look like it had when he first busted it open.

Stacks took the repackaged kilo of coke and put it on the scale, which read 1003.08 grams. He knew that it was an accurate key because the extra 3.08 grams was the weight of the Saran Wrap. Stacks then took the plastic and spread it out, only this time he didn't tear it. Instead, he laid the kilo at the tip of the plastic.

"Come here," he said to Vanessa. "Hold this. When you see me running out of plastic, roll some more out until I tell you to stop."

"Alright."

Stacks began to neatly wrap the brick, each time smoothing out any wrinkles, making sure the coke became more compressed the more he wrapped it. He told Vanessa to stop as he tore off the plastic.

"That's it?" Vanessa asked when she thought it was done.

"No, not yet. Almost, though," Stacks answered, looking around. "Where this nigga put them shits at?" he mumbled to himself.

"What?"

"Some pieces of wood."

"You mean these?" Vanessa asked, reaching under the table and pulling out the wood for which Stacks was looking.

"Yeah. Let me get them."

Vanessa handed them to him. "What are those for?"

"I told you, you'll see." Stacks placed the packaged brick on the floor, putting a piece of wood on each side and another piece, which was the flatter of the three, on top.

"I want you to help me wit' this, a'ight?"

"Yeah, what do you want me to do?"

"Hold on. I'ma tell you in a minute."

Stacks went to the fridge and snatched two clamps off the top.

"I want you to hold these two pieces of wood together while I screw both these clamps on."

Vanessa looked at Stacks like he was crazy, but didn't say anything. She just sat on the floor and did what he asked. "Like this?"

"Yeah, that's good right there. When you feel one side tighten up, hold the other side tighter, and don't let go, or it'll slip."

"I won't."

Stacks put the right clamp on and started screwing it closed until he had it where he wanted. Vanessa held the left side as tight as she could.

It wasn't until Stacks told her that she was doing fine that she began to feel at ease.

"Okay, you can let go now," he told her.

She got up and watched him take over. Stacks took the flat board and placed it back on top of the other two pieces of wood. He put one foot at a time over it, pressing down on the brick. "What does that do?" Vanessa asked.

"It compresses the coke, like you saw it when I first started fucking wit' it. I gotta stand on it because the clamps only compressed the sides, squeezing everything to the top. This'll even it out." Stacks continued to press his weight on the board. "You see this?" Stacks asked, finally showing her the key of coke. "This is how a brick suppose to look."

It looked the same as it did before Stacks had stretched it. Vanessa could tell that he was proud of his work.

"Yeah, I see it. You did ya thing," she said.

"Yeah, it's cool, but I could've done better." He smiled. "I've done better."

"Stacks, you conceited."

"Nah, I'm just playing. Do me a favor, start straightening up some of this stuff while I go wake Don up. He shoulda been in here wit' you learning how to do this shit. Anyway, leave all of that right there," Stacks said, pointing to the acetone, Saran Wrap, and the cake pan, "'cause I gotta whip that quarter up after I give Don this shit."

"Yeah, I can do that, but don't think you got some live-in maid, nigga." Vanessa smiled.

"Nah yo, I know that. I look at you as the queen that you are, your highness." Stacks returned her smile.

"Nigga, save the game for them little country chicks you be hollering at."

"Whatever, V. I'll be right back."

Chapter Twenty-two

"Where the hell is my purse?" Pam screamed. She practically tore her house apart searching for it. It didn't dawn on her until she began to backtrack her steps that she had been without it for the past three days. She realized there was only one place it could be.

"Oh shit. I left my damn purse at the fucking motel with that nigga." Pam remembered the day she had rushed out of the room when she found out the dread was a friend of Don's.

She picked up her phone and dialed the pager number Don had given her to reach him, and punched in the code he told her to use.

Please God, don't let this nigga be the type of muthafucka that searches though people's shit, Pam prayed silently. She didn't want him to see the Rolex she had gotten herself from their last lick.

She hung up the phone and waited for Don to call back. Fifteen minutes went by before her phone rang.

"Hello?" Pam answered quickly.

"What's wrong wit' you, girl?" her sister asked.

"Oh, I thought you were Don."

"Damn, bitch, that nigga got you like that? Tasha asked.

"Tash, not right now. I ain't in no playing mood."

"My bad, sis. What's wrong?"

"Remember the night I called y'all over to my place?"

"Yeah."

"I was in such a hurry to get up outta the room wit' that nigga that I left my damn purse, and it has my ID and shit in there. Not only that, I left the fucking watch I bought up in there too."

"Damn, Pam. How you slip like that? You know you weren't supposed to be traveling wit' all of that shit on you anyway. What if that nigga copied ya info down or something, or worse, what if he started wondering what you doing wit' a twenty-five thousand-dollar watch and put two and two together and think you had something to do wit' that Jamaican nigga murder?"

"I know, I know," Pam whined. "I thought about all of that already." Just as she finished her sentence, her phone beeped.

"Tash, let me go. I think that might be Don on the other line. I'll call you back when I get off the phone wit' him, so don't go saying anything to Keisha and them until I see what's going on, alright?"

"Yeah, girl, I got you, but you better make sure everything's good. And don't forget, we gotta take care of that nigga in Charlotte tonight," Tasha reminded her.

"I won't. Let me go." Pam hung up, stressed.

"Yo, somebody paged me?" Don asked.

"Yeah. How many other females you give this code to?" Pam asked, trying to sound upset. She was glad to hear his voice and had to pull her thoughts together.

"Oh, what's good, love? I didn't know it was you. Ya code didn't come out right. Shit was all bunched up on my pager. That's what took me so long to call back. I been trying numbers for the past twenty-five minutes, 'cause I thought it was a business call. You the first person that answered."

Don's reasoning made sense and explained why he took so long to return her call.

"I'm sorry," Pam said. "I must've been speeding when I dialed it."

"Nah, you don't have to apologize. It's cool. What's up, though? You a'ight?"

"Yeah, I'm okay."

"I was wondering when you was gonna get at me. I was worried about you. You were supposed to call me when you got home that night. I ain't know what to think. It's been like four days now."

"I know. I been meaning to call. Shit just been hectic lately, and I been stressed out. I ain't wanna bother you wit' my problems."

"I understand, yo. Check, though. I got your purse. You left that shit at the tele that day. I almost left that shit in there too. If it wasn't for me dropping my blunt, I wouldn't have even seen that piece lying under the table. It's in my trunk, and you don't have to worry. I ain't go through ya shit. It's just the way you left it."

"I wasn't even thinking about that, boy. You ain't have to say all that," Pam lied, knowing that was her biggest concern.

"Yeah, a'ight, if you say so. I just ain't want you to think I was on it like that, that's all. But yo, you still could've called to let me know what was good that night," Don said.

She tried to think of something quick that didn't sound lame, seeing that he wasn't going to let it go. The first thing that came to mind was what most women used.

"I told you I didn't want to bother you with my problem, plus, I was too embarrassed to tell you anyway. I don't want you to think that I didn't want to call, so I'ma tell you what was really wrong. That morning my period came, and I started getting cramps. That's why I left like that, and when I got home all I wanted to do was take a bath and lay down," she explained.

"Oh, that's what it was?" he exclaimed.

"Yeah."

"You off now though, right? I'm trying to see you."

Pam laughed to herself. She'd just told him she had cramps and was on her period, and the only thing he was concerned about was getting some ass. Even if she was lying, she took offense to Don's lack of compassion. These three niggas were no different than others they'd dealt with. They weren't shit and deserved whatever they had coming to them.

"You might as well say I'm off because right now I'm just spotting, but that ain't nothing a hot bath won't cure. Why? What you want to get into?" she asked, trying to sound like she wanted to hook up with him.

"You," Don said jokingly.

"That can be arranged," Pam replied and faked a laugh. "How about I call you back in about a half an hour, after I get out the tub?"

"That'll work," Don said.

"Okay, I'll speak to you then."

After Pam hung up with Don, she dialed Keisha's number. She knew that Keisha would understand that she wouldn't be able to accompany them to Charlotte tonight. After all, it was business.

Chapter Twenty-three

"Yo, how everything going?" Stacks asked his business associate, Jalon.

"Shit good, dawg. I got half that for you already and should have the other half by next week, like you said."

"That's good. Go get that change for me so I can breeze up outta here. I'ma be at the car, a'ight?"

"Alright. I'll meet you over there."

Stacks pulled out his cell phone and dialed as he walked toward the rental.

"Hello?" a female said.

"What's the deal, sexy?"

"Hey, Stacks," Desiree said. "I thought you forgot about me."

"Never that, sweetheart."

"I can't tell," Desiree joked.

"Don't make me feel bad," Stacks said.

"Why not?" Desiree teased.

"'Cause I really have been thinking about you."

"Okay, I believe you. So what's up? Did your cousin go back to

New York yet?" Desiree asked.

"Nah, she's still here," Stacks replied, wishing he was able to tell her Vanessa was gone. He didn't know how much longer she'd be there. Not that he really wanted Vanessa to leave. In the past week they'd gotten closer than ever. But during that time, Desiree was also a constant thought on his mind.

"Oh," Desiree said, detecting Stacks' disappointmemt. "Well, what's up anyway?"

"Not much. What you doing today?"

"Not too much either. Probably take a shower, cook me something to eat, puff an L, and watch a movie," she said.

"By yourself?" Stacks asked.

"Yeah, basically."

"What's up? You want some company? I can come through."

"That would be nice, but what about your cousin?" Desiree asked.

"She'll be a'ight. She's been down here for a week now, so she's pretty much settled."

"Alright then. When you wanna come?"

"Right now," Stacks replied.

Desiree couldn't stop smiling after hanging up from Stacks. She knew that this was a night of opportunity, and she was going to take full advantage of it. After the night was over, she was sure things between her and Stacks would never be the same. She picked up her phone and speed dialed Keisha's cell phone.

Let the games begin, Desiree thought. She was finally getting what she wanted.

Chapter Twenty-four

Vanessa tossed lightly in her sleep, dreaming. Things between her and Stacks had gone in a direction she never thought possible. The past few days were the best in a long time, involving someone of the opposite sex. Although she and Stacks hadn't slept together, Vanessa had visions of making love to him. That night was the sixth recurring dream. She found herself looking forward to her night fantasies because they seemed so real. She didn't think they would ever become a reality because she didn't believe Stacks looked at her that way. Besides, the last thing she wanted to do was blow their friendship over a one-night stand that shouldn't have ever happened. She decided to harbor these thoughts and feelings out of respect, but her imaginings were so heartfelt that it was becoming difficult to shield how she felt on the surface.

Vanessa believed there was some type of truth in dreams. The way Stacks touched her body, and made her feel in her dreams had to be how he would make her feel in real life. Vanessa longed for his touch. She remembered the day Stacks caught her dancing naked. His eyes scanned her body sensually. He made her aware of her womanhood.

Her nipples stiffened, her stomach fluttered, and between her thighs became moist, but she maintained that night.

In her dreams, Stacks never made love to her the same way, but they all ended the same. He'd whisper in her ear, "Vanessa, you make me feel so good," to which she'd reply, "I never felt like this before either, baby." Then he'd repeat her name each time he thrust inside of her.

"Ooh. Vanessa! Vanessa! Vanessa! Vanessa!"

"Yes," she whispered seductively.

"Wake up," Stacks said, watching her enjoy her dream.

When Vanessa opened her eyes, she saw Stacks standing over her with a smile on his face. She flinched as she grabbed the blanket to cover her partially exposed breasts.

"Boy, you scared the hell out of me."

"My bad. I don't know why you covering up. I already seen your whole body," he said, smiling.

"That's 'cause you been sneaking around, like you doing now," Vanessa retorted.

"I don't be sneaking nothing. I live here too. I can't help it if I always catch you when you naked, enjoying yourself." Stacks laughed again.

"What you mean, always enjoying myself?"

"Yeah, enjoying yourself. First I catch you dancing in ya birthday suit, now I catch you dreaming about something good."

As soon as Stacks mentioned her dreaming, embarrassment came over Vanessa, but she tried to play if off. "How do you know whether it was good or bad?" she asked.

"It couldn't have been bad if you're talking about, 'I never felt like this before either, baby,' " Stacks imitated her.

Vanessa couldn't believe she had said that aloud. She wondered what else he might have heard.

"I don't remember nuthin' like that in my dream. You making that up." She tried to sound convincing.

"I know what I heard, and when I was waking you up, I was shaking you and calling ya name, and you started answering, 'Yes, yes,' all sexy and shit."

"Boy, shut up," Vanessa said, laughing again at Stacks' imitation of her. "I knew I felt something on me. You probably were trying to cop free feels while I was sleep."

"Oh, you real funny, but yo, check. The reason I woke you up was to let you know that I gotta make a move, and I'm gonna be gone for a while. I might not be back 'til the morning, so don't expect me."

"You sure you alright to drive? You just got off the road. You want me to come wit' you?" Vanessa asked, concerned.

"Nah, I'm good. I got it. I'm use to this shit. Besides, it's best that I ride alone wit' this shit in the car," he lied.

Stacks' conscience began to eat at him, and for a brief moment he thought about canceling his date with Desiree. Things were good with him and Vanessa as friends, but he knew that things could get even better with Desiree, and at the moment, that's what he needed. Vanessa was his peoples, but he needed more than a good friend tonight.

Chapter Twenty-five

"Desiree?" Keisha yelled into her phone.

"Yeah, it's me."

"Bitch, where the fuck you at?"

"I'm still at home."

"Home?" Keisha asked, upset. "What you doing home when you supposed to be in Charlotte? Come on, Desiree. How you gonna do this shit?"

"I know, I know, but it wasn't intentional," Desiree explained. "Right when I was about to leave, Stacks called. He wanted to know what I was doing, so I played it like I was going to cool out at home and watch a movie. He asked if he could come over to keep me company, and I couldn't tell him no, could I?"

"Nah, you did right," Keisha conceded. "You know the funny shit about this?"

"What?"

"The bitch Pam just called me right before you did and cancelled too. That other nigga Don wanted to hook up with her tonight."

"Damn."

"Yeah, so now it's just me and Tasha, with her scary ass. If she knew it was just the two of us, she'd be shitting on herself right now," Keisha joked.

Desiree laughed. "Keisha, you know I wish I could be there to watch your back, but—"

Keisha cut her off. "Don't worry about it. I got this. I'll call to let you know what went down, a'ight, so stop worrying about me and handle your business."

A'ight," Desiree said, concerned.

"Now let me go before this bitch start getting paranoid."

"Ooh, yeah, that shit feel good as hell. Suck dat shit, shorty. Yeah, right there, like dat," the kid known as Jersey moaned, palming Tasha's head, pushing it down onto his dick.

Jersey sexed Tasha's mouth rhythmically as she deep-throated all ten inches of his manhood. Releasing Jersey's hand from her head, Tasha tickled his nut sack with her tongue as she simultaneously jerked him off, wondering why her crew hadn't burst into the room. She was expecting them at any minute. Tasha had been dealing with Jersey for the past two months and had been giving him head long enough to know he couldn't resist closing his eyes from pleasure whenever she went down on him. She told Keisha, Desiree, and her sister that this was the best time to run down on the him. Tasha had been delaying Jersey's orgasm for nearly fifteen minutes and wondered how much longer she could keep it before Jersey shot his load. She knew if that happened, as instructed by Keisha, she would have to resort to plan B, taking matters into her own hands and subduing Jersey by any means necessary. Tasha wasn't sure if she was up for that.

Licking all around Jersey's shaft, Tasha was startled when her hair was pulled.

"Ouch!" Her scream alarmed Jersey, causing him to open his eyes. Instinctively he went to reach under his pillow.

"Gimme a reason to blow ya muthafuckin' face off," a deep voice threatened.

Jersey stopped all movement. He looked in the direction of the voice and saw someone standing beside the bed wearing an army-green ski mask, a green-and-tan camouflage army jacket, baggy blue jeans, and a pair of combat boots. The person held a fistful of Tasha's hair.

"Yo, just chill, kid. It ain't got to be no violence, baby boy," Jersey said, holding his hands up in the air, revealing he had no type of weapons. He was so calm about the matter that his thick, large dick still stood erect.

"Nigga, where the paper at?" the deep voice asked.

"It's over there in my inside jacket pocket. It's like eight Gs. Take it and roll, my man, so a playa can get back to handling his business. Feel me?"

"Muthafucka, you think I'm playing with ya punk ass?" the deep voice barked. "Don't make me blow this bitch fucking head off. Now, where the muthafuckin' stash at?"

Tasha started to evaluate the robbery. Could it be that someone else had been scheming on her vic? At first, she thought the masked assailant was one of her girls, but the voice didn't match any of them. Besides, there was only one person instead of three. For the first time, Tasha was actually afraid.

"Please don't kill me. I don't have nothing to do with this," she pleaded.

"Bitch, shut the fuck up." The perpetrator smacked Tasha upside the head with the snub-nosed .357 revolver.

Then, Tasha realized it wasn't a game. Unless Jersey coughed up some more paper, neither of them would make it out alive.

"What's it gonna be, nigga?" the assailant asked.

Jersey lay there helpless. "Yo, fam. Breathe easy. Shorty ain't got nuthin' to do with nuthin'. You ain't gotta take that route. How I know you ain't gonna do me dirty and flip if I tell you where my stash at?" Jersey asked.

"You don't, but I'll count to five, and if I still don't know, I'ma do this bitch."

Tasha stared at Jersey with pleading eyes.

"I got fifty stacks in my Beamer," Jersey said. "The keys are over there on the table."

"That's more like it. Bitch, get up!" the robber commanded.

Tasha complied. How could her partners leave her for dead? Where the hell were they? The only thing she could think about was making it out of the situation alive so she could scream on her homegirls.

"Get them keys," the robber instructed. "You got three minutes to get that shit and bring it back in here or I'ma kill this nigga, and if I hear a car start up, I'm coming out shooting, you hear me?"

"Um-hmm." Tasha nodded.

"Where at in the car?" Tasha asked as tears raced down her cheeks.

"The trunk," Jersey answered.

"A'ight go," the robber instructed.

In less than two minutes Tasha was back with the Timberland shoebox filled with money.

The robber was pleased. "Good, now I want you to tie that nigga up, then you got five minutes to get your stupid ass outta here."

Tasha looked at Jersey. "Yo, just do it, shorty," Jersey assured her. "I'll be alright."

Tasha took a sheet from the bed and tied Jersey's legs, then took another and did the same with his hands.

"Okay, now get the fuck outta here," the robber barked.

Without even looking back Tasha bolted out the house and jumped in her Prelude.

Tears streamed down Tasha's face as she sped down the dark street toward the highway. She frantically pulled out her cell phone and punched Keisha's number.

"Yeah, hello?"

"Bitch, where the hell y'all at?" Tasha screamed.

"Where you at?" Keisha retorted.

"Where the fuck y'all suppose to be. In Charlotte!"

"Tasha, calm ya ass down. What the fuck is wrong with you?"

"What's wrong with me?" Tasha asked in disgust. "What's wrong is why y'all left me hanging? Some muthafucka ran up in that nigga Jersey crib and robbed him and shit, and pistol whipped me."

"Bitch, ain't nobody pistol whip you." Keisha laughed.

"What the fuck is so funny, and how the hell you gonna tell me what the fuck just happened?" Tasha barked. She didn't see the humor in the situation.

"Bitch, I should've pistol whipped ya scary ass. That was a love tap," Keisha replied, still laughing.

"What?" Tasha thought she heard wrong.

"You heard me. That was me. I got the money," Keisha said, disguising her voice in the deep tone she had used during the robbery.

Tasha nearly crashed as she realized what had really happened. As angry and upset as she was, Tasha couldn't help but crack a smile. If Keisha hadn't told her, she would've never guessed it was her. Her girl never ceased to amaze her.

"I bounced a minute after you sped your fraidy cat ass outta there, and I left that nigga tied up," Keisha said.

"I wasn't scared," Tasha replied, trying to play it off, "but you ain't have to hit me with that damn gun, either. Bitch."

"Whatever. I see why you been giving that nigga free pussy all that time. That nigga had a big dick."

"Fuck you, Keish," Tasha shot back. She had wondered if Keisha had noticed Jersey's dick.

"Yeah, I know. Anyway, Desiree and Pam had to cancel, so I had to handle shit on my own. Where you at now?"

"I'm about to jump on the highway."

"Okay. Meet me at the spot. I'll fill you in on the details."

Chapter Twenty-six

"Thank you for holding my purse." Pam clutched the purse to her chest in relief.

"I told you, it was nothing, but you're welcome," Don replied as he exhaled the smoke from the blunt while making some of it come through his nose.

"Can I ask you something?"

"Yeah, what up?"

"Do you have a girlfriend back home?"

"Nah, why?"

"Damn, you answered that kind of quick. You sure you ain't got one?" Pam asked again.

"I ain't got no reason to lie. I'm positive," Don confirmed. "Why you ask?"

"I was just asking to be asking, no particular reason. It wouldn't matter to me anyway, 'cause she's up there and you're down here, so what she don't know won't hurt her."

Pam's answer caused a smile to spread across Don's face. He was definitely feeling her reponse and knew there was a reason why he felt he could fuck with her.

Pam talked like a gangsta bitch who would ride or die with a nigga, and that turned Don on. He figured she'd be the closest thing to a wifey for him, if he ever decided to hook up with a chick.

"It wouldn't work anyway if I had a shorty up top and I was always down here. No chicks back home would go for her nigga being gone this much without fucking around on him. And once I found out, I'd probably fuck around and kill her ass and him, too. I don't need the unnecessary drama bullshit in my life. Chicks don't ride for their niggas no more like that," he said.

"I do," Pam said, trying to get him to trust her.

"Yeah, you probably do, but you one out of a billion though," Don said.

"What about Stacks' girl? Does she ride for him?" Pam asked, hoping she didn't cross the line.

"What? Stacks ain't got a girl," Don replied.

"Oh. I heard my partner say he had a girl coming down from New York, and I assumed it was his wifey or something," Pam quickly retorted.

"You talking about Vanessa. Nah, that's not his wifey. Shorty like family. We grew up wit' her. She from around the way. She just down here on some visiting shit, that's all. Vanessa is a thorough-ass chick. If she had a man, she'd definitely ride for him," Don replied with admiration.

Now Pam knew the chick Stacks claimed to be his cousin was no relation at all but most importantly, she wasn't his girl. For that information, Pam intended to give Don the best sex he ever had, and she couldn't wait to tell Desiree the good news.

Chapter Twenty-seven

Stacks came out the bathroom after talking to Vanessa on the phone. He figured he'd be at Desiree's all night, so he told Vanessa he'd get a room after he handled his business. He hated lying to Vanessa about Desiree, but he was in too deep, so it was only right that he continued to flow with his string of lies. Desiree was still in her silk robe when he came out. She was preparing a plate of food for him in the kitchen. Stacks could smell the flavors and spices from where he stood. The aroma made him realize just how hungry he was. He was brought up that the way to a man's heart was through his stomach, and he believed that. The two most important people in his life, his mother and great grandmother could throw down in the kitchen.

Desiree sensed his presence and turned around, flashing him a smile.

"Do you want to eat in here or in the living room in front of the television? I got trays if that's what you want," she said.

"Yeah, it's cool. We can eat in the living room."

"Okay, well you can go in there and sit down. I'll bring ya plate to you."

"Yes, Mommy," Stacks said, smiling.

"Boy, shut up. I ain't meant it like that," Desiree said, laughing while he went into the living room.

Desiree reappeared with a tray bearing Stacks' plate and beverage. She quickly went back into the kitchen to retrieve her tray. The meal was steaming hot, and the scent of good food filled the air. She handed Stacks the plate, and he readily accepted. Stacks smiled, rubbed his hands together, and immediately dug in.

Stacks finished the macaroni and cheese and last piece of fried chicken and knocked off the rest of his Corona while he and Desiree watched *Love Jones* on DVD.

"Yo, that meal was banging. You did your thing," Stacks said.

"Thank you. I do a li'l sumptin' sumptin'," Desiree said modestly.

"Nah, it was more than that. I like a shorty who can burn in the kitchen 'cause a brotha love to eat."

"Yeah, I see that 'cause you got ya weight up."

Stacks smiled. "Yeah, you gotta feed the muscle."

"I wouldn't know about that 'cause I ain't got none," Desiree said. "And I definitely ain't working out."

"Maybe not, but you got the body, and ya looking right, too, so I know that food be going in the right spots."

"If you say so."

"I know so."

"Oh, here comes my favorite part." Desiree grabbed the remote to turn up the volume. "I love when Larenz Tate, with his fine self, freestyle this poem about Nia Long."

"No doubt. He do his thing, and Nia Long is a sexy muthafucka too," Stacks commented.

Desiree picked right up on his statement about Nia Long.

"You only said that because I called him fine." Desiree smiled.

"Okay, you got that. No more lusting over the actors for either one of us, deal?"

"Deal."

By the time the movie reached the middle, Desiree was laid across Stacks' lap, fast asleep.

Stacks didn't bother to disturb her because he didn't mind. Who would complain about a beautiful woman lying across them? No one in his right mind. He sat there watching the rest of the movie but was distracted by Desiree's silk nightgown, which hiked up each time she tried to find a comfortable position. He could see her long, smooth legs, from start to finish and occasionally the side of her apple-shaped bottom would reveal itself, causing his manhood to become alert. He wondered if she could feel it while she was asleep. There was no way he could hide it, not with her lying across him.

Desiree enjoyed this part of their evening and was good at what she did. She knew Stacks was convinced she was asleep, and her playful teasing was doing the job. It took all her strength to keep from laughing, especially when Stacks' dick was damn near poking Desiree in her ear. She hadn't worn any panties underneath her nightgown so that once she started working her magic, Stacks would get an eyeful.

Stacks debated on whether to slide Desiree's gown up or leave it be. He didn't want her to wake up and see the gown hiked above her thighs and think he'd been looking, even if it were true. He was just about to fix her gown when Desiree rolled onto her back and placed her hand between her legs. He couldn't believe his eyes. From the waist down, he could see Desiree's flesh, and what a sight it was. Her manicured hand barely covered the small patch of hair between her legs. Stacks' heart rate began to increase, and his joint was ready to burst through his jeans. He didn't know whether to wake her up or try to slide his dick out of the way, although the way Desiree's hand was positioned would make it difficult. Stacks had never been in a freaky predicament like this before, so he was stuck trying to decide what to do with a half-naked woman. He wished Desiree would change her sleeping position and roll over or something.

"Damn," he said under his breath.

Desiree was almost in tears, dying inside with laughter. She felt bad for Stacks, for having to go through the torture she was putting him through. She was surprised he didn't catch her smiling a few times.

Desiree could hear his rapid heartbeat from his stomach. She figured he'd suffered enough. Besides, the movie was about to go off. She heard Nia Long reciting the poem at the club for Larenz Tate, so she decided to bring her teasing game to an end, but still turn up the heat.

Just as Desiree was about to open her eyes, she felt Stacks pull his arm from under her, causing her to wait and see what he was trying to do. For a brief moment, the thought crossed her mind that he might be some type of pervert and was trying to cop free feels, but she erased that thought quickly because she knew he wasn't like that.

She realized Stacks was actually trying to pull her gown down. Most niggas would've been trying to pull it up as high as they could. Admiration and respect filled Desiree's heart for him, but she wasn't going to allow him to defeat her purpose. She clasped a fistful of her gown, causing Stacks' hand to slip onto her bare skin. His touch sent a chill through her body, triggering a warm, tingling feeling between her legs. His hand felt strong, but smooth like he had never done a hard day's work in his life.

Desiree felt the heat emanating from his hand circulating all through her. She wondered why he hadn't moved it away yet, but it didn't matter because she intended to move it for him.

Stacks continued to let his hand rest on Desiree's thigh, not knowing why. This was the second time in a couple of weeks that he had been mesmerized by a woman's beauty. First, it was when he had seen Vanessa in the nude and now with his hand glued to Desiree's thigh. He couldn't believe how he went from not being involved with anyone to wanting to be involved with two beauties. Both of them were bad pieces to him, and there was no doubt he was feeling them both.

Stacks knew he had to move his hand before Desiree eventually woke up and saw it, so as gently as possible he began lifting it from off her body, but he did it a little too late. Desiree's eyes opened, and she grabbed his hand.

Desiree looked dead into Stacks' eyes, and he couldn't imagine or predict what was going to happen. Though he tried, he couldn't read the look on Desiree's face. He wanted to at least explain before she thought the wrong thing. Just as he was about to say something, Desiree placed a finger to her lips and guided Stacks' hand between her legs.

Stacks was fucked up and couldn't believe his luck. All night, since he had been looking at her half-naked body, he had wondered how it would feel and taste down there, and now his curiosity was about to be satisfied.

Desiree was on fire when Stacks' finger entered her secret den. She eased closer to him and began kissing Stacks while he kept his finger inside her warmth. After kissing him on the mouth, Desiree moved her attention to his neck. She removed his finger from her pussy so she could straddle him. Stacks lay there, going with the flow as Desiree seduced him. He was used to being in charge, but liked how things were going and knew that he could take over anytime he felt the need.

Desiree lifted Stacks' shirt while kissing and admiring him. She liked the way he was put together, everything nice and solid. Both his chest and abs were hard, but she could tell that his drinking was catching up to him. Nonetheless, she hadn't been with a man this much in shape in a long time; although the whole night was about business, she was looking forward to the pleasure part. She began to unbutton his jeans, and even before she had them fully open she could feel his erection ready to bust out. Stacks lifted up so that she could slide down his pants.

Desiree was impressed when she removed his gray boxer briefs, which matched his tank top and T-shirt. She grabbed his dick and skillfully took him into her mouth. When it came to pleasuring a man orally, Desiree's props were up. Her whole crew had official head games. They used to sit around at one of their cribs, smoke weed, drink, and discuss the best way to go down on niggas for hours straight. Keisha was notorious when it came to the best head, but Desiree came in a close second, and that night she was putting down her best head game.

Stacks had been trying to refrain from busting off, but Desiree was making it real difficult the way she was handling her business on his joint. He had gotten head from some of the best in the business and placed Desiree as number one. She had him going crazy, and he thought it felt better than some of the chicks he had sexed in the past. As much as he would've liked to let go, he held it down a little longer.

Just when he thought he couldn't take it anymore, Desiree stopped. She attempted to straddle him, but he stopped her. Enough was enough. Stacks had laid back long enough allowing her to drive. Now it was his turn to take the wheel. In one swift motion, he laid her on the couch. Desiree was caught off guard. She was use to being the dominant one sexually, even to the most aggressive nigga, but Stacks was too strong, and her position was too awkward for her to regain control. Stacks spread her legs wide enough for his head to fit between them.

The entire time Desiree was doing him, Stacks fantasized about doing the same to her. Desiree's scent was a mixture of an exotic body spray and her natural sweetness. Stacks began to go to work. Desiree thought she was the only one who knew what she was doing when it came to handling her business. The way Stacks attacked her clit with his lips and tongue had Desiree climbing the walls. She no longer cared about Stacks not stopping. She hadn't been with a man sexually since the last nigga she set up, and that was almost a year ago. Desiree realized just how much she needed a tune-up, and Stacks was definitely the right maintenance man for the job. After multiple orgasms—four to be exact—Stacks came up for air.

"Now you can take back over," he said with a devilish grin.

Desiree was still recuperating from Stacks' official tongue lashing and said nothing. Instead, she got up and straddled him again, this time guiding him inside of her. Desiree rode him until they both reached their peaks.

Desiree sat there with her arms wrapped around his neck. They both breathed uncontrollably, lost in their own thoughts.

Stacks was thinking about how intense the sex was and wondered how he was going to deal with both Desiree and Vanessa now that he and Desiree had crossed the line to another level.

Desiree thought about how hard it was going be to go through with her clique's initial plan since she had officially fallen for Stacks. Nothing ever felt this right to her, and a meaningful relationship with a man like Stacks was all she really ever wanted.

Desiree got up and moved to cuddle beside Stacks. He drew her closer and kissed her on the forehead as they drifted off to sleep.

Chapter Twenty-eight

It was a little after eleven o'clock when Vanessa woke up. She heard noises coming from the kitchen and figured Stacks had returned. She climbed out of bed and went to the bathroom to brush her teeth. For some reason, she couldn't wait to see Stacks. Vanessa had missed him all night. When she stepped in the kitchen, disappointment immediately covered her face.

"What? You thought I was Stacks?" Styles asked, noticing the change in her expression.

"Actually, I did, but I ain't mean to look like it's not good to see you, though. You know you my peoples too, nigga." Vanessa didn't want to hurt his feelings.

"It's cool, yo. I know the deal. You want some breakfast?"

"Look at you, up in here cooking and shit. No wonder they call you Styles," Vanessa teased.

"Yo, go ahead wit' that. You want something to eat or what?" Styles asked again.

"Yeah, I'm hungry. What you make?"

"Some eggs, home fries, and turkey sausage."

"I'll take some eggs and home fries. I don't eat turkey," she replied.

"Word? I ain't know that. How come?"

"I just don't mess wit' too much meat. I don't eat no red meats and no turkey, only chicken and fish."

"Damn. No wonder ya shit stay looking right. I don't think I could do that shit."

"Yes, you could, if you tried."

"Like I said, I couldn't do it, 'cause I ain't doing it," Styles said. "I love my Mickey D's and my White Castle's too much for that shit."

They both laughed.

Styles made Vanessa's plate, and they sat at the table to eat.

"Yo, can I ask you something?" Styles inquired.

"Yeah, you know you can. What's up?"

"What's the deal wit' you and my brother?"

Vanessa was stuck. She didn't expect that to be the question, but she knew it was obvious to anyone around that there was something there between her and Stacks.

"Why you ask me that?"

"Come on, yo. I ain't stupid. A nigga got eyes and don't forget, that's my brother. I know him like a book, and that nigga digs the shit out of you."

Vanessa smiled. For sure, if anybody knew how Stacks felt or thought about her, it would be Styles.

"I'm digging him, too, but we just cool. I don't wanna mess up our friendship over no bullshit. If he ever tries to step to me in that way, I'm wit' it. I met some real niggas in the game before, and I think your brother is one of the realest I've ever come across. I know he trying to get his paper right, and I ain't trying to come between that because I know how important it is for him to be on top, so I'ma play it by ear and see where it goes. I haven't seen him wit' no wifey since that bitch Alicia shitted on him back when he got knocked. That right there tells me he ain't trying to be wit' no one chick, and I ain't trying to fuck wit' no nigga who's fucking wit' every bitch. He my boy and everything, but

I ain't trying to hear it. You better not tell him we were talking about all this either, Styles," Vanessa stated.

"Yo, don't worry about that. He ain't gonna know."

"Give me your word."

"Come on, yo."

"Styles, give me your word," Vanessa repeated.

"Okay, you got my word, but yo, let me tell you something about my brother. That nigga ain't starving for paper. He could stop hustling right now and never have to hustle again. Stacks hustles 'cause it ain't nothing else to do. This shit ain't number one to him, and he ain't got no shorty 'cause he ain't found one he thinks is a rider. It ain't too many chicks out there that get down like you. I ain't just saying this 'cause he my brother, but that nigga don't be fucking wild chicks. You should see how tight he gets about me and Don running through these down-south chicks. Stacks is a picky muthafucka when it comes to the shorties he let in or even sleeps wit'. I banged more chicks than that nigga, and he older than me, so the shit you worried about ain't even about nothing."

"What she worried about?" Stacks asked, entering the kitchen on the tail end of their conversation.

Styles and Vanessa both turned around, stunned to see Stacks. They had been so engrossed in their conversation they didn't even hear him enter.

"Nothing. Some small shit. Vanessa thought that work she brought down here interfered with what we doing," Styles said, winking at Vanessa.

"Yo, I told you before, that's nothing. We good, but even if it did, so what? Shit gonna move regardless," Stacks replied.

"I know. I know. It's just that I been down here almost two weeks, and it seems like you been waiting on me hand and foot, like I'm slowing y'all down or something."

"You bugging," Stacks said.

"Yeah, you bugging," Styles repeated, laughing. "You the only one slow rolling."

"How did everything go?" Vanessa asked Stacks.

"Huh?" Stacks asked, almost forgetting his excuse for leaving her.

"Last night. How did everything go?"

"Oh. Everything's good. I was just wild tired, that's all. I'm about to take a shower and take it down now. Try to get like a quick five hours or something."

"Do ya thing, bro. I'm about to step out anyway. I gotta shoot out to Raleigh and handle something. V, you wanna ride?"

"Nah, I'm gonna stay here, but thanks for the offer."

"Yeah, no doubt. Bro, I'll holla at you later."

"Alright. Yo, where's Don?"

"Last time I spoke to him, he was wit' that shorty Pam. You want me to get at him while I'm out?"

"Yeah, do that. We need to poly about some things, so make sure you here by ten."

"I'll be here, and I'll make sure he's here too."

"Stacks, what time you wanna get up?" Vanessa asked.

Stacks looked at his watch. It was almost one o'clock.

"Wake me up around six. I should be good by then."

"Okay."

Stacks went into the bathroom and hopped in the shower.

Even though Stacks had only been away for a half of the night, Vanessa thought it was still good to see him. Still, something wasn't right, but she just didn't know what it was.

Chapter Twenty-nine

"Yo, before I drop you off, I gotta take care of something right quick, a'ight?"

"That's cool," Pam replied.

She and Don had spent the night together again, and they had just as much fun as they had on their last encounter. They sexed each other for half the night and talked the other half. Don had done most of the talking, but Pam listened and learned a lot about him. Although she didn't pick up on any tension between them, she could tell that Don was somewhat envious of Stacks on the low by the way he spoke of him. Every time he mentioned Stacks, he would emphasize the word *always* as if Stacks did something he wished he could have done but didn't have the heart to, or just didn't know how. He spoke with great respect for him, but also wanted to be him, and Pam picked up on that. She wondered if that could be somehow used to her advantage to get closer to Don and get him to trust her more.

"Wait here. I'll be right back," Don said, hopping out of the SUV.

"I'll be here when you get back. I ain't going anywhere," she said with a smile.

"Funny. Real funny," Don shot back at her as he reached under the seat and pulled out a nine-millimeter, then shoved it in his pants.

Pam didn't say anything. She was used to niggas she dealt with carrying guns, so that didn't faze her. She watched as Don approached a group of young guys in front of the pool hall. She didn't know any of them because it wasn't the part of town where she hung out, and she really didn't associate with any small-time dope sellers anyway.

She figured they had to be some of the niggas that Don and them had working for them. Pam took Don as the type of nigga who didn't play when it came to taking care of business, and it turned her on to see a nigga in action. She wished she could've heard what he was saying, to see what type of G he spit at niggas to get them to pump for him. Usually niggas came from up north and promised southern niggas the world, and most of them fell for it. If she were a guy, she would be robbing every nigga who came to her from up top who wanted her to pump for them. Since she was a female, she settled for robbing any nigga from up top who was getting money, and Don was no exception. It didn't matter how cool he was and how good he made her feel when they were together. It was strictly M.O.B.—money over brothers. That's how Pam and her crew rolled.

"Yo, BB, where Marcy?" Don asked the short, brown-skinned kid.

"He inside," the kid answered.

"Go get 'im. I need to holla at you two niggas."

BB paused for a minute and looked at Don.

"Yo, you heard me? Go get that nigga Marcy, son."

BB went inside the hall to get Marcy while Don waited outside. Other niggas who were standing outside when Don pulled up, were either stepping off or went inside, sensing there was some tension in the air. They all knew who Don was and who he rolled with, and though they all had reputations for being thorough niggas, Don was known as the extreme hot-headed one out of the three-man clique.

Don saw Marcy through the window of Karoll's Pool Hall walking toward the door, but he didn't see BB. He knew right then and there these two niggas were playing games, because he had just told BB that he wanted to holla at both of them.

"Yo, where BB?" Don asked Marcy.

"He using the bathroom. He coming."

Don didn't believe him for a second. The way Marcy kept sucking on his gold tooth told Don that something was up. He could feel it. He had been in the game long enough to know when niggas was on some bullshit, and he wasn't going to let a couple of country muthafuckas play him.

"Yo, where my paper at, kid? You the only niggas that give me problems with mine. Let me get that, or bring me the rest of the shit you got," Don said.

Marcy chuckled. "Damn, dawg. Why you bugging?" Marcy asked. "We got ya paper. I thought we was cool? You on some flip shit right now. How you gonna come at us like this?"

"Nigga, you heard what I said," Don yelled, getting upset now. "Get me my paper. Where is it?"

Marcy's jaws tightened as he started sucking his gold tooth again. "BB got it. He in the bathroom counting it up," Marcy said, with a smirk.

"Y'all must think I'm some stupid muthafucka. I'm not in the mood to be playing with you or BB. I suggest you go get him, because shit ain't gonna be good if I have to go inside there," Don said as he began to corner BB.

"Yo, it's all good. Just be patient," Marcy said with a smug look.

Pam saw the area thinning out and immediately got on point. She could sense when danger was near, and something inside her told her this was one of those times. She reached for her handbag to get the .380, which she carried with her at all times.

There was no doubt in Pam's mind that the conversation between the dark-skinned kid and Don was getting heated. She could tell by their body language—really Don's—that the other kid wasn't feeling what Don had to say. She knew she had nothing to do with what was going on. It was some street shit between a worker and a boss, and since she wasn't Don's girl, Pam wasn't obligated to hold him down, but still she remained on point. After all, Don was her investment, and she wasn't going to allow anyone to mess that up. She had her .380 cocked and took off the safety. She watched the heated conversation between Don and the kid. Pam didn't understand how Don appeared oblivious to the change in the kid's attitude. A wide grin spread across the kid's face as he looked over Don's shoulder. Pam followed his eyes, and even before she could zero in, she noticed someone coming from behind the pool hall on Don's blind side. When Pam looked, she saw the boy Don had spoken to earlier when they first arrived. He had a gun and was aiming it directly at Don.

"Oh shit!" Pam yelled as she struggled to get out of the truck. She leaned over the driver's seat and hit the power-lock button then jumped out with her .380 in hand.

"Don. Don, he got a gun," she yelled but not before the boy was able to start busting.

The first bullet caught Don in the right arm, forcing him to jerk. The second one ripped through his pants and went straight through his calf, making him to fall to the ground.

The only thing that was in Don's favor was the distance from which the boy was shooting. If he were any closer, Don would've been a dead man.

Pam saw Don go down and started shooting at the boy who had just shot him. She could tell she had caught the boy off guard, especially when he saw that she was a woman.

Pam unloaded the first clip and was glad she always carried a second with her. She knew the boy wouldn't be able to hit her from behind the truck. He was at a disadvantage being out in the open. She was distracted by more gunshots, but she witnessed the dark-skinned kid go down after Don shot him. When the boy heard the shots, he also saw his partner in crime hit the pavement. He began blasting in Don's direction again. That was Pam's cue to make her shots count. The boy was searching for cover while firing at Don. Pam maximized the moment and fired at the boy. The first two shots missed, but the third one hit him in the leg.

When Don saw what was happening, he began bucking shots in the boy's direction as well. The boy knew he was outnumbered and outgunned and took flight. Sirens could be heard from afar, and both Pam and Don knew it was time to get up out of there.

"Don?" Pam yelled.

"Yo, I'm over here," he answered, waving his gun in the air.

"Hold on. I'm coming."

Pam jumped in the truck and drove to Don's location. She opened the door and Don climbed in as Pam peeled off. The only thing remaining outside was the kid's body.

Chapter Thirty

"Stacks, you getting up?" Vanessa asked him as she shook him until he opened his eyes.

"I'm up," Stacks answered. "What time is it?"

"Six o'clock."

"Damn, I was out."

"Yeah, snoring like a grizzly bear, nigga." Vanessa laughed.

"I don't snore," Stacks said, grinning.

"That's what they all say. I knew I should've recorded you."

"Yeah, whatever." Stacks changed the subject. "Did Styles or Don call?"

"No, not on the house phone, but your cell phone been ringing all day. Maybe it was them and they left a message. I wasn't gonna wake you up for that, when I know you was tired and they'd be here by ten anyway. Besides, you looked so cute sleeping, even if you was snoring."

"Knock it off with the snoring jokes, and hand me my phone. Let me see if they called."

Vanessa handed Stacks his cell phone, and he checked his messages.

He had four—three from Styles and one from Desiree. But none of them were from Don. Styles let him know he hadn't been able to get in touch with Don. Desiree's message was short and to the point. She said she enjoyed the night before and that she was thinking about him. He didn't react because Vanessa was right there, but he smiled on the inside as he deleted all his messages.

Pam pulled to the back of the motel and went to get a room. She didn't know what else to do, so she figured getting a room would be her best bet. Don had blacked out while they were driving. He had lost a lot of blood. His phone had been ringing off the hook, but she didn't answer it because it wasn't the time to be explaining anything to anyone. Once she got Don into the room, she'd call her girls and let them know the deal.

It was almost nine o'clock when Styles pulled up to the trailer. He had just moved two bricks out in Raleigh, at thirty-two Gs a piece, so he had been traveling with a lot of dough. He was happy as hell to be home, after being scared to death on the highway with a burner, sixty-four Gs, and a brick that one of the dudes reneged on copping. If he had gotten pulled over by DTs or state troopers, it would have been a wrap.

Stacks heard the engine turn off and assumed it was Don and Styles, but when the front door opened, Styles was alone.

"Yo, where Don at?" Stacks asked.

"I don't know. I never got in touch with the nigga. He ain't call you?"

"Nah, I ain't heard from him either. Where was he supposed to be going wit' that chick?"

"I don't know. He ain't say, but more than likely he at some tele, though."

"You try to holla at that chick Keisha you be fucking wit'?"

"Nah. I ain't think it was that serious, but I can holla at her if you want me to," Styles replied.

"Yeah, do that, because it ain't like Don not to check in or answer his jack."

"A'ight, I'ma call her right now."

Chapter Thirty-one

"Hello, who this?" Keisha answered her phone.

"Keisha, it's me. Pam."

Keisha sat up in the bed, hearing the panic in her friend's voice. "Pam, what's wrong?"

"What's wrong?" Pam replied. "I was just in a muthafucking shootout, that's what's wrong."

"What? Stop playing. What the hell are you talking about?" Keisha wasn't sure if she was hearing right.

"I ain't playing. I'm for real, and I don't know what the fuck to do."

"You hurt?"

"No, but Don is."

"Don? Who? That nigga that be in Dunn?"

"Yeah."

"What happened? Where you at?"

Pam provided Keisha with full details about what happened at the pool hall as she kept close watch on Don.

"Don't let him pass out like that. Try to wake him up," Keisha told her.

"I've been trying, but he keep going in and out."

"Still, try to keep him up. Did you check to see how bad he was hit?"

"No, but I think the bullets might've went straight through."

"Check and see."

"Alright. Hold on."

Pam tried to take Don's blood-soaked shirt off to check the shot to his arm. Each time she tried, Don moaned loudly from the pain, so she tried to figure out another way. Remembering the box cutter in her pocketbook, Pam retrieved it and cut the shirt off him. When she checked his arm, she realized that the bullet had gone right through his tricep and out his bicep. Although it was still bleeding, the blood had begun to dry up around the wound. After checking Don's arm, Pam cut off his pants and found that the bullet had also gone straight through his calf muscle.

Don is one lucky muthafucka, Pam thought.

"You still there?" Pam asked when she picked up the phone.

"Yeah, I'm here. What's up?" Keisha responded.

"Both them shits went straight through like I thought, but he still losing blood. What the fuck should I do?" Pam asked, getting upset.

"Calm down, baby girl. Everything's gonna be alright. Just listen to me, and do what I tell you. You got money on you?"

"I just spent most of my money on this room, but I got a few dollars."

"Nah, that ain't enough. Check that nigga pockets for some dough."

Pam grabbed Don's cut-up pants and did as Keisha said.

"Yeah, I got it. Now what?"

"Write this shit down I'm about to tell you."

Pam snatched up a pen and pad from off the desk. "I'm ready."

"Alright, I want you to go to the store and get some peroxide, iodine, and some gauze pads. Make sure you get the big ones. Get about four boxes of gauze, some Q-Tips, and a bottle of Motrin," Keisha ordered. Pam wrote everything down and repeated everything she wrote to Keisha.

"Is that it?"

"Yeah, that's it, but do you know what to do once you get all that shit?"

"Yeah, I think I do, but…"

"Hold on. My phone beeping," Keisha said and clicked over.

"Hello?" Keisha answered.

"Hello. This Keisha?"

"Yeah, who's this?"

"This Styles."

Keisha couldn't believe how out of all the people in the world, it had to be this nigga calling, especially at that moment. She had a funny feeling his calling somehow had something to do with Pam being with his boy Don.

"Hey, what's up?" Keisha asked, trying to sound surprised.

"Ain't nothing. Everything's love. What's up wit' you?"

"Nothing. Got my tired ass in the bed, trying to take it down for the night," Keisha lied, in case he wanted to hook up that evening.

"Oh, my bad. I ain't mean to disturb you," Styles apologized.

"No, you ain't disturb me. It's alright."

"Oh, a'ight, but yo, the reason I called was to see if you heard from one of your partners."

"Who?" Keisha asked, knowing to whom Styles was referring.

"Your home girl, Pam."

"Nah, not since yesterday. Why? What's up?"

"I don't know yet, but I know my man Don said he was supposed to be hooking up with her earlier, and we ain't heard from that nigga since. He ain't answering his cell, and I thought shorty might've told you where she was at or something."

Lying came naturally for Keisha, so it wasn't hard for her to convince Styles she was being straight with him. She could tell that Styles really hadn't heard what happened to his boy yet, but eventually he would. Then he and his brother would know that Pam was with Don and he'd be calling Keisha back again.

"I hope everything is alright wit' your man, but like I said, I haven't heard from Pam today."

"A'ight, that's cool. Well yo, I'ma let you go, but when can I see you again?"

Keisha smiled. She knew she had him open from their last encounter. She had him right where she wanted him. Still, she would just have to string him along until they cleared up the situation with Pam.

"I don't know, but we'll set something up," she said.

"No doubt. I'll holla. If you speak to your girl and she's wit' my man, can you tell her to tell him to get at either me or my brother?"

"Yeah. I'll tell her if she calls me," Keisha answered.

"Good looking."

"No problem. Bye." Keisha clicked back to the other line. "Pam?"

"Yeah. What took you so long?"

"That was Styles, looking for Don and you."

"Shit. They know already?"

"No, not yet."

"So how they know we're together?"

"Don told them earlier that he was gonna hook up wit' you."

"What you tell him?"

"Fuck you think I told him? I ain't heard from you, and I don't know where you at. Fuck that though. Just get to the store and get that list of stuff, and after you done, call me back, and we'll take it from there."

"Okay," Pam replied before she hung up.

Pam returned to the motel after getting everything on the list that Keisha had given her. Don was still unconscious when she got back. Before she left, she got him to open his eyes and drink some water to help cool him down. His skin was burning hot, and he was perspiring heavily. She put a towel full of ice under his head to keep cool while she was gone. Apparently it worked because he felt cooler than he did earlier. She dumped the supplies onto the bed and began to prepare to clean and patch up Don's injuries as best as she could. She checked both wounds again to see how badly he was still bleeding and to her surprise, the blood flow had slowed down. Pam shook Don in an attempt to wake him, but he didn't move. She shook him again a little harder, but still no movement.

"Don," she called while shaking him. "Don. Don," she yelled louder, but there was no answer.

Pam panicked as she grabbed his wrist and rested her head on his chest in search of a pulse or a heartbeat, but she was breathing so hard and her heart was beating so fast she could only hear herself. She didn't know what to do. She tried shaking him and calling his name again.

"Don? Don?" Pam continued to scream as tears began to well in her eyes. "No, please God," she cried. "Don? Don?"

As if God had answered her cry, she heard a noise.

"Huh?" was all Don had the strength to let out, but that was enough. Pam wiped her eyes and smiled.

"Nigga, you scared the shit out of me. I thought ya ass was dead."

Don managed to flash a little smile to let Pam know he was coherent.

"Don't worry. You gonna be alright. I got some stuff to hook you up until you can get to a hospital."

Don shook his head, as if to say no.

"What do you mean no? I gotta clean your wounds before they get infected," Pam said.

Don shook his head in agreement.

"Oh, you mean the hospital?" Pam asked.

Don nodded.

"Yeah, you right. If we go to the hospital they'll ask a whole bunch of questions, and then get the police involved. I feel you, but you gotta see somebody. Here, I got you some Motrin to help with the pain. Open your mouth."

Pam fed him four Motrin and made him drink some water to chase them down.

"Okay, now I'm gonna need you to bear with me, so I can clean this shit up. It's gonna hurt, but I got to get it done."

Don tried to say something, but he was so weak that only a whisper came out.

"Save your strength, baby. I got you," Pam said. "Just keep your eyes open to let me know you still wit' me."

Don smiled again.

Pam went to work on Don's wounds and knew it was painful when he flinched and his expression changed. She could tell he was a strong dude by the way he continued to fight to stay alive. After she dressed his wounds, she got up and went to call Keisha again.

"Yo, what she say?" Stacks asked Styles.

"She said she ain't speak to shorty and she don't know where she at."

"Why you ain't tell her to call the chick?"

"I wasn't even thinking like that, but I told her if she heard from her, to tell that nigga to get at us."

"Yo, something ain't right, son. Let's go look for this nigga, kid."

"Yeah, a'ight, no doubt," Styles said.

"You want me to come wit' you?" Vanessa asked.

"Nah, stay here just in case he call the crib. We'll be back," Stacks said.

"Alright."

"Yo, you got ya heat on you?" Stacks asked Styles.

"You know that."

"Hold up then, let me go get mine. We might as well take both cars. Ain't no need to ride wit' two burners in one whip."

"Where we going first?"

"We gonna go through Benson, then hit Dunn and bounce out from there and check all the spots and tele's."

"A'ight, cool. I'll follow you."

When they arrived in Benson, Stacks and Styles began to check all the places that Don could've possibly visited. They started with his favorite spots—the motels. They went to every one in town, but had no luck. They didn't see Don's truck anywhere. They headed over to the projects they controlled and where Don frequently hung out. Don was practically sleeping with every chick in the complex. They asked every person who knew them and knew Don, but nobody had seen or heard from him. Stacks and Styles left Benson and headed for Dunn.

They had no luck in Dunn either, and once again they visited all of Don's favorite spots. Then they decided to shoot to Karoll's Pool Hall on Broad Street. All the young hustlers hung out there. They were sure somebody there had seen Don. He always made it his business to check up on the little niggas who were hustling for them and chilled at that spot. They turned on Broad Street, and as they approached they saw a crowd of people, along with police cars and ambulances. Stacks couldn't believe his eyes. Without knowing what had occurred, he figured somehow Don was involved.

Stacks continued driving in the direction of the commotion. He wanted to get as close to the scene without leaving his car. He didn't want anyone to point him out and he didn't need the cops to ID him. He rode around looking for Don's truck, but didn't see it anywhere. The ambulances pulled off when Stacks and Styles got close enough to see what had occurred. Stacks saw the owner of the pool hall talking to one of the officers, and assumed the man was spilling his guts about what took place outside his spot. *Probably trying to protect his fat ass* Stacks thought.

Stacks knew a shootout had taken place because he saw the officers combing the area. He didn't see any of the niggas who normally got money around, so he knew the crowd had to be people who lived on the street and old timers who hung around the pool room. Stacks turned off the main street, and as he turned the corner he was flagged down by a familiar face. It was Pee-Dee from Elm. Stacks stopped the car, and Pee-Dee hopped in.

Chapter Thirty-two

"Keisha, it's me again," Pam announced.

"What took you so long to call back? I thought something went wrong."

"No, everything's okay. It only took long because Don was in a lot of pain, so I tried to take my time. I'm done, though, and I gave him a lot of Motrin."

"Is he alright?"

"Yeah, he's doing better, but he lost a lot of blood. I think he needs to go to the hospital, but he said no."

"Hell no. You don't want that, either. The police will be all over that muthafucka looking for somebody with bullets up in their ass. You don't think that shit's all over Dunn by now? I just hope none of them niggas knew who you was 'cause we don't need no shit like that."

"You right. So what are we gonna do about this nigga?"

"I was thinking while I was waiting for you to call. I figured this would be an opportunity for them to trust you, and you can get closer to where they lay their head at."

"Huh?" Pam asked, confused.

"Just listen. I want you to give it a couple of hours, then I want you to call that nigga Styles, 'cause the nigga Stacks might catch on. When you get in touch with him, let him know what went down. He'll probably know or done heard about what happened today, but you fill him in on how you held his man down and saved his ass. Most likely he'll wanna know where y'all at, but don't tell him. Pretend you're scared and it wouldn't be safe or a good idea to tell him because Five-O is hot in the area. Tell him to give you his address and you'll drive Don to them. If he gets suspicious, tell him that Don's unconscious and whenever he is awake, he can't talk, that's why you didn't ask him where they lived. Make sure they know how much blood he's lost and how bad he needs a doctor. They should go for it, and that'll get you to the crib at least, if not inside, and that'll be more than we know now about where they stay. If you do get in, you know to keep ya eyes open at all times and try to peep what you can. See if it looks like any wall or floor safes up in there. When you get there, tell them that you gotta call somebody and let them know you alright, like that's your first time calling anybody, and then call me. Everybody should be here by then. I'll fill them in on what happened when they get here. After you mapped out all you can, tell them to drop you off at a bogus area, and I'll come get you from there, alright?"

"Okay, I got you," Pam responded, as she took mental notes.

"The nigga Styles' cell phone number is 718-555-1876. Just say you got the number out of Don's cell phone."

"I'ma call soon as I hang up wit' you."

"Alright, talk to you soon. Be careful," Keisha cautioned.

"What's up, Pee-Dee?" Stacks asked as he drove toward Elm.

Pee-Dee appeared anxious when Stacks stopped to pick him up near the pool hall. "Yo, don't go through the hood. It's hot over there right now. Jump on 95 or something," Pee-Dee suggested.

Stacks did as he was told while looking through his rearview mirror, hoping Styles was still following him.

"Yo, what's the deal, son?" Stacks asked him again.

"Man, Stacks, shit done gone crazy, dawg. Ya boy Don was up at the pool hall shooting out wit' BB and Marcy. I was up there when Don rolled up, but I don't really know what the fuck happened. All I know is Don asked BB where Marcy was at, and BB said he was going to get 'im, he was inside. Niggas started rolling out or either going inside 'cause they thought some shit was gonna kick off. I went inside instead of leaving though 'cause money was coming. When I was going in, Marcy was coming out, but I ain't see BB though. Niggas was up in the pool hall talking about how Marcy and BB fucked y'all money up and was gonna get fucked up now. That was my first time ever hearing about it. I was looking out the window, and I saw ya boy Don letting that nigga Marcy have it, all up in his face screaming on him. Everybody was watching. Just when it looked like Don had calmed down and it was about to be over, all of a sudden we heard shots, and ya boy went down. Nobody ain't know what the fuck was going on or who was shooting. We just knew it wasn't Marcy or Don, but then somebody yelled out that it was BB who was doing the shooting," Pee-Dee said.

"Was that Don in the ambulance back there?" Stacks asked.

"Nah. That was Marcy."

"Marcy?"

"Yeah. When Don went down, Marcy tried to finish him off, but ya boy pulled out his gun and busted Marcy a few times and killed 'im." Pee-Dee replied.

"So what happened to my man?"

"I don't know, 'cause shots started coming through the glass, and I went for cover, but I heard a couple of different stories. I heard some other dude jumped out ya boy truck and started busting at BB, even hit him too. But then somebody else said it wasn't a dude, it was a girl. Mike Wind said he saw her come over the hood and unload and then reloaded another clip, but don't nobody believe him. Whoever it was, though, drove the truck over to a parked car next to where Don was laying and let him in. By the time the shots stopped and I looked up, Don was jumping in and they were pulling off."

"What they say about that nigga BB?" Stacks asked.

"They said BB flew like a bat outta hell when he heard the shots coming from the jeep."

"Yo, what muthafuckas was saying when po-po was questioning them?" Stacks asked.

"Far as I know, ain't nobody saying shit, but you know it's just a matter of time before somebody says something," Pee-Dee answered.

"Yeah, no doubt. Good looking though. I owe you one, kid. Where you want me to drop you off at?"

"You can drop me off at home. Ain't nobody gonna be able to make no more money today, anyway."

As Stacks drove, he thought about what Pee-Dee had told him, and he believed that Mike Wind really saw what he said he saw because he was a stand-up dude. Besides, from what Styles had told him, he knew that Desiree's friend Pam was supposed to have been with Don, but Stacks couldn't believe that she held it down like that. When they got to Pee-Dee's house, Stacks filled Styles in on what he heard and figured it was time to give Desiree a call to see what she knew.

Chapter Thirty-three

"Keisha, where she at now?" Tasha asked, concerned about her sister.

"Bitch, calm down. Didn't I tell you she a'ight and she in a room wit' that nigga?"

When Tasha and Desiree arrived at Keisha's place, she put them on to what went down with Don and Pam out in Dunn. They both listened intently with serious expressions. All Tasha could think about was what her sister must be going through. Tasha wasn't sure whether Keisha was withholding information from her in order to keep her from getting upset, but she felt she had a right to know everything. Pam was her flesh and blood, and if shit really went awry, Tasha wanted to know the truth.

"Keisha, don't tell me to calm down! That's my muthafucking sister, and I wanna make sure she really a'ight. I don't give a fuck about that nigga or how much money him and his fucking crew got. If you hiding something about my sister, you better come clean." Tasha boldly stepped to Keisha.

"Tasha, I'm telling you right now, you better back da fuck up and sit down before you regret it. If something was wrong wit' Pam, I would've told both of y'all. You know ya sister a thorough-ass bitch, and she gonna hold her shit down. We talked about what she gotta do, and she got it covered. She should be calling soon to let us know the deal, so don't worry. Trust me," Keisha said, understanding Tasha's concern, but she would not allow her to overstep her boundaries and blow up at her the way she did.

Tasha calmed down a little as she sat down. She knew that on her best day she was no match for Keisha, but her worry for her sister overpowered her and caused her to come at Keisha the way she did. Although she didn't like it, Tasha respected the way Keisha handled the situation instead of getting into a fistfight, which she could have easily done because Keisha loved to fight.

"Keisha, how long has it been since you last spoke to Pam?" Desiree asked.

"About an hour and a half, maybe two hours ago."

"That bitch Pam is gangsta," Tasha said, proud of her sister. "I can see her ass now, shooting her damn .380 like she Cleopatra Jones or some-fucking-body."

They all laughed a little, easing some of the tension.

"Yeah, I know, right? Wit' her crazy ass," Desiree said, smiling.

"We ain't gonna be able to tell that bitch shit now," Keisha commented. "When I talked to her, she was still shaken up about the shit, but I know when she get that weed and that drink in her ass, she gonna think she the baddest bitch in the Carolinas," Keisha said, laughing.

The tension had officially been cleared as laughter filled the room. They could never stay upset at one another for too long. It never lasted more than fifteen minutes, with the exception of the time when Pam was mad at Keisha for fucking a vic with whom she had wanted to sleep with.

"Des, roll a damn blunt," Keisha said. "My nerves is shot right now, and I need something to get my mind right."

"I got one already rolled," Desiree replied. "I was just about to smoke it when you called me, so I waited 'cause I figured y'all wanted to smoke too."

"You damn right I wanna smoke. Light that shit and stop playing games," Keisha told her.

Desiree shook her head and smiled as she reached in her purse to retrieve the blunt. Just as she was about to fire it up, her cell phone rang.

Chapter Thirty-four

"Talk to me," Styles said, answering his phone.

"Is this Styles?"

"Why? Who this?" he asked.

"This Pam, Keisha's friend."

As soon as Styles heard the name, he became serious.

"Yo, what up, shorty? You a'ight?"

"Yeah, I'm okay, but Don's not doing so well."

"What's wrong wit' 'im? Where he at?" Styles asked impatiently.

Pam was careful in choosing her words, like she and Keisha discussed. She needed things to go the way they had planned.

"You know what happened already?" she asked, knowing the answer.

"Yeah, we heard what went down, but not everything. How bad is he hurt?"

"He lost a lot of blood. He got hit in the arm and in the back of his leg. He was unconscious for a while, but I been keeping him up, and I brought some stuff to clean his wounds and dress 'em up. He's a strong nigga, but he still be in and out, and when he up, he be so weak he can't even talk. That's why I had to call you."

"Yo, you did well. We been waiting to hear from you, and we heard how you went all out too. We appreciate that, but what took you so long to get at us?"

Pam knew that question was coming, and she had prepared herself for it.

"I was so scared at first, I ain't know what to do. I didn't know whether he was gonna die or not, and I didn't wanna be the one to tell y'all. You the first person I called all day. I knew it would be better if I touched base with his peoples first, and he didn't want me to take him to a hospital. I was just glad to get away and get him to a place where I could help him before he died. Nobody don't know where I'm at, and I know my peoples just as worried about me as y'all were about him."

"Where you at?" Styles asked again.

"I'm at a motel."

"Which one? Let me know so we can come scoop you two."

"No, I don't think that's a good idea," Pam replied.

"Why not?"

"Because, it wouldn't look right if you came here and we all left together. The lady at the desk thinks I'm by myself, and I hit her with a fake ID. If she sees you pull in here, she may get suspicious and start watching the room or even call the police. You know how they are when they see young black people in new cars and stuff."

Styles thought about it for a second and agreed that Pam was right. He liked the way she was thinking and was a little envious of Don for having a chick like Pam with him at the time when he got into something. He wondered if her friend Keisha was as thorough as she was. "You right, and we don't need that, but this is what we can do. You know how to get to Smithfield from where you at?" Styles questioned.

"Yeah."

"A'ight, you know where the self-service carwash at?"

"Yeah, I know where it is," Pam answered.

"Okay, I'm gonna go there right now. By the time you get there, I'll be there waiting for you. I'll be in a burgundy Intrepid. When I see the truck come through, I'm gonna pull out, and you can follow me to our crib."

Pam began to feel at ease, seeing that her mission was just about accomplished. Soon she would know where they lived.

"That sounds good. It should take me about a hour and a half to get there 'cause I gotta straighten up and clean up this room, then get Don up to get him in the Jeep."

"Do what you gotta do. I'll be there waiting."

"Alright. I'll call you if there's a problem."

"No doubt," Styles said. "Yo, Pam?"

"Yeah?"

"Be careful, yo," Styles said.

"I will," she replied, and they hung up.

"Hello?"

"Desiree?"

Desiree recognized the voice. She knew it was just a matter of time before Stacks called. She put her finger to her lips to quiet her friends as she attempted to speak.

"Hey, what's up, stranger?" she said in a happy-to-hear-from-him kind of way.

Normally, Stacks would've joked around for a minute, but this wasn't a social call, and he needed some answers.

"What's up, Desiree? Listen, right, I'm calling you 'cause something happened wit' my man, and I think one of ya partners might be involved. I need to know if you heard from her today or not."

Desiree heard the concern in Stacks' voice. She was prepared to answer, but hated that she had to lie to him.

"Who? Which partner?"

"Your girl Pam."

"No, I haven't heard from Pam all day, but what happened, and why you think she involved?"

Stacks didn't want to say too much about what jumped off with Don and Pam because he didn't want to alarm her. Still, he had to tell her something.

"I don't really know the details of what popped off, but my man got into something out in Dunn, and he told my brother earlier that he was hooking up wit' Pam today. We think she might've been wit' him when it went down."

If Desiree didn't already know what really happened, she would've pressed Stacks until he told her more. She knew that he was holding back, but she understood and respected how he was trying to spare her just in case her friend was hurt. She knew Pam was fine, but still she faked her concern.

"Is Pam alright?"

"Yo, as far as I know, yeah, but I was hoping you knew something."

"Nobody ain't called me and said nothing."

"Yo, could you do me a favor and call her, or call one of ya other partners and see what you can find out?"

The more Stacks talked, the more Desiree felt him. To her, he was a thorough and smart nigga from the streets, and she knew his love and loyalty wouldn't allow him to stop or give up until he got to the bottom of the situation. She admired his strength.

"Yeah, I can."

"Hold on. My phone beeping," Stacks said.

"Okay."

Stacks clicked over. "What up?"

"Yo, bro, it's me," Styles replied. "That chick Pam just hollered at me. She said Don's fucked up, lost a lot of blood and shit. I'ma meet her out in Smithfield at the carwash and take them to the crib."

"Where they at now?" Stacks asked.

"At some tele, but she wouldn't say which one. Shorty a little fucked up behind that shit and was all paranoid about me coming to scoop them. That's why I'ma meet them at the carwash. She said the nigga Don was unconscious for a minute, but now he's going in and out, and he too weak to talk." Styles said, giving him all the info he knew.

"Word?"

"Yeah, son. Shorty said she cleaned his wounds and dressed him up, though. That bitch a trouper, B."

"Yeah, no doubt," Stacks agreed.

"Yo, meet me back at the crib. I should be there probably within the next hour and a half to two 'cause shorty said it's gonna take her a minute to get there."

"A'ight, yo, I'll meet you there. I got the chick Desiree on the other line."

"Oh, word? You told her what went down?" Styles asked.

"Not really. Just that something happened and her homegirl might've been wit' Don when it did."

"Yo, shorty said I'm the only person she got at, so you might wanna let her know now that we know what's good," Styles advised his brother.

"Nah, not yet," Stacks said.

"A'ight, whatever. You make the call. I'll catch you back at the hut."

"Yeah, no doubt. One."

"One."

Stacks returned to Desiree's call. "Pardon me for that. It was my brother."

"Is everything alright?" Desiree asked.

"Yeah. I ain't mean to get you all upset. I just thought you might've known something. I'm sure everything's good, and they probably together laid up somewhere, knowing that nigga. You got my word, if I find out something, I'll let you know what's up, and you do the same, a'ight?"

"Yeah, okay."

"A'ight, well, I'll holla at you." Stacks ended the conversation.

As soon as Stacks and Desiree hung up, Keisha filled her in on the conversation she just had with Pam about meeting Styles at the carwash and following him to where they lived. As Keisha talked, Desiree recognized the familiar look in her friend's eyes. The time was coming for them to score another lick. Only Desiree wasn't sure whether she was up for this one.

Chapter Thirty-five

"Yo, son, I'm at the crib. Where you at?" Stacks asked his brother when he answered the phone.

"I'm still at the carwash. Shorty called me about twenty minutes ago and said she was on her way. She should be here in about another ten or fifteen minutes, and we'll be on our way."

"A'ight. See you when you get here," Stacks told him before they hung up.

"You alright?" Vanessa asked Stacks. She noticed he was sitting on the couch with his head down while he massaged his temples.

Stacks was surprised to see her. He thought she was in her bedroom sleeping.

"Yeah, I'm a'ight. Just a little tired. I thought you were resting."

"How can I sleep when one of our peoples is missing?" Vanessa answered as concern spread across her face.

Stacks smiled. Her beauty almost made him forget just how thorough she really was when it came to the game. Vanessa wasn't the type of woman with whom you could associate the word *soft*, unless you were referring to her body. Even then, Stacks knew there was nothing soft about her only firmness came to mind.

"Oh, he's not missing anymore. We know what happened," Stacks said.

Vanessa immediately picked up on his tone and knew something was wrong. "What happened?" she asked.

Stacks clued her in on what took place in Dunn. Any other female probably would have cried or become emotional, however, Vanessa knew the game, and she understood that what happened to Don was just part of it.

"Don's strong. He'll be alright," Vanessa reassured Stacks.

"I know. I ain't even worried about that. I just wanna make sure he don't get knocked for that shit and no heat is on us. We definitely gonna have to get him up out of here and back to the yiddy."

"Where's he at now?" Vanessa asked.

"Him, Styles, and shorty that held him down should be on their way here."

"How you gonna get him back to New York?" Vanessa asked.

"Most likely, I'll probably have to drive him up there 'cause he can't get on a plane or nothing. C-Cipher gonna be everywhere, and they'll peep something's wrong and be all on us. Once they get here, I'ma get situated to be out tonight."

Vanessa pondered Stacks' last statement. She wanted to convince Stacks to let her roll with him.

"Stacks, I wanna ride with you. I think it would look better on the highway if you have a female with you. Don will probably be out the whole trip, and it'll look like you were driving alone. You know how those troopers are on 95, especially when you get to Jersey and hit the turnpike. All that racial profiling and stuff going on out there, it ain't safe. The last thing you'd need is to get pulled over and for them to see that Don's hurt. They'll really get suspicious then, but if they see a nigga and a chick, they may not bother us."

Stacks considered what Vanessa said, and felt it made sense. He was aware of how crazy it got with the troopers on the highway and decided to play it safe.

"I feel you, V. You right. It would be better if you took that ride with me. That's good looking because I didn't ever think about that."

"Two heads are better than one," Vanessa replied.

Stacks laughed. "No doubt." His cell phone rang, and he answered it. "What's good?"

"Yo, bro, shorty just pulled up, so we'll be there in a minute, alright?"

"Yeah, alright. See you in a few."

After they hung up, Stacks stood and stretched to relieve some tension. "That was Styles. They'll be here in a minute. Just get ready to make that trip. You don't need no clothes or nothing 'cause we coming right back the next day. Just take ya dough that you need to re-up with and drop off the shit you made down here to wherever you gotta take it. Ain't no need of going up without copping, when we gonna have to re-up in a couple of days anyway."

This was Vanessa's first time ever running and getting money with Stacks, but she dug the way he handled his business. She realized Stacks was the type of dude who didn't let anything get in his way when it came to taking care of his priorities. She knew that he loved Don and that was his man, still, what happened to him didn't affect Stacks' money-making decisions. He was focused and definitely staying on top of his game.

"Okay, I'll be ready. I'ma go hop in the shower right quick."

"Cool. If you need any help, let me know," Stacks joked.

Vanessa shot him a look as she walked toward her room. "Whatever."

Styles flicked his high beams when Don's rental truck pulled up.

He started to pull out so Pam could follow him to their trailer but noticed she was flicking the lights on the truck, trying to get his attention. Styles threw his rental in reverse and pulled alongside the truck as Pam rolled down the driver's side window.

"Yo, what up, shorty?" Styles asked.

"Something's wrong wit' Don. Ever since we left the motel, he's been screaming crazy and sweating again. He's really in pain, and I think he needs to go to the hospital. I know there are risks involved, but I don't wanna see him die."

Styles was feeling how concerned Pam was about his boy and respected chicks like her in the game.

"Yo, we can't take him to any hospitals down here, but we'll get 'im to one. Don't worry. Just follow me to the crib so we can take care of him," Styles said assuringly.

"Alright, but I just wanted you to know."

"Yeah, that's good looking. I appreciate that," he said before he pulled off.

Chapter Thirty-six

"Yo, Styles and them ain't here yet?" Stacks yelled from the room where he was counting his money.

"No, not yet," Vanessa said, looking out the living room window. "Hold up, I think that's them pulling up now. Yeah, that's them. They here."

Styles was lifting Don out of the truck just as Vanessa was opening the front door of the trailer. She saw the girl who drove the truck standing next to Styles, waiting for him to help Don out so that she could close the door to the truck.

Styles cradled Don as the woman followed. Vanessa was standing in the doorway when they reached the trailer.

"What up, V?" Styles greeted Vanessa as he passed her and carried Don to the bedroom.

Vanessa greeted him in return while keeping her eyes on the woman.

"Hi," the woman said to Vanessa.

"Hey," Vanessa replied.

The women stared at each other long and hard, both forming an immediate opinion about the other. There was something about the woman that Vanessa didn't like, and the feeling was mutual as far as the woman was concerned.

Pam broke the stare, not wanting to stir up any unnecessary bullshit with Vanessa. Now was not the time to be confrontational, but when the opportunity presented itself, she would find out why Vanessa was grilling her like that.

Vanessa was glad the woman had broken the stare first because she knew she would've stood her ground. She had mastered the art of grilling a person, male or female, so it was just a habit. She was grateful the woman saved Don's life, but there was definitely something about her that didn't sit right with Vanessa.

Styles returned from Don's room just in time to break the ice. "Yo, where Stacks at?"

"He's in the room, getting ready," Vanessa answered.

"Ready for what?" Styles asked.

"We're taking Don home tonight."

"Oh, word? I figured he'd wanna do something like that."

"Yeah, it's for the best," Vanessa said.

"Oh, yo, V, this Pam. Pam, this my peoples Vanessa," Styles introduced.

They shook hands and plastered fake smiles in front of Styles.

"I heard about what you did for Don. I'm glad you was with him to hold him down like that," Vanessa said sincerely.

"I'm glad I was there too. Don's a good guy and didn't deserve to go out like that," Pam returned.

Stacks finished counting the money he was going to flip, drop off, and leave behind in New York. He put three hundred and fifty grand in G stacks of hundreds in the duffle bag—two hundred Gs for the eight bricks he intended to cop and the other one hundred and fifty Gs to drop off to his stash crib back home. He put the other five hundred Gs back in the floor safe, along with one of his twin .40–caliber guns, tucking the other one in his pants. He closed the safe, put it back in the floor and slid the bed back over it.

When he appeared from the bedroom, Styles, Vanessa, and Pam were holding a conversation.

"Yo, what's the deal?" Stacks interrupted them. "Where Don?"

"I laid him in the room. He burning the fuck up, and those bandages shorty put on him are starting to soak," Styles told his brother. "She told me on the way to the carwash the nigga was screaming like a muthafucka out the blue, sweating crazy. I felt his head, and he feel like he got a fever or something. That nigga BB must've hit him with some rusty-ass bullets because I never heard of shit going straight through, fucking niggas up like that, kid."

"It happens," Stacks said. "Yo, Pam, I appreciate what you did for my peeps and everything. That's my word."

Pam looked at Stacks and smiled. She could see why her girl was attracted to him. The nigga definitely had it going on. He had a look of strength about himself, and he was as handsome as they came. Pam secretly wished she was the one to get close to him instead of Desiree. Not only did Stacks look good, he also looked like he knew how to fuck. It was a shame things had to go down the way they were because Pam still would've tried to give him some, but now that would never happen.

"Don't worry about it. I'm just glad he's alright," Pam answered.

"Yo, you still got more of that dressing?" Styles asked.

"Yeah, it's in the truck. You want me to go get it?"

"Yeah," Stacks answered. "Could you reapply them?"

"I could do that." Pam headed for the door.

"V, help her out while I holla at Styles for a minute." Stacks wanted some privacy with his brother.

"I got you," Vanessa said.

Pam came back inside with the gauze pads, and she and Vanessa went in the room to fix Don up.

"Yo, son, that nigga Don ain't looking too good. I don't know if he gonna make it," Styles said to Stacks.

"Don't say that, son. You know that nigga Don a strong muthafucka.

We just gotta get his ass up top and to a hospital. After that, he should be good. We can't take no chance taking him to no doctors down here 'cause they gonna report that shit."

"Yeah, I feel you, but it's gonna take you at least nine hours to get to the yiddy. You think he can hold on that long? The nigga still losing blood."

"Yo, I told you, he'll be a'ight. The nigga's strong. You know that. Remember when we was kids, and the nigga got hit by that car and was laid up in the hospital with two broken legs and a broken arm with tubes and shit all in his ass? The doctor said he'd have a permanent limp. One year later the nigga was running around like shit ain't never happened." Stacks laughed at the memory.

"Yeah, that nigga a funny muthafucka, B, trying to get everybody to start calling his ass Super Don, the Man of Steel." Styles laughed with his brother. "Yo, while me and V up top, I'm gonna go ahead and cop 'cause we low right now. I'ma drop some of this dough off, too, but I'm leaving five hundred here and those two bricks we had left. I already whacked them. You know where they at, right?" Stacks asked.

"Still in the back of the trailer up under that big rock?"

"Yeah."

"A'ight. I got 'em, but when you coming back?" Styles inquired.

"I'm trying to come right back tomorrow night. No later than two days."

"That's cool. I should be good until then."

"Yo, when me and V bounce, make sure you get shorty to wherever she needs to go. Ain't no need for her being up in here like this. Take her to get something to eat somewhere and drop her off at her home or something."

"Yeah, I'll make sure she gets home safe," Styles said.

"A'ight. I'll hit you up on the jack when I get up top."

"No doubt."

Styles decided to tell Stacks what was on his mind. "Yo, bro?"

"What's good?"

"Dig, right, I wasn't gonna say nothing 'cause I gave her my word, but you my brother, and I think you should know," Styles said.

Stacks looked at him, puzzled. "Know what?"

"Yo, don't say nothing 'cause then she gonna know I told you, but Vanessa feeling you like a muthafucka."

Stacks was stunned. "What?"

"You heard me. V feeling you, son, but she ain't wanna step to you 'cause she ain't wanna fuck up y'all's friendship. She ain't trying to be second to no next chick."

Stacks was dumbfounded. All this time he had been feeling Vanessa, but was afraid to express it for fear of rejection, and she was actually feeling him the same way.

"Word? She told you that?" he asked, smiling to himself.

"Yeah, she told me that, and I know you feeling her, too, bro, but like I told you, she ain't trying to be second to no next chick."

"Come on, son. You know I wouldn't even try to play V like that. I got too much love and respect for her, and it ain't nobody for her to be second to, anyway."

"You sure about that, kid?" Styles asked.

"Yeah, I'm sure. Why?"

"Son, you can't tell me you ain't feeling that chick Desiree. That day V was talking to me in the kitchen, you was just coming in from being with that broad. You can't front on me, nigga, 'cause I know. I smelt ya ass, and V probably did too. I know you fucking her, and she a bad piece, just like Vanessa. All I'm saying is, if you can't keep it official with V, then don't even fuck with her like that, son, 'cause you gonna fuck something up," Styles advised.

Stacks didn't reply because he knew his little brother was right. He was feeling Desiree just as much as he was feeling Vanessa. If he tried having both of them, eventually someone would get hurt, and he didn't want that, especially if it was Vanessa. Stacks had known her far longer than Desiree and understood that Vanessa deserved a nigga's loyalty when they fucked with her. There was no doubt that Vanessa gave a hundred percent, so Stacks agreed with Styles when he said if he couldn't keep it official with Vanessa then it was best not to even cross that line and try to deal with her on that level.

"Bro, I'm glad you slipped that to me, and you got my word I ain't gonna say nothing. If I can't keep it funky with Vanessa, I wouldn't try to fuck with her like that," Stacks said.

"I know that, bro. That's why I told you, so you'd know what's good, 'cause if I didn't, neither one of you wouldn't have said nothing, and I think shorty the one for you, B."

Stacks smiled. "Oh, you think she the one, huh?"

"Yeah, nigga, that's what I think," Styles answered.

"A'ight, nigga. Point taken. If it's meant for us, then shit'll fall into play, nah mean? Yo, let me get situated for this trip. Check and see if they almost done wit' Don up in there, 'cause I'm trying to be on the road within the next half hour."

"A'ight. I'ma go see what's up," Styles said.

Vanessa and Pam put new bandages on Don's wounds in silence. The tension hovered in the air. Vanessa was no dummy and had been in the streets long enough to recognize a snake when she saw one, and Pam's vibes were indicating she had reptilian in her blood. Although Vanessa was grateful for what Pam had done for Don, Vanessa was not impressed. She made a mental note to question Don about what really happened at the pool hall.

After they had finished wrapping the bandages, Pam broke the silence. "That should hold him till y'all get him back to the city," she stated.

"Yeah," Vanessa replied dryly.

"Will you be coming back down when Stacks returns?" Pam asked. "Maybe we can hang out or something if you do."

"Probably not. I think I had enough of the south to last me a lifetime," Vanessa replied.

Pam caught the sarcasm in Vanessa's voice but let it ride. She knew there was a reason she didn't care for northern women, and now she knew why. Pam didn't like when northerners tried to shit on the south. She wished Vanessa was in fact returning to North Carolina so she could make her pay for the disrespect she had just displayed. Since this was Pam's last time having an encounter with Vanessa, she decided to have a little question-and-answer session. "It must be hard on you being up there and your man being down here and all."

Vanessa's reaction was a little slow, but then she realized what Pam was insinuating and brought a smile to her face.

"You mean Stacks? Oh no, sweetheart. Stacks is like a brother to me. They all are," Vanessa clarified.

"Oh, I just thought…well, my girlfriend'll be glad to hear that," Pam slyly remarked.

Vanessa knew she was trying to be funny, but she ignored Pam's slight since Stacks wasn't her man.

Styles entered the room. "Yo, V, Stacks told me to tell you he'll be ready in a minute."

"Okay."

"Aye yo, Pam, I'ma drop you off wherever you want. We can stop off and get something to eat before that, though."

"That sounds good to me," Pam replied. "Vanessa, it was nice meeting you. I hope you have a safe trip back home." She tried her best to sound sincere.

"Thanks," Vanessa replied sarcastically.

The entire scene between Vanessa and Pam went unnoticed by Styles.

"Aye, yo, Stacks. Help me carry Don to the car," Styles hollered.

"Give me a sec," Stacks replied from his room.

"I can help," Vanessa said, volunteering.

"You sure?" Styles asked.

"Yeah, I'm good. I won't break," Vanessa teased. "Stacks, I'ma help Styles, so don't worry about it."

"A'ight. Cool," Stacks replied.

Come on then, V," Styles said.

"I'll get the door," Pam volunteered and headed to the exit.

As Pam stepped out of the room, she and Stacks collided into each other. "Oh, excuse me," she said.

"Don't worry about it, shorty," Stacks said as he moved on.

Pam noticed the navy duffle bag Stacks was holding, and instantly a bell went off in her head. She knew the contents of the bag had to be either drugs or money.

"Yo, like I said before, I appreciate how you held my man down," Stacks said.

"I'm just glad I was there for him," Pam replied in her most feminine tone.

"Yeah, me too. Yo, tell ya partner I'll see her when I get back."

"I will."

With that, Stacks was out the door.

"Yo, take care of my boy," Styles told Vanessa. "And my brother," he added with a smile.

"Shut up, nigga," Vanessa retorted, playfully punching Styles in the arm.

"Nah, for real though, do me that favor," Styles said seriously.

"You know I got you, boy. Do me a favor too."

"Anything, sis. Name it."

"Watch out for that bitch in there. I don't trust her ass."

"Who, shorty?" Styles asked, surprised. "Nah, yo, she a'ight," he added in Pam's defense.

"How you know? Just 'cause of what she did for Don?"

Styles was clueless as to why Vanessa was acting so tight with Pam, but the last thing he wanted was to get in a debate with Vanessa over something he felt she was overreacting about. To put her mind at ease, he submitted. "A'ight, sis, I feel you. If you say she ain't right, then she ain't right. I'll be on point."

"Thank you." Vanessa hugged Styles.

"You ready?" Stacks asked Vanessa as she exited the trailer.

"Yeah."

"Stay out of the town until I get back," Stacks instructed Styles. "We'll check on that BB shit when things die down."

"A'ight, yo."

Styles watched as Vanessa, Stacks, and Don pulled out of the driveway. Once they were out of sight, he went back inside the trailer.

"So what you wanna eat, shorty?"

This was better than Pam expected. "How 'bout we just cool out here for a little, order some Domino's, and smoke a blunt before you take me home," Pam suggested.

Pam's seductive tone didn't go unnoticed. Styles felt the vibes she was giving off as he peeped her wandering eyes zeroing in on his crotch. His manhood began to stiffen at the thought of what could possibly jump off between them.

"Sounds like a plan to me." Styles had dealt with enough females to know when they wanted to cool out together. He had no problem with accommodating Pam because she was definitely a bad piece to him, and it wasn't like she was Don's girl, he thought.

On several occasions Styles and Don had switched and shared chicks, so this would be no different, he reasoned. Styles allowed his little head to do the thinking and overpower his big head without hesitation.

Pam smiled and knew she had Styles right where she wanted him. She used her sex as a form of manipulation to entice Styles and was looking to hit payday. His hunger, greed, and lust for her would cost him dearly, she thought.

Chapter Thirty-seven

Vanessa slept for the first two hours until she felt the cold air hit her. When she woke up, she realized Stacks had rolled down all the windows.

"Boy, what you doing?" she yelled at Stacks playfully.

He laughed at the way Vanessa jumped out of her sleep.

"Yo, I was dozing off, and I needed some air. You over there knocked out and shit, and this nigga back there snoring his ass off. Y'all was making me tired."

Vanessa laughed. "You could've woke me up if you needed company. You ain't have to try and freeze my ass out, nigga."

"Oh, next time I'll do that." Stacks smiled.

"Where we at?"

"Virginia. We just hit Richmond."

"Damn, it don't even seem like it was that long."

"You was out, that's why."

"Shut up," Vanessa retorted.

"Yeah, a'ight. Yo, look back there and check on Don. Make sure the nigga still breathing. He's been out for a minute."

"Okay."

Vanessa turned around and leaned over to check on Don. She grabbed his wrist to check for a pulse, and thought she felt something, but wasn't sure, so she put a finger under his nose and felt air on it. He was still breathing.

"Yeah, he alright, just sleeping," she told Stacks as she turned back around.

"Good."

"You want me to drive some?"

"What? Nah, I got it. You ain't gonna kill me," Stacks joked. "I ain't never seen you drive."

"Whatever, Stacks. For ya information, I can drive. I probably been driving longer than you, and better too."

"Yeah okay, if you say so, but we won't find out tonight." He smiled.

"You think you so funny."

"No, I don't."

"Yes, you do."

"No, I don't."

"Stacks, shut up, boy."

He laughed at her. "I'm just playing with you."

"I know that."

"Seriously, though, I got it, but I appreciate you riding with me."

"You welcome."

"Yo, let me ask you something."

"What?"

"Have you been enjoying yourself down there?"

Vanessa couldn't believe Stacks had to ask her that. She thought he could tell she was having the time of her life. She wished she had the nerve to tell him that not only was she enjoying herself being down there, but she also liked being around him.

"What kind of question is that? I thought you could tell. Coming down was the best move I made in a long time. It's a little slow sometimes, but it's nice. Better than having to deal with all the nonsense up north. And the money's not bad, either.   Where else could I go and have fun without having to hustle and still make money? Yeah, I could get used to being in the south."

That was the type of response for which Stacks was looking. He was glad Vanessa had been enjoying herself. He thought about what Styles told him before they left and wondered how he should approach the subject.

"I'm glad to hear that. I figured that, though. I just wanted to hear it from you." Stacks looked over at her. Vanessa caught him staring, and there was a quick connection.

"You the one who's gonna get us killed," she said, to him.

"What?" he said, puzzled.

"You gonna get us killed if you don't keep ya eyes on the road."

"Oh." Stacks laughed, returning his focus to the road.

They still had a few more hours before they reached home, so Stacks had some time to figure out how to step to Vanessa. In the meantime, he needed to focus and get Don some medical attention immediately. At the rate that Don was bleeding, there was a good chance that he would die.

Chapter Thirty-eight

"This bitch should've called by now," Keisha said, concerned. "I know she ain't fuck up and blow that shit."

"Keisha, calm down. You know how slow Pam is when it comes to making her move, but you know she get it done," Tasha said, defending her sister.

"Yeah, Keisha, I'm with Tasha on that. Pam know what she doing," Desiree added.

"Yeah, y'all right. I'm bugging the fuck out. I know she be handling business properly," Keisha relented.

"If she ain't called within the next hour, then we'll just call her," Desiree suggested.

"Yeah, that's what's we'll do," Keisha agreed.

"That pizza came right on time 'cause that weed gave me the munchies," Pam said to Styles.

Styles and Pam had been puffing and sipping Hennessy, and immediately demolished the large pie as soon as it arrived.

"You still wanna smoke, or you done?" Styles asked.

"You can roll another one. I wanna call my girlfriends and let them know I'm alright, and I gotta use the bathroom."

"Yeah, do ya thing. The bathroom's back there." Styles pointed down the hall as Pam got up and retrieved her cell phone.

"I'll be right back." She walked to bathroom and hit a speed-dial button the minute she closed the door.

"Hello?"

"What's up, girl?" Pam said to Keisha.

"Bitch, where the hell you at?"

"Where you think I'm at?" Pam whispered. "I'm at these niggas' crib."

"You alright?"

"Yeah, I'm alright. Why? What's wrong?"

"Nothing's wrong. We was just worried about ya ass, that's all."

"Oh, nah, everything's okay. Listen, I'm here with that nigga you was getting at."

"Who, Styles?"

"Yeah, him. Anyway, his brother and that chick left about a couple hours ago to take that nigga Don back to New York, so they gonna be gone for at least a day or two…well, Stacks is, anyway, 'cause that bitch said she wasn't coming back. I wish she was, though, so I could get her muthafuckin' ass. She thought she was hot shit with her whack-ass accent slamming the south and shit."

"Pam, fuck her," Keisha said. "What's going on?"

"Oh, yeah, like I was saying, before Stacks left, I saw him carrying a duffle bag, and I'm positive it wasn't filled with clothes. I think the nigga's gonna cop while he up there. I saw what room he came out of with the bag, so I'm sure that's where they keep their paper. Me and the nigga Styles been getting high and drinking since they left. I been fronting, blowing the smoke out instead of inhaling, 'cause he got some strong shit and I don't wanna get too fucked up. You know how that Henny fucks with me, and I couldn't fake like I was drinking that. This nigga Styles feeling me right about now, and I think I'ma have to slip him some ass in order to stick around long enough for y'all to get here, but I wanted to run it by you first."

"Do what you gotta do. You know I don't give a fuck. You know how we do, and the nigga got some good dick too," Keisha said.

"It don't matter. He could be whack in the bed. I'm just buying time."

"I feel you, girl. Where they stay at?" Keisha asked.

"You know where those private trailers are past the carwash?"

"Yeah."

"They live right in that area. You know how they space out. I counted how many it was from the carwash, and it's the seventh one. I don't know the address, but it's a straight-away, so it shouldn't be hard to find. If you're not sure, just look for a Jeep and a burgundy Intrepid parked out front."

"Okay, I got you. We'll be there as soon as we can. Make sure you see where that nigga put his gun when you fuck him."

"He already got it out, lying on the coffee table. I'm on point. You know that. Oh, and tell Desiree that bitch that was down here wasn't Stacks' wifey. She like a sister to him. They grew up together."

"How you know that?" Keisha asked.

"'Cause I was milking her ass for info on the low, and she told me. I know she wasn't fronting by the way she was acting."

"I'll tell Deisree, but it doesn't matter because when he comes back, we'll be waiting for Stacks' ass too."

"I figured you'd wanna do that. It's whatever, though."

"That's right."

"Alright, let me go. I been in here too long. This nigga might start getting suspicious."

"Where you at?"

"I'm in the bathroom."

"Bitch, you shot out."

"Fuck you, Keisha. Let me go."

"A'ight, hoe. Enjoy the dick."

Keisha filled Desiree and Tasha in on the latest with Pam and explained how everything was about to go down. They got up and pre-pared to roll.

"Des, Pam told me to tell you that bitch wasn't Stacks' chick. They're like sister and brother."

"How she know that?" Desiree inquired.

"She got the bitch to tell her. You know Pam's a sneaky-ass bitch. She know how to get somebody to open up to her ass. Fuck him, anyway. Pretty soon, he'll be just another nigga that got got, just like rest of them other niggas," Keisha said to her.

"Yeah, you right." Desiree acted like she could care less.

Desiree didn't tell Keisha about the night she and Stacks spent together. She hadn't told anyone. It was her little secret, and she cherished it. No man had ever made her feel the way Stacks did. Desiree couldn't stop thinking about him.

She felt nothing for his brother Styles, so it didn't matter what happened to him that night. She hoped everything went according to plan and nothing ill popped off once they got to the crib, so they didn't have to continue pursuing Stacks because he didn't deserve what was intended for his brother.

"Damn, I thought you fell asleep in there or something," Styles said as Pam straddled him and took the blunt from his mouth.

"Blow me a shot gun," she told him.

Styles took the blunt, turned it around to the part that was lit, and began blowing smoke from the back. Pam put her hands on the sides of her face and took the smoke in her mouth and up her nose. She filled her mouth with more smoke and closed her lips to hold it in. Afterward, she took the blunt from Styles then pressed her lips against his and blew the smoke into his mouth. Styles took all the smoke, inhaling it and swallowing what didn't seep out.

Pam slipped her tongue in his mouth and began kissing him, and Styles returned the favor. Pam began to unfasten Styles' pants while they continued to kiss. Once his pants were open, Styles wrapped an arm around Pam and lifted her off the couch. When he stood, Pam wrapped her legs around his waist. Styles moved the coffee table to create more space and laid Pam on the living room carpet. The night had just begun.

Chapter Thirty-nine

"V, wake up."

"Huh?"

"Yo, I'm stopping for a minute," Stacks announced.

"What's wrong?"

"Nothing. I just gotta use the bathroom and splash a little water on my face."

"Oh. Where we at now?" Vanessa questioned, still groggy from sleep.

"I'm about to pull into the Maryland House."

"Okay. I gotta use the bathroom, too, and my stomach's growling, so I'ma get something to eat."

"Yo, I'm hungrier than a muthafucka," Don said from the backseat.

Stacks and Vanessa were surprised to hear his voice.

"Yo, what up, son? Damn, it's good to hear ya voice, kid. You a'ight back there?" Stacks said, looking at Don through the rearview mirror.

"I'm a'ight, just sore as hell, that's all. How long have I been out?" Don asked.

"This time or before?" Stacks asked.

"Damn, it's like that?"

"Yeah, son. You been scaring the shit out of us for damn near twenty-four hours. You was on some in-and-out shit."

"My bad, dawg," Don apologized.

"Nigga, fuck you mean, ya bad? Ain't nothing you could've done about that. I'm just glad ya ass alive."

Vanessa listened to them talk. The love between them was apparent. She felt like she was intruding on a sentimental moment.

"Hey, Don, it's good to see you up," she finally said.

"Thanks, V. Yo, where we at?" Don asked.

"We about to pull into the Maryland House."

"The Maryland House? What we doing way out here?" Don asked.

"We taking ya ass back home, that's what. You need a fucking doctor, nigga. You lost a lot of blood and shit," Stacks told him.

Don's head hurt, and he felt the pain shooting through his body, but he didn't remember why. He almost forgot what happened to him until Stacks mentioned the blood loss.

"Damn, I was wondering why I was feeling so weak and sore and shit. Them bitch-ass niggas BB and Marcy tried to get at me."

"They did get at you, nigga, but you got at one of them too. The right way, though. It's a wrap for that nigga Marcy, and the nigga BB's days are numbered, too, son. Believe that. Luckily, shorty was there to hold you down. She said she hit that nigga once or twice too."

"Oh shit, Pam, right?"

"Yeah."

"I forgot shorty was with me," Don continued. "That's a thorough-ass chick, son," Don said, giving Pam her props.

At the mention of her name, Vanessa decided to tell Stacks her instincts about Pam.

"And sneaky too," Vanessa added.

"What?" Stacks and Don said simultaneously.

"You heard me. Something ain't right about her. I know it and feel it. I was getting bad vibes off her the whole time she was at the house.

Then, when we were wrapping Don's wounds again, the bitch tried to question me on some slick shit."

"About what?" Stacks wanted to know.

"About where I was from, if I was coming back, and shit like that, and about us."

"Us?" Stacks asked, surprised.

"Yeah. She thought I was ya wifey."

"Word?"

"Yep. Don't worry, I ain't fuck ya thing up with her girlfriend, if that's what you wanna know," Vanessa said with attitude.

"What you talking about? I don't fuck with her girlfriend." Stacks knew that Vanessa was referring to Desiree.

"I don't know, V," Don rejoined the conversation. "Whenever me and shorty was together, it was all good. She was the only chick down there that I was really feeling. She ain't give a fuck about what I had or what I could do for her," Don said.

"Of course you not gonna see it. You a guy, but a bitch can pick up on when a bitch ain't right."

Stacks thought a moment. "Yo, I ain't saying you wrong about shorty. I'm just saying, maybe you going over the top. Just to be on the safe side, I'ma call Styles and see what's good, and make sure he got rid of her, a'ight?"

"Whatever," Vanessa replied, being nonchalant. "Whatever."

Chapter Forty

Styles had his face buried between Pam's thighs when the phone rang.

"Why you stop?" Pam asked, enjoying the moment.

"Hold up. My phone ringing."

"Let it ring," she said, trying to push Styles' head back down.

It had been a while since a man had gone down on her and knew what he was really doing, so Pam wanted to take advantage of Styles' tongue sexing while she still had the chance. The last two guys that she was with had left her unsatisfied. The dread didn't eat pussy and Don tried, but he didn't know what the fuck he was doing.

"Nah, I gotta get that. It might be my brother."

When Pam heard that, she immediately got back on point. She remembered Stacks telling Styles that he'd call him when he got to New York. It had only been about six hours since they left, and they couldn't have possibly made it there yet, Pam thought. Something might've happened to Don on the way up.

"Okay, but don't take so long." She really wanted him to finish what he started.

Styles jumped up and ran to the kitchen to answer the phone after the fourth ring.

"Hello?"

"Yo, son, what up?"

"What's good, bro?"

"What took you so long to answer the phone?"

"I was using the bathroom."

"Oh, yo, everything a'ight?' Stacks asked.

"Yeah, everything's good. Why? What up?"

"Nah, I'm just checking, that's all."

"Yo, you in New York already?"

"No, I'm in Maryland. I just wanted to make sure you handled your business and dropped shorty off somewhere."

"Yeah, no doubt," Styles lied.

"A'ight, that's cool. Yo, somebody wanna say what up to you."

"What's the deal, playboy?" Don greeted Styles.

"Oh shit, what's good, nigga? How you?"

"You know, I'm alive," Don replied.

"I feel you, but yo, don't even sweat that, B. That nigga's time running out. Feel me?" Styles said.

"I know that. You ain't gotta tell me. Yo, I'll holla at you later though. We about to get something to eat, a'ight?"

"Yeah, take care, kid."

"No question. Here go Stacks."

Stacks came on the line. "Yo, bro, just watch ya self down there. Don't even go out until we get back, a'ight?"

"I hear you, yo."

"A'ight, catch you on the come back."

"One," Styles ended.

"One."

Styles hung up and went back to finish his job with Pam.

"How many of them shits we passed already?" Keisha questioned.

"I think that was the fourth or the fifth," Tasha answered, uncertain.

"Shit. Desiree, how many you count?" Keisha asked.

"I wasn't even paying those shits no mind. I thought you had the count."

"I did, but I lost track. Fuck it, I'ma turn around and start again from the carwash."

Chapter Forty-one

Stacks replaced his cell in his hip holder. "Everything's good down there, V. Styles already got shorty up outta there, so that's a done deal, a'ight?" he said as he looked at her briefly.

"A'ight, if you say so," Vanessa said, sounding uneasy.

Stacks looked at Don through the rearview mirror, and they exchanged a quick look. Vanessa's reply left tension in the air, but no one bothered to further address the issue.

Vanessa and Stacks took Don's food order and went inside the Maryland House. They returned shortly after, filled up at the gas station and hit the road again. Traffic flowed smoothly, and within another hour-and-a-half, they were entering the New Jersey turnpike.

"I hate the fucking New Jersey turnpike. This shit long as hell," Stacks complained.

"We'll be home in a minute," Vanessa assured him.

"Yeah, I know. I just hate driving through this muthafucka with my burner, 'cause they be buggin' in Jersey. They'll pull you over for D.W.B. out this piece," Stacks said.

"D.W.B.? What's that?" Vanessa asked.

"Driving while black."

Vanessa laughed. "You shut up, boy."

"I ain't playing. I'm for real."

"You ain't never lied, kid," Don spoke as he woke up. "Jersey don't be playing no games, especially if you black or Hispanic."

"Well, like I said, we almost in New York, so we alright," Vanessa said.

"Shit, we ain't a'ight 'til we get to our destination," Stacks stated as he searched the highway for state troopers in the cut.

Chapter Forty-two

"The next one coming up should be the one," Keisha said

"What kind of rides Pam said to look for again?" Tasha asked.

"A burgundy Intrepid and an SUV," Desiree answered.

"There they go right there." Tasha pointed to the trailer they were pulling up to.

"Yeah, I see 'em." Keisha killed the lights on the car as she turned on to the path that lead to the trailer. When she got within fifteen feet of the house, she turned off the engine. "Alright, it's showtime. Y'all ready?"

Desiree and Tasha nodded.

"Alright, let's get this money then," Keisha said.

One by one, they exited the car and headed toward the trailer. They knew the front door would be unlocked. Whenever they did a home invasion, it was mandatory for whoever was fucking the victim to leave the door open. Keisha led the way. When she grabbed the knob it opened with ease.

"*Ssh,*" she warned her partners. She slowly cracked the door just enough to see inside. When she stuck her head in, the first thing she saw was Styles and Pam.

Styles had just finished going down on Pam, then they switched positions so she could return the favor. She had given him head for at least an hour, trying to buy enough time for her girls to arrive. She figured by the time they started sexing, Keisha and their crew would be pulling up. Pam took her mouth off Styles and wrapped her hand around his joint. She climbed on top and guided him inside her. He grabbed her by the hips to meet her pump for pump. Pam removed his hands from her hips and placed them on her breasts as she slowly grinded her hips into him. Pam had been doing everything in her power to keep Styles occupied. She even allowed him to fuck her raw, though the last thing she wanted was to catch some shit or make a baby with some random nigga. But Pam was caught up in the heat of the moment and also needed to kill time until her girls came.

Pam knew Styles was open off the sex from his expression. As she rode him, she realized his gun was within arm's reach, so she lay on top of him and began licking his ear and kissing him on his neck.

Pam continued to ride Styles and fondle his ears and neck with her tongue. She tried to reach for his gun, but was unsuccessful. She even tried pumping him harder in order to get him to slide back, but he didn't budge. Instead, Styles met her stroke for stroke, giving her all he had until something broke his concentration. A light shone across his face, and he opened his eyes. When he opened them, he noticed shadows behind Pam and quickly reached for his gun, but he was too late.

I couldn't have arrived at a better time, Keisha thought, seeing Pam riding Styles. She knew men were most vulnerable when they were in a piece of ass. She entered the house first and waved Desiree and Tasha in. The two of them entered and steathily closed the door behind them. They all witnessed Pam working Styles' dick like a pro. They all had their guns out, cocked and ready for whatever. They spread out, careful not to be seen or heard, but just as Desiree was moving to the right, Styles opened his eyes and caught her. Desiree froze long enough for Styles to push Pam off him and reach for his gun. Styles came up emptyhanded, and when he looked up, Pam stood there naked, pointing his gun dead at him.

Chapter Forty-three

"Yo, son, wake up. We here," Stacks yelled to Don.

"Where we at? This ain't the projects," Don said, looking around.

"I know. It's Dr. T's crib," Stacks replied. "Ya ass need a doctor, nigga, and he the only muthafucka we can take you to without the police getting involved. You know if we take you to the hospital, they gonna call it in. When po-po get there, they gonna ask you a million questions then lock ya ass up. I already called ya mom's crib and spoke to ya sister and 'em. They should be here already. V gonna help you in. You know I can't stay, B. I gots to take care of some shit, but before we go back down, I'ma stop by and check on you. So yo, handle ya business, and don't worry about nothing else 'cause we got you, son. You know how we do. But you know it's over for you in the south, for a while anyway."

"Yeah, no doubt, but yo, be careful when you get back down there, a'ight?" Don said.

"Always, baby boy." Stacks reached in the backseat to give Don a pound. "I love you, son."

"I love you, too, kid," Don said.

"Tell Moms I said hi. I'm sorry I couldn't tell her myself."

"She'll understand," Don said as Vanessa helped him out the backseat.

Stacks sat in the car as he watched Vanessa help Don into Dr. Thompson's office. They had dealt with the doctor on many occasions to avoid going to jail after being in shootouts, beefs with other blocks and boroughs, and sustaining gunshot wounds. Dr. Gary Thompson—aka Dr. T—was good peoples. He was an ex-doctor who crossed over and tried to sell legal drugs to the street people in the hood for affordable prices. Unfortunately, he got caught and lost his license. Since then, he'd been exercising his medical skills on those who couldn't take the risk of going to a real hospital, and he made good money at it. In the hood somebody got shot or stabbed every day and just wanted to pay cash with no questions asked about where they got the money or how they acquired the injury. Even though what Dr. Thompson did was illegal in a court of law, he was considered one of the good guys.

Stacks was really bothered by the incident that occurred down in the dirty, but he was grateful Don only lost blood and not his life. Just the thought of how those dudes tried to get at his man infuriated him. The only thing on his mind was revenge.

A few minutes later, Vanessa returned and broke his train of thought.

"Don's moms said hey, she loves you, and she understands," Vanessa informed Stacks.

"I knew she would," Stacks replied. "Yo, how 'bout we shoot uptown right now and go cop this shit so we ain't gotta be rushing later. Then we can go eat, get a room, and cool out 'cause I'm tireder than a muthafucka. I ain't really trying to be up here too long, but we gots to go see Don later at his crib, and from there, we can be out."

"I'm wit' whatever you wit'," Vanessa said.

"A'ight, that's cool. So we'll do that, then I'll drop this paper off and take you to drop yours off. Then we'll go cop a room so I can situate the shit, plus I wanna take a quick shower to wake me up."

"Yeah, that'll work," Vanessa agreed.

"A'ight, that's what we gonna do then." Stacks pulled off.

Chapter Forty-four

"Nigga, don't fucking move," Pam yelled.

Styles complied with Pam as he saw the familiar faces surrounding him. He let out a little laugh as he looked at them one at a time, making sure they were who he thought they were. If looks could kill, they'd all be dead.

"I got him, sis. Put some clothes on," Tasha said as she stepped closer to Styles. She pointed her nine-millimeter Beretta at him.

Pam gathered her clothes and got dressed.

Keisha came closer and knelt beside Styles' head.

"Where the money at, nigga?" Keisha asked.

Styles put on a weak grin. "So, that's what this is all about, huh?"

"Nigga, I'm asking the questions up in here, but yeah, that's what this is about. What you thought, we just came up in here pulling guns on ya punk ass just to see you naked, nigga?" Keisha snarled.

"Hah. I can't believe you bitches. Setting us up the whole time. I don't know why we ain't see this shit coming," Styles said.

"I'll tell you why, nigga. 'Cause you was only thinking wit' ya damn dick, that's why," Pam said as she returned to the room, fully dressed.

"Fuck you, bitch," Styles yelled.

Keisha busted him in the face with the butt of her black .380.

"You ain't in no position to be calling somebody names. Now I'ma ask you again, where the money at y'all got stashed in this muthafucka?" Keisha placed the barrel of the gun alongside Styles' head.

"Go ahead and shoot. I ain't telling you shit. You gonna kill me anyway, bitch," Styles said.

Keisha laughed. This wasn't the first time a nigga they robbed cursed her like that, and it wasn't the first time one ever refused to assist them. She found humor in their so-called going-out-like-a-gangsta attitude, when in reality, they were really scared to death.

"Yeah, a'ight, gangsta. I know ya type, and I got something for ya ass," Keisha said.

Desiree watched everything go down, but was a little uncomfortable. Any other time she would be in the midst of everything with the questioning and threatening, but she didn't want to participate in badgering Styles. The more she looked at Styles sitting there naked, the more he resembled Stacks, and she couldn't bring herself to participate in Keisha's antics.

"Fuck that nigga, anyway," Pam stated flatly. "That's the room right there I saw that nigga Stacks coming out of wit' the duffle bag, so most likely that shit in there."

Styles looked at Pam. He couldn't believe how reckless he and his crew had been and how stupid they were for not recognizing the setup. He had suggested they bring Pam to their crib, and it was his fault for not listening to Vanessa when she warned him not to trust the country chick. The icing on the cake was the lie he told Stacks earlier when he called to ask Pam's whereabouts.

Keisha belted out instructions. "Okay, well, Pam, go check that room. Tasha, you check that room down the hall, and Des, you help me tie this nigga ass up." Pam and Tasha did as they were told without hesitation. Desiree stalled for a moment.

"Desiree?" Keisha called as she watched her friend stand motionless.

"Huh?"

"Snatch up one of those chairs in the kitchen so we can tie his ass up."

Desiree looked at Keisha, then at Styles who stared hard at Desiree. It sent a shot of guilt through her whole body. She broke the stare and went to retrieve the chair. Keisha pulled out rope as Desiree held her gun on Styles.

"Nigga, get up," Keisha barked.

Styles started to get up.

"Slowly," Keisha yelled as she backed away, careful not to give him a chance to try some superhero shit.

Styles got up and sat in the chair in which they intended to tie him down.

"Des, come tie him up while I hold you down. Gimme ya gun so this nigga won't try no funny shit. Nigga, I'm telling you right now, if you try anything while my girl tying you up, I'm gonna blow ya fucking head off," Keisha informed him.

Desiree began to tie Styles up, and he tried speaking to her without Keisha hearing.

"Yo, why you doing this? You not like them. I can tell, and I know you feeling my brother on the low," Styles acknowledged, hitting a nerve deep inside Desiree who didn't flinch at his remark. Instead, she continued to tie him up, temporarily suppressing her feelings for Stacks.

"Make sure them shits tight," Keisha said. "He looks like he waiting for the opportunity to try something, and we can't be having that."

"They tight," Desiree replied.

After they finished tying up Styles, Pam came out of the room she was searching and called her girls. "Yo, I found something. Come in here," she said.

Within seconds they were all walking toward the room Pam was searching.

"Des, stay here and watch him. I'ma go see what Pam found," Keisha said.

"Go ahead. I got him," Desiree said, heading back toward Styles.

Chapter Forty-five

"What you find?" Keisha asked, entering the room.

"Look." Pam pointed to the floor. She had moved the bed and discovered the floor safe beneath the rug.

"Damn, bitch, how you find that?" Tasha asked in admiration.

"I don't know. I was just searching and decided to move the bed, then I saw this rug, and shit just didn't look right. Why would a rug be under the bed and nowhere else in the crib?"

"Good job, baby girl," Keisha congratulated her. "Let's get at this nigga and see if he gonna give up the combination."

Desiree kept the gun pointed at Styles while trying to hear what was happening in the other room. However, a noise grabbed her attention. She quickly turned toward Styles and caught him trying to move closer to the couch.

"What the hell are you trying to do?" Desiree asked, walking up on him. "Styles, please don't make me hurt you because I will if I have to." She walked over to the couch to feel between the pillows. "Is this what you was looking for?" Desiree asked, revealing the snub-nose .44 Bulldog.

"Yo, shorty, why you going out like this?" Styles asked in a heartfelt tone. "Yo, I know you a good chick. I can tell, just like my brother could. That's my word, my brother was feeling you like a muthafucka, on some real shit, and this how you going out on him? You think that a little bit of paper them chicks in there might've found is something? I could easily give you the combination, but what's in there ain't shit. My brother looked at you on wifey status and you wouldn't have wanted for nothing, straight up!"

Desiree knew Styles was trying to get in her head, and she couldn't help but hear what he said about what Stacks felt about her. She knew that everything Styles said was true because she and Stacks definitely made a connection the night they slept together. Unfortunately, the events of the day had gone much too far, and it was too late for Styles. As for Stacks, there was still hope for him to come out of this unharmed, she thought. There was nothing she could say to Styles to assure him that his life would be spared.

"Just be quiet. It'll all be over soon, and we'll be up outta here," she said.

Styles shot Desiree a look of disgust and laughed at her last comment. He found it funny how Desiree tried to pacify him, like everything would be alright, as if he were naïve enough to believe her. The more he stared at her, the more heated he became. Styles had visions of wrapping his hands around her pretty little neck and strangling the life out of her body. If only he could get one arm free he would have a chance to get at least one or two of them before they killed him. The girls didn't know the house the way he did. The gun in the couch was just one option out of many for him.

Styles shifted from side to side, hoping to loosen the ropes, but he stopped when he saw Keisha and the others reappear.

"What's up?" Desiree asked as they came back into the living room.

"Pam found a floor safe up in there," Keisha answered, "but we weren't as lucky this time for it to be opened like the dread shit was."

Keisha's comment about the dread caught Styles' attention, and he couldn't believe his ears. *So these bitches are the culprits behind the dread getting bodied and robbed,* he thought. There was no doubt in his mind they intended to murder him. He remembered just how dirty they had done the dread. He knew the only thing that would buy him time was his knowledge of the safe's combination, and Styles had every intention of using that leverage for as long as he could. He planned to stall them with the hope that Stacks and Vanessa would be on the highway headed back down to the dirty.

Chapter Forty-six

"Stacks, you been in there for damn near an hour, boy. Hurry up," Vanessa yelled. When she received no answer, she yelled, "Stacks, did you hear me?"

Vanessa waited patiently for Stacks to come out the shower as she sat in her towel. It had been a long ride for both of them, and she wanted to freshen up before they hit the road again. She headed to the bathroom to find out what was taking Stacks so long. She opened the door to scream at him, but was at a loss for words when she saw his silhouette through the clear glass shower door.

A good hot shower was just what Stacks needed to calm his nerves. Lately he had been bearing too many heavy loads, and they were beginning to take their toll on him. Between making sure things were going right with their down-south flow; trying to watch his, Styles, and Don's backs; dealing with Desiree; and having Vanessa down there, he was constantly on point. After the Don incident, he realized he couldn't control everything around him like he thought he could. Stacks felt like he was losing his edge and began to think that maybe it was time for him to leave the game. He definitely had more money than he knew what to do with, so there really wasn't a reason why he needed to stay. The more he thought about it, the more he convinced himself that this would be his last and final trip to the dirty. After all of the work he had purchased was gone, he would be done, for good. He began to think about all the things he could do and would do once he stopped hustling but became distracted when he heard the shower door slide open.

When Stacks turned around, he couldn't believe his eyes. Vanessa was climbing in the shower with him. His attention immediately zeroed in on her as he stared at her body the way he had the first time he caught her in the raw. Vanessa returned the favor and gazed at Stacks. She had never seen him naked before, but she liked what she saw and was amazed at his bulk. They stood in silence, admiring each other's bodies.

"You were taking too long, and I couldn't wait," Vanessa said nervously.

Stacks grinned. It took a lot of nerve for Vanessa to step to him like that, putting herself out there, not knowing what to expect. Instead of responding verbally, he decided to make it easy so there would be no mistake about it. He grabbed Vanessa by the waist and covered her soft, pouty lips with his before he eased his tongue in her mouth. Vanessa relaxed into his kiss as Stacks took control. She didn't know where their relationship would lead, but at this point she really didn't care. Vanessa was only concerned about the here and now and how long she had wanted Stacks. Night after night she dreamed about his touch, and now his hands were gently caressing her, and his hard body was presssed against hers. This was much better than her dreams, and she planned to enjoy every bit of it.

Chapter Forty-seven

"Now I know you know the combination to that safe in there," Keisha said to Styles.

"You don't know nothing 'cause I don't know that shit," Styles said defiantly.

Keisha laughed because she'd anticipated his answer. Their vics never made it simple. She wished just for once, niggas would cooperate and stop procrastinating.

"Nigga, don't give me that shit. There ain't no way in hell you don't know the combination to ya brother safe. That's bullshit," Keisha yelled.

"Believe what you wanna. I told you I don't know it, so do what you gotta do."

Keisha wasn't buying it. *Whop.* She busted Styles in the head with her pistol. A stream of blood rushed down the side of his face. "Do what I gotta do, huh? Nigga, I'ma do what I gotta do if you keep trying to talk slick and play these fucking games. Now if you wanna make it outta this shit alive, you better stop acting like you bulletproof and give me the numbers to open that muthafuckin' safe."

"Ha, make it out alive. Bitch, who you think you faking out? Not me. You think I don't know you gonna kill me? You must be crazy. Ain't no way in hell you gonna let me live, coming up in here with no masks on, letting me know who you are. Yeah, a'ight." Styles laughed.

Keisha decided to play it cool. Styles was right. They were going to have to relieve him of his life, and if he continued with the smart talk, it would be sooner rather than later. Before they did that, they needed the combination to the safe. Otherwise, they would have done all of this for nothing, and there wasn't enough time to retrieve their tools or purchase new ones. This safe didn't look as easy to crack like the others.

"Look, if you give us the combination, we gonna be up outta here. We don't care about you seeing our faces 'cause we leaving North Carolina anyway, and you'll never find us. So if you wanna keep ya life, you'll give up the digits to the safe," Keisha lied.

"Yo, I told you, I don't know it. Only my brother knows it," Styles repeated.

"Maybe he's telling the truth, Keisha," Pam said. "If he is, then we can just wait here until that nigga returns from New York and get him to tell us, plus get him for the shit he coming back with. The way that duffle bag looked filled, he probably bringing back at least ten to fifteen keys back down wit' 'im."

Desiree shot Pam a dirty look. That was not how she intended for their scheme to go down, and that was not what she wanted to happen. Desiree didn't know how they were going to pull off the robbery so she could still get with Stacks, but she didn't like Pam's suggestion.

"That nigga know the combination," Desiree said, "just like he know it's dough up in that muthafucka."

Everybody looked at Desiree.

"How you know he knows that?" Keisha queried.

"'Cause he said it when y'all was in the room."

Styles remained quiet. He took a chance trying to get in Desiree's head, and it backfired on him. Styles didn't know how much longer he could stall them, but he would continue to hold out as long as he could with the hope that Stacks would return in time to save his ass.

Chapter Forty-eight

After their passionate afternoon, Stacks jumped up from his brief nap. He and Vanessa had fallen into a light sleep in the hotel room, exhausted from two hours of pleasure. They'd sexed in the shower and ended their session in the bedroom. The sudden movement startled Vanessa from her slumber.

"Stacks, what's wrong? You okay?" she asked with concern.

"Yo, I just had a fucked-up dream, V. Something ain't right," Stacks said.

"What was the dream about?" Vanessa sat upright, fully alert.

"Yo, honestly, I can't remember, but it was crazy. You know how a dream be jumping from scene to scene and shit?"

"Uh-huh." Vanessa nodded.

"It was like that. It was just wild: blood, drugs, guns, and shit everywhere, and we were together with Styles and Don and a couple other people that I can't remember. Shit was just crazy."

"Maybe you were just tired, and all that driving is catching up to you. Lack of rest can make you sleep hard and dream about all types of crazy shit," Vanessa replied.

"Yeah, maybe, but yo, I got a bad feeling about shit. I want to change our plans," Stacks announced. "Instead of us driving back together, I want you to hop on the train and take this shit down. If my gut feeling is right, ain't no need for us to be together and get pulled over and we both get knocked. Whenever I start to feel like this, bad shit happens, and I don't want you to get caught up in the mix. I don't think it's good for me to ride back dirty at all, so I'ma need you to take my burner wit' you too. If you don't want to hop on the train like that, then we can just cancel the move and drop everything off. I'll come back and get it some other time."

Vanessa made her decision before Stacks had even finished his statement.

"We don't have to cancel. I'll hop on the train. We trying to get this money, right?" She wanted to assure him that she was down with him, no matter what.

"No doubt, but I ain't want you to think I was trying to play you or nothing, like you some mule. You know I got love for you."

"I know you do, and I got love for you, too, Stacks. That's why I ain't got no problem wit' it."

Stacks looked at Vanessa's naked body while she spoke. This was the type of woman he always wanted in his life: beautiful, street smart, and thorough. Vanessa was all three. It was no secret he was feeling Desiree, but after spending time with Vanessa, his mind was made up. Stacks was no longer torn between two women because without a doubt, he wanted Vanessa to be his other half, his sidekick and partner in crime.

"Yo, V, I need to say something to you before we leave here."

"Go ahead. What's up?" Vanessa asked.

Stacks really didn't know where to begin, so finally he said, "You know we been knowing each other for a minute now. Chilling since we was kids."

"Yeah," Vanessa agreed.

"We been friends from day one, and I always had respect and love for you, even back then. You know I'd never do anything to jeopardize our friendship or to hurt you because having you as a friend means more to me than you'll ever know. Besides, I'd feel fucked up if I messed that up. That's why it's hard for me to say this shit right now because I know once I do, ain't no turning back." Stacks paused to pull his thoughts together. He didn't want to spit the wrong words out his mouth.

"Stacks, what? Just say what you trying to say." Vanessa was anxious to hear what he had to tell her.

"Remember that day we was kicking it around the way?" Stacks asked.

"Yeah, the day you invited me down?"

"Yeah, that day."

"What about it?" Vanessa asked curiously.

Stacks took a deep breath. He couldn't believe how nervous he was trying to tell Vanessa what was on his mind. This had been the second time in less than a week that he had choked around a woman. This was the first time he ever had to express his heart, his true feelings.

"I don't know, but that day, things between us just changed, on my part anyway, but I tried to put it in the back of my mind," he said.

"Stacks—"

"Hold up, let me finish. I gotta get this off while the timing is right," Stacks interjected. "That day we were talking, I saw you in a way I had never looked at you before. I remember when you used to be up in the clubs doing ya thing on the dance floor. I use to check you out and all that, but that was as far as it went, and I ain't talking about that. I'm talking about seeing you in a way that a nigga is attracted to a chick."

Vanessa remained silent and waited for him to finish discussing his feelings for her.

"V, I dealt wit' mad chicks in the past and all of that. I ain't even gonna front, but I only been in one real relationship wit' a female, and that was because it was convenient, not because I loved her or was in love wit' her. I cared about her and had love for her, though, until she did me dirty when I was doing my bid up north, so I ain't never really been in love or loved a chick, and I didn't even know what it felt like. Then you came down, and we started spending time together and shit. You started being a constant thought on my mind when I was in the streets and you at the crib, but I gotta keep it gully though. I had some other shit on my mind that was blurring my thoughts, and at first I thought I was feeling the next chick like I've been feeling you, but shit ain't the same.

"Right now, I can't even believe I'm telling you this, but I want to keep it real wit' you on the strength of our friendship. I know I'm not supposed to know this, and I gave my word I wouldn't bring it up, but Styles told me about the conversation y'all had. Don't be mad at the nigga. He was just pulling my coat to what was good. And seriously, I'm glad he did because it helped me to get my mind right before it was too late and tonight, how it went down wit' us, made it official for what I already wanted to do. I want to know if we can make it happen wit' us," Stacks said.

Vanessa gathered her thoughts before she spoke.

"Stacks, everything you just said is how I've been feeling. That day back home, I felt the same way, and I ain't gonna front either, I was digging you like a grave. That trip down south was the best thing for me. Not only because I got a chance to get away from New York, but because I got a chance to get closer to you. Do you remember that day you caught me dreaming?"

"Yeah," Stacks replied.

"That dream was about you, like all my dreams were while I was down there. If I wasn't dreaming about you, I was thinking about you 24/7. You made me feel alive again, just being yourself, and for that I'm grateful. Many times I wanted to come into your room and climb in bed wit' you, but never worked up the nerve. Plus, I know you were wit' someone down there."

"It wasn't—"

Vanessa interjected, "You don't have to explain. It doesn't even matter now. What's important is that you were honest, and I respect you for that. I respect you for respecting me like that. If you meant everything you said, then my answer is yes," Vanessa exclaimed.

"I meant every last word," Stacks said as he leaned over to kiss her. They made love one last time before they got ready to be on their way.

Chapter Forty-nine

Keisha had been torturing Styles for hours, but it was no use. He refused to talk. She had never beaten a man as bad as she beat him. She had used the butt of her pistol to split Styles' lip and both of his eyes, closing the right one, and she gave him a busted nose, along with a deep gash on his forehead. The others watched as Keisha went to work on him. Desiree felt sick to her stomach at the sight of the blood leaking from Styles' beat-up face. The pounding he had taken changed his whole appearance; he no longer resembled his brother. He looked more like a piece of raw, bloodied meat. The average man would've broken down, but not Styles. Desiree wished he would just give up the combination to the safe so they could be on their way. Not for his sake, but for Stacks'.

"Nigga, I'm getting tired of beating ya ass," Keisha yelled. "Why don't you just do yourself a favor and give me the damn digits to that safe?"

Styles couldn't talk, even if he wanted to. His mouth was sore and his throat was dry. During the course of the pistol-whipping, he had swallowed two of his teeth. It didn't matter what these bitches did to him, he was never going to give up the combination. Styles didn't care whether he lived or died. He only wished he lived long enough to see his brother kill all these grimy-ass bitches. And even if he didn't, he knew that his death would not go unavenged.

"I don't think he gonna give it up," Tasha said.

"Me neither," Pam said.

Desiree remained quiet. She waited to see what Keisha was going to do or say.

"Fuck it, then. We just wait for his muthafuckin' brother to come back and get him to tell us. If he don't, then we'll just body both these niggas, dig that shit up outta there, take the shit he bring down wit' 'im, and be out," Keisha suggested.

Desiree didn't like Keisha's idea and started to question her about it, but thought better of it. None of them had ever questioned Keisha's authority or direction in the past, and she didn't want anyone becoming suspicious about her behavior. As much as she liked Stacks, her team came first. Desiree decided to put her personal feelings aside and roll with her girls.

Chapter Fifty

It was a little after one when Stacks got up. He didn't realize just how tired he was until he and Vanessa sexed and his head hit the pillow a second time. Stacks couldn't believe he'd been asleep for five hours. All the traveling back and forth, along with all the partying and drinking had finally caught up to him. His body must have shut down on him because of exhaustion due to his heavy workload and fast lifestyle. It was like that when you ran the streets, though. No sleep 'til Brooklyn because the game was a 24/7 job. As long as you put work in the game, it was your boss. It was the one who did the hiring and the firing, and if you didn't get the job done or were caught sleeping and it felt that your services were no longer needed, you'd be replaced by someone else. Like the saying went: *The game never changes, only the players.*

Stacks felt rejuvenated. A few hours of rest did him good. He figured that would hold him for at least a couple more days before his body shut down again. He got up to stretch, then woke Vanessa.

"Wake up, sleepy head."

Vanessa rolled over and threw the covers over her head. Stacks snatched both the blanket and the sheet off her, exposing Vanessa's beautiful bare body.

"Boy," she yelled as she tried to cover up.

In spite of her beauty, like most women, Vanessa was self-conscious.

"What you trying to hide? I seen every inch of you already," Stacks said with a smile.

"So," Vanessa responded. "Gimme the sheet so I can go to the bathroom."

"What? You're bugging. Let me find out you really shy on the low," Stacks said, laughing.

"I'm serious, Stacks. Stop playing and give me the sheet."

Seeing she was for real, Stacks threw Vanessa the sheet. He couldn't understand why she couldn't just get up and walk to the bathroom in the nude; but then again, he had never really been able to understand women. He didn't think any man did, for that matter, so he figured he never would. Vanessa got up and went to the bathroom, closing the door behind her. Stacks just smiled, grabbed his cell phone, unplugged the charger from the wall, and turned it on.

After they showered and dressed, Stacks gave the room a thorough check to make sure they didn't leave anything behind.

"V, you got everything?" he asked.

"Yeah."

"A'ight. I'ma call Don and let 'im know we on our way over, then I'ma hit Styles up and let 'im know that we should be home tonight. Go turn the key in while I load the car. I'll be out front."

"Okay."

"By the time we leave Don's crib, your train should be coming."

Chapter Fifty-one

"Who is it?" a woman asked from the opposite side of the door.

"I'm here to see Don," Stacks said.

"Girl, open the fucking door," Don yelled. The woman quickly unlocked the door.

When it opened, Stacks immediately recognized the pretty red-boned chick. She was wearing Don's Dallas Cowboys Emmit Smith jersey. Felicia and Don had been dealing with each other off and on for years. She was practically wifey, or in Don's case, the closest thing he could get to it. Stacks noticed Vanessa grilling him out the corner of his eye, and he smiled as he walked toward Don.

Vanessa and Felicia had known each other since they were from the same hood, but it was apparent they didn't share any love and only exchanged pleasantries out of respect for the fellas.

"Yo, go put some clothes on. You see I got company," Don instructed Felicia while pausing his Xbox 360.

Felicia shot him a dirty look but did as she was told.

"Yo, what it is, son?" Stacks asked as he gave Don a pound and hug.

"Everything's good," Don replied.

"I see you still into video games and shit." Stacks pointed to the game Don had on the big seventy-inch screen TV.

"You know it. Yo, what up, V? You ain't got no love for me no more?" Don joked.

"Nigga, what you talking about? You know you my dawg," she said.

"Well, come give me a hug or something. Damn, you know a brother just escaped death," he said, smiling.

Vanessa smiled as she walked to where Don was seated. When she leaned to give him a warm embrace, Don looked at Stacks.

"Oh, my bad. Is it alright, son?" he asked Stacks with a smirk.

"Fuck you asking me for, nigga?" Stacks tried to act nonchalant.

"Yeah, a'ight, nigga. You ain't faking me out. I saw it all over your face when y'all walked through the door. Something is definitely different with you two."

Stacks tried to resist the grin tugging at his lips but it was useless. "Nigga, shut the fuck up," he said.

They all laughed as Vanessa hugged Don.

"Yo, what Dr. T say?" Stacks asked.

"He said I should be good in a couple of weeks. The bullets ain't hit no bones or arteries, so I'm a'ight. He shot me up with some shit and gave me some pills for the pain. He told me to keep changing my bandages and shit. That's why I got shorty over here, because I ain't wanna have my moms and them all up in here preaching to me and shit. You know she was crying like a muthafucka after you left. I called Felicia up, and she said she'd come over and hold me down until I get better, so I'm good."

"That's good. At least you got somebody to take care of you. Plus, you got some live-in ass, unless you can't get it up no more, nigga," Stacks said, laughing.

"What? Nigga, on a bad day my shit still rock up," Don shot back.

"Okay, you two, that's enough of the pissing contest. Stacks, you shouldn't be talking about that girl like that, anyway," Vanessa said.

Felicia returned to the living room with a pair of shorts to accompany the Cowboys jersey and sat beside Don.

"So when are you leaving?" Don asked.

"We bouncing as soon as we leave here. I'll probably hit the turnpike at least by five, once I drop V off at the train station."

"Train station? Why? What's up?" Don asked.

Stacks shook his head. "Nothing really. I just don't want to travel back dirty like that. I ain't feeling it right now. I been having some fucked-up feelings, like something's wrong. I just don't know why. In my heart, I think this shit starting to get the best of me, kid. I'm losing my focus. I'm getting tired of this shit, B. I ain't trying to do this too much longer, especially after what happened to you. I ain't trying to stay in this shit long enough to let it happen to me or Styles or let po-po knock us. I ain't ever going back to jail, son. That's my word. I'll hold court in the streets before that happens again, nah mean? Look at all the shit we escaped already, anyway. We've been some lucky muthafuckas."

"I hear you, B, and I know what you saying. You know it's whatever with me, and I'm riding wit' you no matter what," Don said.

"I know you are, son."

"What up wit' Styles, though? You hollered at him today?" Don asked.

"Nah, not since we dropped you off when we were bringing you up here and you spoke to him. I called the nigga before I left the hotel, but I ain't getting no answer at the house or his cellie."

"Hotel? Yeah, now I know why y'all came up in here looking all crazy and shit," Don said with a smile on his face.

"Nigga, stop trying to play Sherlock Holmes," Stacks warned.

Don couldn't help but laugh. "A'ight, a'ight, go ahead, but I know you two fucking."

Vanessa smiled, but Stacks ignored Don's comment.

"Like I was saying, nigga, I ain't been able to get in touch wit' son. Matter of fact, I'ma try him right now again." Stacks pulled out his cell phone.

Stacks dialed the house and Styles' cell phone numbers, and there was still no response. He held the phone out to make sure he was dialing the right numbers because it was strange for his brother not to pick up.

"Same shit, no answer at the crib or his cell."

"Yeah, something's funny because that ain't like son—maybe me, but not him, "Don said.

"Stacks, tell him about your dream," Vanessa said.

"What she talking about, B? What dream?" Don asked curiously.

"Nah, like I was telling you, I been having these funny-ass feelings that something is wrong. Then I had this crazy-ass dream, and we was all in it—me, you, and Styles, and some chicks, but I can't really remember what the shit was about. Shit was crazy," Stacks said.

"Damn, dawg, you sure you not just stressing? That's why you feeling like that and had that dream." Don said.

"I might be a little stressed, but that ain't it, though. It's more than that, I know it."

"Who were the chicks in the dream? You can't remember them?"

"Man, I don't know. I knew who they were in the dream, but when I woke up, I couldn't picture their faces. Shit got me fucked up, but let me think." Stacks shut his eyes, trying to recapture his dream, but he drew a blank.

Don, Felicia, and Vanessa remained quiet as Stacks tried to think.

"Pam—I mean Felicia—go get me something to drink, my throat dry," Don said, trying to play off calling Felicia by the wrong name.

"What the fuck did you just call me, nigga?" Felicia asked, visibly upset.

Don stuck to his guns and continued to try to play it off.

"What? Fuck you think I called you? The same thing your mother named you," he said.

"No you didn't, muthafucka. You called me another bitch name. Some bitch named Pam."

"Fee, you bugging," Don replied with a straight face.

At the sound of Pam's name, images began to appear. Stacks saw the women's faces as vividly as he had in his dream.

"Yo, that's who it is," Stacks yelled, opening his eyes.

Everybody looked toward him as if he'd lost his mind.

"Who it is? What, nigga?" Don asked.

Stacks turned to face Don and looked at him like he was supposed to know what he was talking about.

"The chicks in my dream, nigga."

Both Vanessa and Felicia wore confused expressions, but Don was able to fill in the blanks and pick up on who Stacks was talking about.

"Word?"

"Yeah, son, that's who they are. All of them."

A few seconds went by, and Vanessa finally caught on. She knew how Don could have easily made the mistake of calling Felicia Pam, especially since Pam had saved his life. Vanessa didn't know who the rest of the chicks were, but she was aware that Pam had a little clique. She just listened as Don and Stacks politicked.

"Why the fuck would they be in ya dream like that?" Don questioned.

"I don't know, B, but that's who they was though."

"You think maybe 'cause of what happened with me or something, or from us partying with them?"

"Nah, I don't think that's it because none of that shit was in the dream. But yo, did you know shorty had a burner on her when you went to holla at BB and Marcy?" Stacks asked, sorting things out in his head.

"Nah," Don answered.

"Did you ever see her with one before?"

"Nah, son, never, but why you ask that?"

"I don't know. I'm just trying to backtrack a few things. Yo, did shorty ever do anything funny around you or make you second-guess her about anything?"

"Yo, I don't know if this shit means anything, but now that you mentioned it, one day me and shorty was in the tele puffing on some trees, and I told her that the trees tasted like the shit we blow up top, and reminded me of the smoke the dread used to sell. Then I said God bless the dead. When I said that, shorty got real interested in the dread and how he died. I told her the story and how they found him and shit, and that was that. I ain't give that shit a second thought—not until now anyway," Don said.

Stacks thought for a minute as he tried to gather all of the pieces of the puzzle. None of this was sitting right with him. He never had a reason to suspect Pam, but Stacks didn't understand Pam's interest in some dude she didn't even know.

"Oh shit. I just remembered something," Don yelled, pulling Stacks from his thoughts.

"What?"

"Right after I told shorty about the dread, she said she had to bounce home cause her asthma was acting up. I offered to ride with her to make sure she got home safe, but she said she'd be a'ight and promised to call when she got in, but she never did. Then after she left, I noticed she had breezed so quick she forgot her handbag. I almost didn't see that shit, but I had dropped my L and noticed it. When I picked it up, it was open. I wasn't trying to look in the shit, but on a quick glance I saw something shiny that made me take a closer look. That's when I saw the Rolex in there. The official shit too. At the time the smoke had me comatose, so I ain't think nothing of it, and when I hollered at shorty again I ain't say nothing 'cause I told her that I ain't even look in her joint. But the funny shit was when I asked her why she didn't call me when she got home that night, her story changed from rushing up outta there cause of her asthma to her being on her period. I ain't really give a fuck because I was more concerned about whether she was off that shit or not so I could hit again, but yeah, shit sounded real suspect now that I think about it."

Felicia looked pissed off as Don openly spoke about his affair with Pam, but he ignored her and continued.

While Don hashed out the details of his encounters with Pam, Stacks began drawing his own conclusions. He was quickly beginning to realize that these broads were definitely shady. Before Stacks could utter a word, Vanessa beat him to the punch.

"I told you that bitch wasn't right. I knew it," Vanessa said, hyped. "I knew that bitch was a snake."

"Yeah, you were right, baby," Stacks agreed. "Yo, son, why you just now bringing this shit up? You knew how things were going down with niggas getting bodied and shit down in the dirty, especially that shit with the dread. I'm willing to bet money on it that those chicks had something to do wit that nigga's death. I knew that broad was too good to be true," he said, referring to Desiree. "That's why she ain't have no man."

"That's the chick you were telling me about?" Vanessa asked.

"Yeah, that's her," Stacks answered.

"That's gotta be the one that bitch Pam was talking about when we was wrapping Don's wounds. No wonder she was so concerned about whether I was coming back down or not. They probably were trying to set y'all up all this time."

"Yo, you think they got Styles down there?" Don questioned.

"I don't know, B, maybe. The only way they could get him would be at the crib. He said he dropped that chick off when I called him on our way up here, so it's a possibility she got with them other chicks and doubled back," Stacks said. "Unless," Stacks paused for emphasis, "he never dropped her off and she was still there when I called."

"Why would you think that?" Don asked. Stacks shot him a look while he played the entire setup in his head. "Oh, word. Maybe."

"I think she was, 'cause I remember Styles took a long-ass time to answer the phone when I called him, and normally he does that when he's up in some guts or something," Stacks said to Don. He knew his brother and Styles became easily distracted when it came to pussy.

"Yo, if that shit is true, then you gotta get down there ASAP, B," Don advised.

"Yeah, you right. V, we outta here. I'ma drop you off at the train station, and I'ma hit the highway."

"Okay, I'm ready," Vanessa said, preparing to walk out the door.

They said their good-byes, and Stacks and Vanessa exited Don's crib. Don sat helpless, cursing himself for his present predicament. He was unable to ride with Stacks, to see what was up with Styles. All he could do was hope their assumptions were wrong and everything was fine.

Stacks cruised across the Delaware Memorial Bridge when he made his first attempt to call Styles to let him know he was on his way back. He called the house, and the phone just rang. When he dialed his brother's cell phone the voice mail came on automatically. Stacks tried to convince himself that Styles was probably asleep, but he knew even if he were the phone would have woke him because he was a light sleeper. Then Stacks figured that Styles might have stepped out briefly, but he would never leave without his cell phone, which served two purposes: It was his lifeline for business and his booty service, and Styles never wanted to miss a booty call or a maintenance call.

Stacks knew his brother too well, and there were only a few things that would prevent him from staying in touch: being in the middle of a business transaction on which they needed to be focused in case someone tried to get funny, being incarcerated or in the presence of the police, or if there was some major shit going down and they just couldn't get to a phone.

He automatically erased the first thought because he told Styles to chill while he was gone, especially with the shit that went down with Don. That left him with options number two and three. His gut was telling him more than likely it was number three. *Either way, five hours from now I'll know,* Stacks thought as he accelerated on the gas pedal.

Chapter Fifty-two

Two hours had passed, and Styles still refused to cooperate. Keisha was growing tired of cursing and beating him. At one point, Styles had blacked out. It didn't make sense to kill him because they still wouldn't know the combination, and if his brother arrived and saw him dead their plan would still be squashed.

Keisha could tell her girls were becoming aggravated, but their only other option was to be patient and hope that Styles either got tired of the beat down or his brother returned.

"Pam, go move the car from where it's at," Keisha ordered.

"Where you want me to park it?"

"I don't know, just move it. Take it down the road and park it on the side or something and walk back. I don't want that nigga Stacks to see it when he pulls up. We gotta make sure everything set when his ass get here."

"A'ight."

"Tasha, you and Desiree finish searching the house and see what you come up with that's worth something, and make sure ain't no guns stashed around this muthafucka."

"Got you."

"Des, where you wanna start?"

Desiree was not in the mood to be searching, but she had no choice but to participate. Her mind wandered, and images of Stacks filled her head. She prayed Keisha would just change her mind and break open the safe so they could leave. They would still have to kill Styles, but that wasn't of major concern.

Desiree knew better than to believe in fairytales. When you were in the game and played it, you took whatever came with it—the bitter with the sweet—and Desiree knew that. She knew it was a dirty game, and they played for keeps. Unfortunately, those rules she lived by applied to Stacks as well. Still, she hoped to avoid what appeared to be the inevitable.

"Let's start in there and work our way through," Tasha said, pointing to Stacks' bedroom.

Desiree was not ready to enter Stacks' room and go through his personal belongings. She felt like she would be invading his privacy and betraying his trust. Desiree was at the point of no return, and there was no turning back. The damage was done, and she would never be able to right this wrong.

The night Stacks left Desiree's place, she thought then things would never be the same between them, but this wasn't what she had in mind.

The only way Desiree could possibly survive the night was to get Stacks out of her system once and for all. *That nigga ain't worth more than my homegirls. Niggas come and niggas go, but friends are forever. They been with me before I met that nigga, and they'll still be with me when he gone, so get ya shit together and forget about his ass.* Her mind said one thing, but her heart said another. It was a tug-of-war, and Desiree didn't know which side was going to win.

Chapter Fifty-three

Stacks tried calling Styles again to no avail. He was finally in Virginia, and he was counting the minutes as he drove. He glanced at his watch, becoming more worried about his brother not answering the phone. The bad feelings he had in Jersey at the hotel were fucking with him. There was no doubt in his mind that Styles was in trouble.

For the past six hours Stacks had driven like a madman and thanked his lucky stars he hadn't been pulled over for breaking the speed limit. He was doing at least fifty miles over the limit and was glad he had given Vanessa his gun. Otherwise, he wouldn't have chanced speeding like a Nascar driver.

Stacks had been so wrapped up with his brother he never bothered to stop and think about Vanessa's safety. She was getting on the train with his piece and other shit that would definitely be just cause for her getting locked if she got caught. The thought of something happening to Vanessa only added to his stress.

I gotta get out of this shit. I gotta get outta this shit before it kills me or someone I love, Stacks thought.

Vanessa was scheduled to arrive in North Carolina approximately one hour after Stacks. His original plan was to wait at the station until her train got in, but his senses told him not to do that. Instead he decided to go to the house, and if Styles wasn't there, he would try to locate him. Stacks knew Vanessa would call him when she arrived, but he intended to be there for her when her train got in.

Chapter Fifty-four

Desiree battled with the feelings she had for Stacks, and being in his room and rummaging through his closet wasn't helping the situation. Instead of searching the closet for pertinent information, she found herself running her hands through Stacks' wardrobe. She was in a daze as she came across the outfit he wore the first night they met.

As she closed her eyes, she could see Stacks approaching her from across the room. She didn't comment on his attire at the time because she was more focused on his physique. Desiree thought Stacks looked like someone straight out of a hip-hop catalog wearing blue Parasuco jeans with a burgundy leather stripe down the side and the shirt to match. He also donned a platinum chain with an iced-out medallion, and had the watch, bracelet, and ring to match. Yeah, she knew instantly Stacks was the real thing as soon as she saw him. He was far from being a fake balla. He was the real-deal Holyfield.

"Desiree?"

"Huh?"

"What you doing, girl?"

Pam's voice snapped Desiree out of her trance.

"What it look like I'm doing? Searching the closet," Desiree said, hoping Pam hadn't caught her slipping.

"That ain't what it looked like to me. It look like ya ass was in la la land or something. I hope ya ass ain't sweet on this nigga, girl, 'cause we got a job to do, and you know we don't let feelings get in the way of our work."

"Pam, miss me wit' that bullshit. Ain't nobody sweet on nobody. I was searching the closet, so calm the hell down," Desiree replied.

Pam eyed her friend suspiciously.

"A'ight girl. You right. I'm tripping. I was just making sure you had ya mind right, that's all."

"Yeah, I understand. Anyway, you know you my girl, so don't sweat it," Desiree said, happy that Pam was dropping the subject. The last thing she needed was for Pam to be running her mouth to Keisha. It was bad enough she was feeling this nigga Stacks hard, but for it to come out and get back to Keisha would be difficult to cover up. Desiree knew she had to do a better job of concealing her feelings for Stacks—at least until this was all over.

Chapter Fifty-five

Stacks couldn't wait to see exit seventy-three for the Smithfield area. He was only thirty minutes away from his trailer, but it felt like it was a lifetime. Stacks made a final attempt to reach his brother, so the uneasiness that he was feeling would subside.

All kind of crazy thoughts ran through his head as the home phone rang. What bothered Stacks most was he knew niggas were gettin' bodied up left and right. He even warned Styles and Don to be careful, but he didn't realize how close to home his words would actually hit.

First, BB and Marcy turned on Don, which would really fuck up their flow. They would be short on manpower, and niggas might begin to view what happened to Don as a sign of weakness and try to get at them. Now his brother seemed to be MIA. He didn't know if the girls were responsible for Styles' unexplained absence, or if Styles simply went against his suggestion to chill and ventured outside and got caught up in some unnecessary bullshit.

Styles had been known for being hard headed in the past, but Stacks hoped this was not one of those times. The last thing he wanted or needed was to lose his brother. Although Stacks occasionally came down hard on him, Styles knew his big brother was merely concerned for his welfare. If Stacks didn't intervene as much as he did, Styles would have been locked up or dead by now.

Stacks wanted to remain positive. The fact that there was no answer at the crib and the voice mail picked up on Styles' cell phone discouraged him.

Stacks cursed out loud as he hung up. He'd know what was up soon enough.

Chapter Fifty-six

Ever since Keisha informed her crew about the new plans, she had noticed an immediate change in Desiree's behavior. Keisha debated whether she should confront her girl or leave shit alone. She changed her mind when Desiree revealed that Styles did know the combination to the safe and there was a lot of money to be had. Still, Desiree's actions put Keisha on alert.

"Pam, where'd you park the car?" Keisha asked when her friend returned.

"I just backed it out and parked it on the side of the main road. Shit, it was too fucking dark to be walking out there like that," Pam complained.

"Bitch, ain't nobody ask you how dark it was out there, and since when ya ass been scared of the dark? What if that nigga comes in the morning and see the damn car out there?"

Pam just looked at her girl, but didn't utter a word because she knew Keisha was right. She was being lazy and sloppy and hadn't taken the time to think about Stacks coming back and seeing a strange car.

"Here. Take ya fucking gun with you if you scared, but you better move that shit away from here."

"I think I saw a flashlight in the kitchen," Pam said as she headed out of the room. "I'll go check again."

"Yeah, get this scary-ass bitch a light," Keisha said, sounding both pissed and frustrated.

Chapter Fifty-seven

Stacks reached Dunn and had another seven minutes to get to his place. He had the travel time down to a science. The closer he got, the more his anxiety level increased. It was killing him to find out what was up with his brother. Stacks hoped everything was copasetic and it was just his paranoia getting the best of him again. He figured he was probably overreacting, but if that wasn't the case and something really happened to his brother, nothing in the world would stop him from hunting down his prey, just as he intended to do with BB for the dumb shit he pulled with Don.

Stacks turned off the exit that read ENTERING DUNN. Stacks was glad he finally made it down in one piece, but was mad that he parted with his gun, although giving it to Vanessa was the best decision at the time. Besides, once he got to the house he could easily get another one from his safe.

Although it felt like the train was taking forever, Vanessa thought this trip was a lot better than her last one down south. She was anxious to learn what the situation was with Styles. After spending time, making love and exchanging feelings, Vanessa had never been happier. It occurred to her that she hadn't smoked any weed or sipped any brown juice since her last train ride. The only thing she was high on was Stacks. She saw good and big things ahead, and she was looking forward to their future together. Vanessa was going to be Stacks' ride-or-die chick, and nothing was going to separate them. In less than two hours they would be reunited.

Chapter Fifty-eight

"Keisha, how long we gonna wait here for that nigga?" Tasha asked. They were all becoming impatient. What was supposed to be an in-and-out job was quickly becoming overtime, and there were no guarantees they would hit payday with what was in the safe. Styles was zoning in and out of consciousness and had already proven that under no circumstance was he going to be helpful, and there was no telling when Stacks planned to return. Still Keisha was willing to ride out the game plan.

"As long as it takes. Why? You got an appointment to be somewhere?" Keisha asked sarcastically. She didn't approve of Tasha's question or the fact that she was undermining her authority. She didn't appreciate how her team was giving her fever. First Desiree started acting shady and now Tasha was tripping.

"Damn, I was just asking. All this time we could've dug up the safe and been gone by now. But either way it don't matter to me," Tasha replied.

Keisha knew she was wrong for attacking Tasha, but she was on edge. They were all restless and tired of being cooped up in the trailer.

They had no clue as to when this nigga Stacks was really returning, and it was getting the best of them. This was the longest they'd ever taken in a robbery, and so far nothing was going as planned.

"I hope Pam was right about that nigga going up north and coming right back," Keisha said. "Otherwise we have no choice but to dig up the safe and kill this nigga." Keisha used the gun to move Styles' head from side to side. He was semiconscious and in horrible pain.

"That's what he told this nigga," Pam replied, pointing to Styles. "I heard him say he was going to try to come right back."

"Let's just hope he does. I wonder why Stacks ain't even tried to reach out to this nigga though," Keisha said curiously.

"He called one time when he was close to New York, but that was it," Pam said.

"Still, he would've called when he got up there. Shit ain't adding up, and something doesn't feel right. Tasha, check the phone and see if it's working," Keisha requested.

Tasha headed to the kitchen where the phone was located. She put the receiver to her ear and heard the dial tone.

"Yeah, it's working." As she placed the phone back into its cradle, something caught her attention. "Oh shit," Tasha exclaimed. "That nigga probably been calling, but he ain't getting through because the fucking ringer is off."

Styles was drifting off, but when he heard Tasha's newfound revelation, which he had known for several hours, he stayed alert. A smile crept across his aching face as he thought, *You bitches ain't as smart as you thought you were.*

"What the fuck you smirking at, nigga?" Keisha barked from across the room. "This muthafucka knew the fucking ringer was off the entire time." She walked over to Styles who was still tied up and punched him in the mouth with a forceful right hook, causing his lip to bleed again.

Styles forced another smile as he spit out blood.

"I shoulda slumped this nigga a long time ago. Where his cell phone at?" Keisha asked as she gave the room a quick once-over.

"Right there," Tasha said, spotting the phone on the floor near the couch.

"Check that shit too."

Tasha picked up the phone and flipped it open.

"Shit," she cried. "This muthafucka is dead."

Desiree, Keisha, and Tasha looked at one another in astonishment and then at Styles. This nigga had been playing them all along. Keisha removed the gun from her waist and shoved it into Styles' injured mouth.

"You really think it's fuckin' funny, huh, nigga?" Keisha asked as she yanked Styles' head back with one hand while keeping the .380 in his mouth with the other. "I guess you not as dumb as we thought you was, but we gonna see who gets the last laugh, nigga. Yo, everybody, tighten up and be on point. If I'm correct, that nigga Stacks is well on his way and may be here any minute, especially if he been calling and ain't get no answer," Keisha instructed.

They immediately sprang into action. Tasha and Desiree went to check the doors to make sure they were locked so Stacks couldn't sneak up on them while Keisha kept her gun trained at Styles' head.

Chapter Fifty-nine

As Pam walked back from moving the car, she saw another vehicle approaching. The vehicle turned onto the dirt path leading to the trailer, killing its lights and stopping short of the house. There was no doubt in her mind that it was Stacks. She increased her pace to head back to the trailer. As she reached the top of the driveway, she saw the male figure looking through the side window of the trailer. Pam wondered why he was peeking in the window instead of entering. Did Stacks know what was going down, and if so, why wasn't he running up in the house blazing his heat trying to save his brother? Pam wondered. Either way, she had the upper hand and began to walk lightly to creep up on Stacks.

"Oh shit," Stacks exclaimed under his breath. He couldn't believe his eyes as he cautiously peeked through the window. The fact that he was witnessing his brother being tortured by those bitches infuriated him. His brother's face had been beaten severely and was barely recognizable. Styles was in dire need of assistance. Stacks figured his brother refused to cooperate with those bitches, and as a result was paying a heavy penalty.

Though he had his suspicions, nothing could have prepared him for what was happening inside his trailer. Stacks' blood boiled and fueled with rage as he watched Desiree and her partners. These must've been the chicks that were responsible for robbing and slumping the other hustlas from up north. Stacks was pissed for allowing himself to be blinded by lust. No kind of pussy was worth this shit.

Stacks watched one of the girls flip open Styles' cell phone, and he saw the other chick run to put her gun in Styles' mouth. Stacks was certain they were aware that Styles had cut off all lines of communications. Now Stacks knew that Styles had deliberately turned off the phones in an attempt to warn him of danger. Judging by their swift movements, the clique was probably aware of his impending return. Stacks collected his thoughts since time was of the essence—he had to act fast because Styles' life depended on him.

His heart was heavy as he watched his brother suffer. Several ideas came to mind as he tried to figure out how to get Styles out safely and kill the bitches. Desiree walked across the room and distracted Stacks from his thoughts. Watching her play a part was really fucking with him mentally. Stacks believed Desiree's feelings for him was genuine, but she had ulterior motives and betrayed him in the worse way. Stacks promised he would make her reap what she sowed.

Looking back, traveling without his gun wasn't the greatest idea. Stacks wanted to run in the trailer and gun down those shady-ass females. Unfortunately, his hands were just as tied as his brothers. He had a few people he could call on for a burner, but he didn't know if anyone could be trusted at that point, especially after what happened with Don at the pool hall. The only other option was to wait for Vanessa, and she wasn't due for another hour. Stacks didn't want to wait that long.

"Damn," Stacks cursed to himself. Why didn't he see this shit coming?

Chapter Sixty

"Nigga, put ya hands where I can see 'em," Pam ordered Stacks, and he complied. "Slowly."

Damn, I'm really slipping, Stacks thought. He hadn't realized that there were only three of them up in the house and the one who helped save Don was missing.

Stacks slowed his movements. He didn't want Pam getting trigger happy and taking him out. He couldn't believe his luck, and how this chick had snuck up on him. He didn't remember seeing Pam in the house, only the other three. She had to come up from the road, which was good. Stacks now had two things in his favor: One, she didn't yell to her friends to inform them of his presence, and two, she was standing too close to him with her gun shoved in his back. He'd been caught slipping when he was younger by stick-up kids and knew it wasn't smart to be all up on somebody like that because it gave them easy access to try you, and Stacks intended to capitalize off her inexperience.

"Take it easy, shorty. I'm showing you my hands," Stacks said calmly as he raised his hands.

"Nigga, where ya gun at?" Pam asked.

Stacks finally found the answer to getting ahold of a gun. All he had to do was play his cards right.

"It's in my waist. You want me to get it?" he asked, already knowing her answer.

"No. I'll get it. Don't you fucking move."

Pam moved and began to reach in front of Stacks with her left hand as she held him at gunpoint with the other. She searched for his pistol. Dumbfounded, she realized Stacks wasn't carrying a gun, but it was too late. Before she could back away, Stacks shifted his weight to his left and caught Pam dead in the center of her face with his elbow. He broke her nose and knocked her out before she was able to pull the trigger on her .380. Stacks quickly turned and retrieved the gun Pam dropped during her fall. He picked up her limp body and placed her in the back of the trailer, just in case one of the other ones decided to step outside. His first instinct was to kick in the door and run up in the crib busting shots like he was Billy the Kid, but he knew he would only be signing his brother's death certificate—and possibly his own—if he emptied the clip and one or two of them were still alive, so instead he decided to sneak into the house and get better positioned, then take them by surprise.

Chapter Sixty-one

Vanessa's train arrived as scheduled, but Stacks was nowhere to be found. An uneasy feeling swept through her. She anticipated him being there when her train came in, especially since he was aware of how she'd been traveling. Her gut told her something was wrong. Stacks wasn't the type of person to neglect his responsibilities or leave someone hanging. There had to be a hell of a reason for him or Styles not to pick her up. Vanessa pulled out her cell phone and dialed Stacks' cell phone, and the voice mail answered. She left a message and proceeded to dial Styles and got his voice mail as well. She cursed herself for not knowing their house number. She noticed a taxi sitting out front of the station and approached it, got in, and gave the driver the address. Something was up, and she wasn't going to sit around and wait to find out.

"What the hell is taking Pam so long?" Desiree asked.

"I know, right? She should've been back by now," Tasha replied.

"She must've parked that shit way down the road. Her dumb ass probably walking back now, scared to death of the fucking dark," Keisha said, laughing for the first time in hours.

Stacks listened as they inquired about Pam's whereabouts. His timing couldn't have been better as he snuck into the trailer unnoticed. He initially thought they saw the light dancing through the crack of the door when he crept in, but they were so caught up in their conversation, they missed it.

However, Styles saw the glimmer of something. At first, he didn't pay it any attention, because he thought it was that bitch Pam returning, but when he focused on the image squatting and creeping on the floor, he knew it could only be one person: Stacks.

Stacks saw his brother looking in his direction, but couldn't tell whether he had seen him. He knew that if Styles knew it was him he would remain calm and keep his cool. To confirm his suspicion, Stacks threw up a number that Styles would recognize. They did this as kids to alert each other that their moms was coming if they were doing something they had no business doing. As they got older, they used it in the streets as a code for danger being near or if one was on the verge of being caught out there by two females.

Styles acknowledged the code aloud.

"Four-zero-one," he said, and immediately everyone directed their attention to him.

"What you say?" Keisha asked first.

Styles remained silent.

"Nigga, what the fuck did you say?" she asked again, drawing her gun on Styles.

Styles decided to play a game with Keisha.

"Bitch, I was trying to remember the combination to the safe until you broke my concentration," he answered.

Keisha's eyes lit up after hearing Styles mention the combination to the safe.

Stacks heard his brother and was proud of his performance. *Way to go little bro,* Stacks thought.

"So what is it, nigga?" Keisha asked, hovering above Styles. Desiree and Tasha stood near, giving him their undivided attention.

Styles paused as he looked straight into Keisha's eyes and spoke slowly.

"Four-zero…go fuck ya self," Styles yelled.

Stacks knew his brother was telling him to pop off. It was either now or never. Do or die. Keisha smacked Styles with her gun, causing his chair to topple onto the floor. Keisha misstepped, minimizing the chances of Stacks shooting his brother or getting him caught in the crossfire.

Stacks came out of hiding and let loose. Boom. Boom. Boom. The muzzle of the .380 Stacks was spitting lit up the room as the shots rang out in a thunderous roar.

Chapter Sixty-two

The taxi drove past the carwash, and Vanessa became aware of her surroundings. She knew they weren't far from the house, but she couldn't see beyond the darkness.

"Can you turn on your high beams?" she asked the driver as she held on to the headrest to sit upright for a better view.

"Sure," he replied and turned on his high beams. Vanessa spotted Stacks' rental parked closer to the top of the driveway than to the house. She found this strange and knew to stay on point.

"Right here," she yelled to the driver. The cabby was barely able to come to a full stop before Vanessa handed him two twenty spots. She quickly grabbed her bags and jumped out the cab. "Keep the change," she said as she closed the door. She ran down the driveway, and as she got near, she heard shots coming from inside the trailer. Panic swept through her, and she froze in her tracks. Vanessa didn't know who was involved, why there was shooting, and there was no way she could call the cops. Aside from that, she knew she had all of the drugs with her. Vanessa also remembered she was carrying Stacks' gun. She was no slouch when it came to beef, and if Stacks was in trouble, she would step up to the plate. She loved him and would ride or die with him and for him. That's just how it went down in the streets. Vanessa unzipped the duffle bag and pulled out the .40 caliber. Cocking it back, taking off the safety, she ran to the house. Before entering, she looked through the side window. The scene before her made her blood boil.

"I knew that bitch was a snake," Vanessa said, referring to her suspicion about Pam. She knew these women had to be associated with her.

Vanessa couldn't see Stacks, but she saw Styles lying on the floor tied to a chair. She couldn't determine whether he was dead or alive, but would soon find out. Based on the position everyone was taking cover in the house, she figured Stacks was shooting to her right. Two of the girls knelt down for safety, but one was in plain view.

"Yeah, bitch," Vanessa said as she raised the .40 caliber and let off four shots through the window. Two of the shots missed, but the other two hit one of the girl head-on as they ripped through her one after the other. She never knew what hit her.

Keisha heard the shots ringing from outside. She felt heat pass through her body and saw Tasha's lifeless body slump over the table and fall with a thud to the floor.

This is not supposed to happen, Keisha thought. Tears of anger rolled down her face as she saw Tasha's dead body on the floor with a bullet to the head. Someone caught them off guard and killed her girl and grazed Keisha who felt a searing pain in her side where blood spilled. She didn't know Desirees's condition, and now she was concerned about Pam. Where was Pam?

Stacks heard the shots, but didn't know from where they were coming. He couldn't see any of the chicks in the house, but he knew the shots weren't coming from inside. He heard smaller calibers being fired at him when he originally set the shootout off, and he received a leg wound.

For the first time in her life, Desiree was afraid of dying. She witnessed Tasha go down and knew that now it was either Stacks, Styles, or her. She knew from the start that it was a bad idea to wait for Stacks, but never voiced her opinion. Now it was costing them dearly. This was more than the value of what was in the safe a hundred times over. Money was replaceable, but their lives weren't. If only she would have made the right choice to choose Stacks over their heist, but it was too late. Desiree made the wrong choice and was about to lose everything—a chance at a relationship, her happiness, and possibly her life.

"Desiree, Desiree," Keisha whispered.

"Huh?" she answered, reality returning with Keisha's voice.

"We gotta get the fuck up outta here."

"How?" Desiree asked, crouched to the ground.

"I don't know."

Vanessa saw the girl fall onto the table and hit the floor. She knew the bullet to the head killed her, but it didn't faze Vanessa. As far as she was concerned justice had been served. Street justice and the girl Vanessa bodied got what her hands had called for. Vanessa knew that if the girl she slumped and her friends killed Styles and Stacks, they would have no regrets either. You live by the gun, you die by the gun, simple as that. Vanessa was thinking of ways to enter the house and assist Stacks when a sharp pain ran up her spine. She fell to the ground and landed on her knees.

Chapter Sixty-three

The shots from outside brought Pam back to consciousness. She stumbled to get to her feet as she noticed blood all over her clothes. Her nose was sore and broken. She staggered to the side of the house and saw Vanessa standing by the same window Stacks was peeking into earlier. Thanks to Stacks, she no longer had her gun, so Pam searched the ground for anything that could be used as a weapon. She spotted a piece of plywood and picked it up, then made her way toward Vanessa. When she got close enough, she drew back and swung, hitting Vanessa in the back, knocking her to her knees. Pam saw the gun fly out of Vanessa's hand as she went down and quickly retrieved it.

Vanessa quickly recovered from the blow when she her assailant going for the gun, which was still within reach. Vanessa remained still. When Pam bent over to get the gun, Vanessa punched her in the midsection, and Pam bent over. Both women were on their knees as Vanessa attacked her. They were rolling on the ground like two female mud wrestlers in a pit. Each struggled to gain the upper hand, but it was like a tug-of-war. Vanessa punched and clawed at Pam, farther injuring her face. Nonetheless, Pam held her own and threw a few damaging blows at Vanessa who made several attempts to regain possession of the gun. Finally, they both reached for the weapon, but Pam was quicker. Again they struggled, only this time it was to possess the .40 caliber. Pam managed to pull it in as Vanessa tried to restrain Pam from being able to aim it in her direction. Pam was strong, but pound for pound, Vanessa was stronger. All four hands were on the gun. They continued to fight for the upper hand until the gun went off.

Everyone heard the shots blast off. Keisha hoped Pam was taking out the mysterious shooter outside while Stacks hoped Vanessa was taking Pam out.

"What was that?" Desiree whispered to Keisha.

"I don't know. I think it's Pam. I hope."

"Shit is out of control," Desiree said with tears in her eyes.

Keisha didn't respond. There was no time for tears. They needed a plan, and she decided to take action. She crawled over to Styles who was still tied to the chair.

"Nigga, I swear to God if you don't throw ya fucking piece over here and call ya fucking man off outside, I'll blow this muthafucka brains out," Keisha announced sternly.

Stacks saw Keisha hiding behind Styles' chair. She pulled it upright and had her gun pointed at his temple.

"Fuck that, bro. Don't do it," Styles yelled.

"Shut the fuck up, nigga," Keisha said, hitting Styles upside the head with the barrel of the gun.

Stacks thought quickly. He knew Keisha would kill his brother without a second thought, especially since her girl was dead. He also knew Styles wasn't afraid to die as long as his death was avenged, but Stacks didn't want his brother going out like that, so he tried another route.

"Yo, how about you and ya partners just roll up outta here, and this shit'll be over?" he hollered back.

Keisha laughed. *Who the fuck does this nigga think he's fooling?* she thought.

"Nigga, you think somebody stupid? This shit'll never be over, not until we dead, or you niggas dead. Nah, fuck that. I ain't trying to hear that shit."

Stacks figured she wouldn't go for that, but he had to try. Then another thought popped into his head.

"Yo, Desiree? Desiree?" he yelled.

Desiree couldn't believe Stacks was calling her. She had no idea what he could possibly want to say to her after all that had happened. She was afraid as well as ashamed to answer him.

"Desiree?" he called again, hoping she would answer.

Keisha looked at her friend, puzzled.

"Answer him," Keisha told her.

Desiree shot Keisha a look, but complied.

"I hear you," Desiree responded.

"Yo, I don't know how it got to this, and I know shit fucked up right now, but you know me, and you know how I get down. My word is my bond, and this is my word on everything I love. We can all walk up out of this shit alive, and it'll all be over. Enough people have been hurt and enough blood been spilled. I ain't trying to die, and I know you ain't either. If you care about me the way I think you do, then you'll listen to me and know that what I'm saying is straight up. You and ya girls can walk up outta here unharmed, without any repercussions," Stacks said, trying to sound convincing.

Keisha couldn't help but laugh, but Desiree believed every word out of Stacks' mouth. She detected his sincerity and felt he meant what he said.

Vanessa rose from up out of the pool of blood that belonged to Pam. She had shot people before, but never at close range, and to see Pam's lifeless body caused chills to run through her. Prior to this evening, she had never killed anyone, and in one night she had taken two lives. After she pulled herself together, Vanessa went back to thinking of ways to enter the house unnoticed. And then it hit her.

Keisha still had the gun to Styles' head. She wasn't trying to hear any of the weak-ass game with which Stacks was coming at Desiree. She knew there was only two ways she was getting out of there: either in a blaze of gunfire or in a body bag. There were no other options.

Stacks waited for a response, hoping what he said sank in. He was really willing to let them walk out alive to save his brother's life. This went against everything he lived by in the game. Stacks strongly believed in the laws and codes of the street. It was either kill or be killed, but that killer instinct as a means of survival was not in full throttle at the moment, and it caused him to be more compassionate.

Desiree made up her mind. She knew that if Stacks gave his word then he wouldn't hurt them.

"Stacks, I never wanted it to turn out like this, but you right, the damage is done. All we wanna do now is get outta here. My homegirl Tasha is dead, and we need to get her body and leave, but I don't know how we gonna do this. Maybe we can untie ya brother and lock y'all in a room until we bounce or something, but you gonna have to throw us ya clip in your gun, just to be on the safe side," Desiree said.

Keisha was furious. She couldn't believe the shit that was coming out of Desiree's mouth. Her partner in crime had gone soft on her and wanted to give up, but Keisha wasn't going to have that.

"Desiree, what the fuck you doing, bitch? You lost ya damn mind? That nigga playing you, girl. Can't you see that or ya ass so blind by that dick you can't recognize game when you hear it?" Keisha hissed.

"Keisha, ain't nobody blind. I know what I'm doing. I'm trying to save our fucking lives. You the one blind if you can't see that our fucking girl is dead because of all this shit, and we gonna join her if we don't compromise."

Stacks tried to listen as they discussed his proposal but couldn't hear everything that was said. For the most part, he knew Desiree was trying to convince her friend that his solution was their only alternative, other than shooting their way out, which he didn't believe they were up to doing.

Keisha wasn't trying to hear Desiree, but she pretended to go along with it. There was a great deal of doubt in her mind that Stacks was on the up and up. She didn't trust this nigga or the one tied up. Nonetheless, she intended to play the situation by ear and improvise as she went along.

"You better be right about this, girl, or else we dead anyway. But if you think you can get us outta here alive, then I'm wit' you," Keisha said. Desiree was relieved to be getting her friend's support.

"Stacks, we gonna untie ya brother, but you gonna have to throw the clip in the gun to me," Desiree yelled.

Stacks thought she was insane. He heard her the first time she had said it, but he didn't think she was serious. There was no way he was going to agree to that unless they did the same.

"Yo, what about your shit? How that sound? You gonna have to throw ya shit down too."

Desiree didn't think of that, but she knew that Stacks was right and that would show good faith on both their parts.

"Okay," she said.

"Bitch, is you crazy?" Keisha whispered.

"Keisha, what choice do we have? He's gonna do the same."

Keisha was on fire. She considered shooting Styles, Stacks, and even Desiree with the intention of getting up out of there. Desiree had betrayed her all in the name of love—or lust, she figured. If they ever made it out alive, this would be the end of their crusade as well as their friendship, Keisha vowed.

When Stacks heard Desiree's response, he was surprised, but if they were willing to unarm themselves, then against his better judgment, he was willing to do the same.

"A'ight, untie my brother," he yelled as he popped the clip out of the .380.

Keisha began to untie Styles as Desiree took the clip out of her nine-millimeter. When she finished untying him, Keisha ordered Styles to go in the bedroom, and he refused. Styles couldn't believe his brother was allowing these chicks to walk out scot-free.

Keisha cocked her gun.

"Nigga, I'm losing my patience," she said.

"Keisha, chill," Desiree whispered.

Stacks saw what was going on. He heard Keisha order him into the bedroom and Styles' refusal.

"Yo, Styles, it's a'ight, son. Go ahead. I'll be there in a minute."

Styles stood there for a few seconds before limping toward the room and closing the door.

"Gimme your clip," Desiree said to Keisha.

Keisha took the cartridge out of her Beretta.

"Yo, what up?" Stacks yelled down to them.

"We ready," Desiree yelled. "Send yours down and we'll send ours."

"A'ight yo, same time."

Stacks tossed his clip to them, and they slid theirs in his direction.

He picked them up and put the clips in his pocket then proceeded toward them. When he got near Desiree, he shot her a look of disgust. Desiree couldn't look him in the eye. The room was silent as they passed each other, and Stacks decided to break the ice.

"Handle ya business. I gave you my word," he said and started toward the room. Just as he reached for the knob, Vanessa's room door flew open. The loud sound of the door hitting the wall startled Keisha. Quickly she snatched up the .44 Magnum on the kitchen counter, swung around, and pulled the trigger twice.

Chapter Sixty-four

The first shot Keisha let off from Styles' gun spit out wildly and caused her wrist to jerk back from the sudden force. In an attempt to better control the firearm, Keisha held the gun firmly with both hands and let off another round.

The shot from Keisha's gun hit Stacks in his back, traveling straight to his heart. He stumbled and fell to the ground. Styles came out of the room to see what had taken place. Nobody moved. Styles scanned the room and saw his brother slumped over in Vanessa's arms. He saw the gun in Keisha's hand and knew she was responsible. He raised the .40 caliber he had retrieved from the safe and emptied the clip into Keisha. She was dead before her body hit the ground.

Desiree lay in pain, unable to believe that Keisha had shot her and Stacks. The bullet tore through her torso, and she was losing massive amounts of blood. Tears rolled down her cheeks as she cried from the pain and her lost love, Stacks. The first and only man she had ever loved.

Vanessa sobbed uncontrollaby as Stacks lay in her arms. The blood pumped out of him like a faucet.

"Stacks," she cried, "please don't die, baby. Hold on. You gonna be alright, just hold on," she said again as Stacks fought for his life.

"V, I-I-I love," Stacks said, trying to get the words out, but he didn't have the strength.

"Don't talk, boo. I know. I love you too. Save ya strength and hang in there. I need you," Vanessa cried, but it was too late. Stacks was quickly slipping away as he choked on his blood.

"No. Stacks, no. Don't leave me. I need you," Vanessa bawled, but her cries went to deaf ears because Stacks was gone. Vanessa's cries could be heard all over the south as she wept for the loss of the man she truly loved.

Styles suppressed his emotions, knowing that his big brother was dead. He had avenged Stacks by killing the person responsible. He stared at Desiree as she lay helplessly in a pool of blood. Styles decided to make her suffer and die slowly.

Vanessa gently laid Stacks' body on the floor and drew her gun on Desiree.

"Bitch, look at me," Vanessa yelled.

Vanessa put the barrel of the gun to Desiree's head, and Desiree stared at her.

"I'm sorry," Desiree gurgled through sobs. "I never wanted to see Stacks get hurt. I loved…"

Vanessa didn't want to hear her sob story. She pulled the trigger at point-blank range, planting one in Desiree's head, causing blood to splatter in her face. Vanessa kept her gun aimed at Desiree as her body lay listless. Styles grabbed Vanessa's arm and removed the pistol from her hand.

"It's all over, sis. He can rest in peace now."

Epilogue

One year later…

After that dreadful night, Vanessa decided to move out of New York. She took the money she had stashed and convinced her grandmother to move out of the housing project with her to Houston, Texas. She enrolled in a local community college because she wanted a brighter future and to make her grandmother happy. She had been through a lot that year, suffering the loss of her lover, her friend, and her baby's father.

On the eve of Stacks' murder, he and Vanessa had conceived a child. Stacks left her with a gift. Vanessa had taken Stacks' death hard, and it took a toll on her body. She was only able to carry the baby for seven months and gave birth to a premature boy.

After isolating herself for four months, her grandmother paid her a surprise visit and gave her a dose of reality. Vanessa began visiting church and found God. Stacks' death was a wake-up call, and she never went back to hustling again. She had finally taken her grandmother's advice and decided to do something positive with her life while she was still young. It was the only way to dispel the nightmares and horrors of her past. She had cut all ties with anyone associated with the game, but she was having a hard time cutting them off mentally because deep down she felt the streets were a part of her and would always be that way. Occasionally, she shed tears for Stacks because he wouldn't be there to see his son become a man and their son would grow up without his father. She believed it was a known fact that in the hood, the good die young. In her eyes, Stacks was one of the good ones and didn't deserve to die. Her faith made her realize that when God feels it's your time, then it's your time. There were no negotiations when it came to death. The last time she had really heard from anyone from her past was when Styles had contacted her on the six-month anniversary of Stacks' death. Initially she was happy to hear from him, but when she found out he and Don still hustled down in the dirty, she had asked that he not contact her anymore. A few months later she read in the *Daily News* that Donnell Porter had been arrested in Queens for the murder of a Brian Brown of North Carolina. Vanessa knew it had to be the kid BB who shot Don, almost killing him. It was simply the code of the game, an eye for an eye.

Vanessa was amazed how after such a great loss Don and Styles continued to operate as if the same destiny didn't await them. She couldn't believe Styles and Don had actually gone back down south to hustle again. She dreaded the thought of her son growing up and choosing the path his father and uncle had chosen. However, she knew from playing the game herself, that sometimes the game chose you and as long as you put work in the game, it was your boss.

Vanessa prayed to God every night that when the time came Little Stacks would make the right decision. She also hoped that Styles didn't fall victim to the barrel of a gun like his brother, but she knew it was a possibility, especially since he was was one of many from up north hustling down in the dirty.

###

Runnin' Game

by Courtney Parker
Available in Stores NOW!

"*Runnin' Game* is urban drama at its best!"
–Nikki Turner, national bestsSelling author of
The Glamorous Life and *A Hustler's Wife*

Now that Carter Turner's athletic career is off the ground and running, he has to beat the women off with a stick. Carter is on top of the world…that is until he receives a telephone call that rocks his track career and changes his life forever.

Carter is no stranger to life in the fast lane, with a career destined for gold and a girl determined to ride or die, fate finds favor with this young couple. Only just as the icing is put on the cake, the cake begins to crumble under the weight of Carter's grimy past. With a string of lies straining his relationship and a possible injury threatening his career, Carter is doing what any young player has to do…*Runnin' Game*.

Morning, Noon & Night:

Can't Get Enough

Available in stores NOW!

Caution: Searing HOT! Do not read this book without a partner or toy nearby for immediate satisfaction.

Sexy, sultry and titillating...*Morning, Noon & Night* will press your hot buttons. Representing a wide range of styles and voices, these narratives offer a steamy assortment of fiction that will fulfill your every fantasy.

"I'd been working at Morning, Noon, and Night, Inc., a place where one just can't get enough, for the past six months.

The real secret to how I make so much money is my ability to get people to call in around the clock. I really can't take too much credit for this because the entire time that I'm getting my callers off, Big Sexy is usually getting me off."

–Natosha Gale Lewis, *Enough*

"Morning Noon & Night features a good mix of fantasy situations, including lesbian encounters, bondage and ménages à trois."

–Michael Presley, author of Black Funk I, II & II

No Strings Attached

Please accept this invitation to:

Event: Termination of marriage
Reason: Misplaced dick in another woman
Time: 3:40 P.M.
Date: May 20, 1999

Felice Jackson is sexy, single, and satisfied—or so she claims. She is an affluent, thirty-something entrepreneur who is partial owner of the successful firm Jackson and Jackson Financial Consultants. The only problem is her very active sexual relationship with her ex-husband and business partner, Bedford Jackson.

Felice is disgusted with men, but not enough to shut them out of her life physically. She enjoys the touch, smell, and taste of men too much to deprive herself. Instead she decides to stand at the helm of life and call the shots in relationships. If a man can do it, Felice can too. She isn't going to shed another tear for these tired-ass men.

Felice enjoys her no-strings-attached creed—until her secret past collides with her present.

There is a revolution in black literature in America. It is nationalist in direction, and it is pro-black. That means, in effect that it is deliberately moving outside the sphere of traditional western forms, limitations, and presumptions. It is seeking new forms, new limits, new shapes, and much of it now admittedly is crude, reflecting the uncertainty, the searching quality of its movement. But, though troubled and seeking, it is very, very vital.

–Mr. Hoyt W. Fuller, author
Addison Gayle Jr's anthology
The Black Aesthetic (1971)

Flowers in Bloom titles are available online and at your local bookstores. If they do not carry your selection of choice, please request that the store order it.
Visit: www.flowersinbloompublishing.com

Thanks in advance for your patronage!